THE DRAGON THIEF'S HEART

ISBN – 979-8-9906947-4-3

eISBN – 979-8-9906947-3-6

CONTENTS

CHAPTER ONE

T he boy grasped the sharp rocks protruding from the steep cliff and hung by his fingertips. With small hands, he pulled himself up. It seemed as if there was no end to the sheer towering wall of rock. Reaching the top was taking forever. He did not dare look down to judge how high he was, or he might grow dizzy and lose his precarious hold. A few pebbles came loose in his hand and tumbled soundlessly into the emptiness far below. Flattening against the rockface, he took a deep breath, and his arms shook with effort, but he kept going.

If he were to make the cave by nightfall, he had better hurry, and if he didn't want to plunge to his death, he needed to be very careful. The trick was to do both successfully at the same time.

Cursing under his breath, the boy continued up. Sweat matted his hair, and his tattered clothing caught and tore on the jagged stones. His fingers began to leave bloody splotches from scrapes and torn fingernails, but he tenaciously held on. Grabbing with one hand above the next, placing one foot after another, he pulled upward. Finally, after what felt like endless hours, he slapped a hand over the top of the cliffside and carefully eased up the last few inches to cautiously peer over the edge.

In front of him was a rocky plateau, and he could see a cave looming a short distance away. Glancing around, he strained over the last few inches of the cliff before he could roll onto his back and lay flat on the ground. Rocks dug into his spine, but he didn't care; he was exhausted and needed a long moment to rest his aching limbs. When he finally could breathe normally, he sat up and dangled his legs over the edge of the precipice as if to say '*HA! I beat you!*' Back turned away from the ominous cave, he looked out into the expanse. A vast mountain range spread as far as he could see, and the thick forest blanketed everything as if nothing existed in the world but trees and towering peaks. Distant clouds rumbled and threatened a storm from darkening clouds.

The boy had been lucky that the rain held off while he climbed, but now he wished it would rain. He wished that torrents of water would drench these mountains because the rain would help disguise what he had to do next. Taking a fortifying breath, he stood up, turned around, and saw his goal.

Before him, there was a massive, black hole that marked a cave entrance in the mountainside. It loomed large, gaping ominously, just like in the tales he had heard. It was about a short distance from the cliff where he now stood. He would have to cross an open plateau to get there, and he watched for any sign of life. Walking forward a bit, he crouched low and ran toward the shelter of a nearby clump of trees. Flattened up against the widest tree trunk he could find, he peeked around and surveyed the landscape ahead. It was very rocky with short, dry grassy patches, an occasional bush, and more trees. Further in, there were mounds of something that looked like dirt, but he could not quite tell what they were from this distance. Burial mounds of those who came before him, his active imagination supplied, and he shivered, nervously licking his dry lips. Glancing behind, he looked toward the west. Darkness was swiftly falling, and he knew that the creature in the cave would come out and go hunting at night. All he had to do was hide and wait.

Crouching down and prodding a loose tooth with his tongue, the boy carefully thought through his next moves. Distracted by various ideas, he reached into his mouth and grabbed it with his dirty thumb and forefinger. Wiggling, wrenching back and forth, he finally gave it a quick yank. He looked at the bloody white thing between his fingers and grinned, and just like that, the last baby tooth was gone. He could taste the metallic tang of blood, and he spit on the rocky ground.

Moving quickly from bush to boulder, to mounds of dirt, he snuck toward the cave. Once he judged he was close enough, he stopped behind a large rock and sat down. A sense of age, the haunting of old things and the ominous past struck him, and he realized this was an ancient place of magic and forbidden to trespass upon. Then, a breeze came up from the north and blew a horrid stench toward him. The boy slapped both hands over his nose and mouth to stifle a retching cough. The foul scent that engulfed him was like nothing he had ever smelled before. It was horrible, like an animal had died weeks earlier after rolling in its own droppings, only worse. The boy ducked his nose inside his shirt to try and block the smell, but then he caught a whiff of his own body odor. Wrinkling his nose, he realized he stunk like sweat, blood, dirt, and any number of awful things.

It had been weeks since his last bath. Recalling it made him shiver as he remembered the cold dredging he had received in a horse trough. He had been begging in one of the many small towns he passed through. A man, rather than giving him a charitable coin, threw him in the trough, complaining of his odor and unwashed state. Once again, he smelled almost as bad as whatever fouled the air around him now. Young boys were supposed to be dirty; up until now, he had not cared much about it, but he was sure the *creature* within the cave would smell him coming. That would not be good if he did not want to end up as a small, tasty morsel in the beast's stomach.

With every inhale, the smell of the place overwhelmed him. After a few minutes, he thought maybe he was getting used to it. Crawling forward on his belly, he approached one of the mounds where the stench was worse. He dug into the stuff and smelled a handful. Rearing back, he studied it in the dying evening light.

Suddenly, it dawned on the boy what this was, and a slow smile spread across his face. He looked around in surprise. Everywhere he saw the mounds of what he had thought earlier were dirt and rocks, but now he knew. It was the beast's *dung,* and it was everywhere! Piles and piles of the stuff were mounded in different sizes, with some appearing old and hard, and some almost fresh. Many of the mounds were covered in grass and some had small trees growing from them. The glint of long white shards or sticks protruded from the muck. Picking one up, he realized the white shards were bones!

The smile grew wider over the boy's face as an idea blossomed. He stood up, braced himself, and took a running leap, jumping feet first into the largest, wettest pile. He sank into the muck until he was up to his chin in it. Dizzy from the horrid stench, he breathed through his mouth and tried hard not to puke. There was nothing in his stomach to bring up except for bile anyway, but he really did not want to make noise by retching. After a few moments, the nausea left him, and he waded out of the pile. Flinging off the larger chunks of filth, he ran his fingers through his messy hair, getting the stuff off his head. Now, all he had to do was find a spot to hide and wait.

After the exertion of climbing the cliff, the boy was exhausted. He leaned against a large boulder and huddled in a tight ball, shivering. If he didn't die from the smell of the dung, the beast could eat him, or the cold might get him, but there was a fire in his blood as he contemplated the prize, which would be located just inside the cave. It was a bit of a mystery what he would find.

One night in a small village, he had been listening outside a tavern door and overheard a bard telling tales of a gigantic monster. He told of treasure to be found in the beast's hoard. The old man had been vague but then he spoke in a sad voice and told a legend that the *last dragon* lived deep in the mountains on the highest peak. Most people scoffed at the old man's wild tales, but not the boy. He believed. Now, as he passed the time with visions of wealth and prosperity racing through his imagination, he conjured fantastic dreams of the future.

The night descended quickly this high in the mountains, and soon the sky was as black as a tomb. The boy waited. A full moon rose in the east, helping him see better as it climbed higher. It was massive, like a huge creamy white ball in the starry sky. It lit the landscape around him with a pale white light that cast strange shadows from the multiple barriers surrounding the boy's hiding place.

Dozing off, head bumping the rock behind him, the boy heard a noise and woke with a start. It was a scraping, slithering sound. Rocks clattered and the ground shook slightly with the footfalls of the huge beast emerging from its lair. Fully awake now, the boy hunkered low and watched from the minimal safety of the boulder that hid him as the last dragon in the land appeared right before him.

Its scaly, horned head was covered in a streaming mane of thick, shiny, black hair. The boy marveled, completely surprised and terrified. The long neck and massive shoulders followed as the beast left the cave. This beast's hair glittered like black water flowing over a diamond strewn field of living flesh. He thought the mythical beasts were all scales, claws, and horns, though this one had those also. Fully emerged, its black hide magnificently reflected the bright moonlight. Ducking down further, the boy realized he could see the beast because of its huge size but that also meant he could be seen in return. Doing his best to stifle the shivers of terror traveling deep through his bones, he peered forward, carefully trying to make out more details.

The *dragon* had long, sharp, dagger-like spikes rising along its spine. As it stretched, spanning black wings out, it was a magical sight to behold. It stepped into a brighter patch of moonlight, and the boy saw that the glimmering scales of its belly were shades of ruby against the black. The dragon shook its long mane, dipped its head, and stuck its front feet out. Its hindquarters arched up like a cat stretching as if it were just waking from a long nap. It yawned revealing long sharp fangs and rows of lethal teeth.

In the moonlight, it was hard to distinguish the beast's eyes and muzzle, but the boy had seen enough to know the dragon was terrifying, but almost beautiful. Gold gilded the ridges of its black scales casting an ominous glow and reflecting the moonlight. The boy's fearful shivers increased as the beast raised its nose and sniffed the air. It began to shudder, its massive sides vibrating in a low hum. Its chest glowed red as it growled and drew in a deep breath. It seemed to suck the very air from the night.

Tilting its head back, its long crimson neck exposed, the dragon opened its mouth wide and expelled a long stream of white fire. It swung its massive head from left to right and lashed its long tail, incinerating the space, around and toward the ground in front of its lair. The flames swept the bushes, the mounds of excrement, and the boulders. As the dragon sprayed its fire in a sweeping half-circle, it blasted the stone where the boy sat huddled, shaking, and terrified. He could feel the intense heat of the dragon flame licking his skin, hair, and clothes, and he ducked, covering his head with his hands. He thought this was how the end of his short life would happen, being burned alive by the massive black dragon. At the same time, he was thrilled with the knowledge that he had found it and was probably the only one in a thousand years who had ever seen one up close.

After a few moments of roaring and breathing white flame, it suddenly stopped, and the dragon gave a long hiss, snapped its dripping jaws, and leaped into the air. The gust of wind caused by the massive wings fanned the white fires that burned the bushes at the mouth of the lair. Then the dragon quickly disappeared into the distant sky.

CHAPTER TWO

A fter the dragon flew away, the boy slowly uncovered his head, dropped his hands, and looked at his arms and legs. He was unharmed! Miraculously, he was not burned or even a little bit scorched. Standing up, he looked himself over in disbelief. Then he looked around, thinking hard about what he had just seen. The nearby bushes were on fire, but the mounds of dragon droppings were barely smoldering. It dawned on the boy's clever mind that by being covered in the dragon's dung, he was *protected* from the dragon's fire. Not surprisingly, it made sense that what came out of the dragon's body would not burn.

With a low chuckle of disbelief, the boy puffed up with confidence and looked out into the night where the dragon had disappeared under the starry sky. It was a large black spot in the moonlit distance. He knew it was only a matter of time until the beast returned, but by then the boy would be gone with the treasure he had come for. Thumbing his nose at the retreating beast, he turned to the matter at hand.

Slinking cautiously toward the cave mouth, the boy reached down and broke a branch from one of the bushes that was still burning. His worn boots were covered with dragon dung, so his footfalls were hushed in the massive, echoing cave. Raising his makeshift torch high, he crept forward cautiously. The bones of animals littered the floor as did rocks and dirt, and things he did not want to look at too closely. Huge deep gouges crisscrossed the floor from where the dragon's claws dug in the ground as it left its cave. Shaking with fear, the boy whispered to himself, listing all the things he would buy with the dragon's treasure. It bolstered his courage to think of the foods he would soon enjoy. He would eat three or more meals a day and he would forever be grateful to the beast. Passing a wide curve, he slunk close to the walls and carefully placed one foot in front of the other while he searched for the dragon's hoard.

Further in, the ground seemed to take on a strange soft quality. Bending low and feeling around, the boy realized that it was a large area covered in pine boughs and tree branches. He scratched his head and wrinkled his nose in thought, not sure of what he found. As he moved forward, he saw that intermixed with the pine boughs were long black strands like thin ropes. The boy realized he was seeing the dragon's long hair that had been shed all over the floor. He got a brilliant idea and reached for some of the longer pieces. Winding it around his waist and looping some over his shoulders, the boy soon looked like a strange furry creature. He moved further in as he wrapped the hair around him, and he began to grow a little more apprehensive.

He had expected to walk right into the cave and find the dragon's treasure hoard glowing golden in a towering, sprawling pile. Instead, all he found was the pine-bough-padded flooring, gouged dirt, and tons of worthless rocks. He swung his torch, peering around, and saw no chests of gold, not a single coin! No jewels sparkled in the faint light, and no magical armor or silver swords glistened from gilded scabbards. He swore angrily under his breath and continued to search.

Ahead, shards of something white caught the torchlight, and the boy bent to pick one up. Dragon teeth! He wanted to dance and shout with glee but knew he had better not push his luck by making a ruckus. He picked up a few of the larger ones that were as long as his arm and a couple of the smaller ones and put them in the bag he brought to carry his loot.

Grabbing another branch from the ground, he lit a new torch as the other was sputtering out. He moved deeper into the cave, deciding he would take a few more minutes of searching, then he would have to leave or risk the dragon returning and trapping him there.

The shadows in the back of the cave were just as frightening as the dragon itself. The boy did not like the enclosed space, and he began to feel *very* apprehensive. He was about to give up, realizing there was no treasure to be found. He would have to settle for the dragon's hair and a few of its teeth. In anger and disappointment, he again cursed under his breath over being denied his riches after all his hard work.

Suddenly ahead, something shimmered faintly. Quickly, he scrambled over the rocks, looked down, and saw a huge crystal. Not sure if it was his imagination or not, the boy scoffed at himself as he imagined it *glowed*. It was just the reflection from the torchlight he realized, as he slunk closer.

The crystal was sort of rounded at the bottom but had faceted edges on the top like a jewel the boy had once seen in a hunter's dagger. Wound up and buried in the dragon's shed hair, it looked milky white, and just the right size to fit into his bag. Wedging the end of the torch into the ground, the boy grasped the sides of the crystal and heaved. The thing did not budge. He pushed and pulled, and it moved just a little in the discarded dragon hair, but it was stuck tight in the ground. The boy thought for a moment and then had an idea. Reaching inside his bag, he pulled out one of the larger dragon's teeth he had collected.

Slashing down, he severed the long hair binding the crystal in place, until they lay strewn around like the shorn locks from a dozen black-haired maidens. The boy worked quickly at it and finally lifted the crystal, staggering back as it pulled free from its spot. Surprised by its light weight, the boy chuckled with glee and stuffed it into his pack. He stuck the long tooth through his worn belt, grabbed his torch, and ran out of the cave like Hell's hounds were on his heels.

Before he left the cave, he hastily ground the torch in the dirt, putting the flame out. Now for the hard part...getting away with his loot and his life.

The boy had planned his escape well. He was not going to risk his life further by climbing back down the massive escarpment that he had scaled earlier, especially not in the dark. He was going to climb up! He hoped that the dragon cave on the mountain top had a backside of the mountain that sloped gently downward and, after a short trek up and over, he could just walk down through the sloping land in the opposite direction. This forest was not called Ten Thousand Mile Forest for nothing, and he knew that by heading east the land would level off. Going in one direction was as good as any other. He had not left his scent for the dragon to follow because he smelled like dragon dung. It should confuse the beast sufficiently if it ever suspected someone had been there. He justified, he had not taken anything of value, just some dragon hair, teeth, and a large crystal. So, why should it follow him at all? He would sell what he found and be able to buy himself something to eat, some new clothes, and perhaps new boots that fit. Then he would be off on his next adventure.

Climbing up the outside slope was not too difficult. The boy scrambled up boulders with his heavy burden and finally reached the top of the mountain. The bag with his loot was scraping his sore back and he had reached a level of exhaustion his body complained about. He stopped to catch his breath and unslung the bag from around his shoulders and looked at it in the moonlight and then had an idea. Carefully, he unwound the dragon hair from around his chest, shoulders, and torso. Not willing to waste any, he laid the strands out in a long pile and arranged them as quickly as he could. It was thick, surprisingly light and strong, silky to the touch, and so black that it was easy to see in the moonlight. Then he hooked the bag around his neck and began to wind the long strands of dragon hair around his middle over the crystal. Once neatly wound up, he tied the ends like a rope. Now, the bag with the crystal was tied snugly against his chest so it wouldn't bang against his back which made it easier to carry while giving his arms a rest.

The terrain changed with short areas of flat ground and clumps of massive rocks. In the open areas the boy ran. Risking a look around, he searched the sky for signs of the dragon. The vast mountain range stretched out beautifully in the moonlight. White puffy clouds speckled a sky gilded with silver moonbeams and glittering stars. The boy grinned, turning in a direction he judged to be northeast. As he had hoped, the mountain terrain gently sloped downward on the backside, and he vaulted over stones and fallen logs. There were no mounds of dragon dung on this side of the mountain, which suited the boy just fine. The stuff still clung to him and had soaked through his clothes. His skin was clammy, and he smelled worse than anything he had ever smelled before. It was all worth it because he had his treasure and had escaped with his life.

Running, sliding, and scrambling down the back of the mountain, the boy judged he possibly had until early morning when the dragon would return to its lair. Again, justifying his actions, he began to rationally believe that he really had not stolen anything at all and did not expect to be pursued. The dragon would come back with a full belly after hunting all night and then it would curl up in its hair and pine-bough bed and fall into a peaceful sleep. It would never even know that the boy had been there.

As he ran, his heart pounded against the crystal tied tightly to his body. It felt almost as if the crystal pulsed in rhythm with his heartbeat, but the boy could not stop and think about such fanciful things now. He had to keep moving and get as far away as possible. The boots he wore were getting too small and the rocks pierced the worn leather. He stubbed his cramped toes more than once. Cursing under his breath, he promised himself that a new pair of boots was the first thing he would buy. Then he would have a hot meal and, even though he was too young, with as much money as he would get, he would buy a pint of ale! Maybe he would even sleep in a real bed in an Inn. There was a mountain village further north of the dragon cave, and he would sell the items he had *found,* and then he would be set for life. His imagination flew as he walked through the forest and thought about how his dream of all dreams would become a possibility. He would buy a sword! A real sword, with a sheath and maybe even a matching dagger. Slowing to a walk, the boy continued to fantasize about all the things that he would buy, compliments of the dragon's lair.

An hour later, stopping to rest, the boy squatted down next to a tree and fought to keep his eyes open. He heard the snap and pop of branches breaking and he shuddered. Something large was heading toward him in the night. He had just outsmarted a dragon, and whatever was coming at him now would not even be remotely as frightening. The low snuffling grunts of a bear reached the boy's ears, and he froze, hoping the beast would move past.

Sure enough, a huge black bear reared up on its hind legs in front of him, and the boy stood up slowly. Looking around, he quickly realized that either way he ran, the bear would catch him. He was contemplating scurrying up a tree when the breeze picked up and blew past him. The bear sniffed, its black nostrils flaring. It seemed to pause, tasting the scent on the air, then it bellowed as if in revulsion and fear, turned, and ran away as fast as it could.

The boy doubled over and burst out laughing. Sniffing himself and wincing, he realized the bear had smelled the dragon on him, and it had frightened him away. He was elated, doing a little jig, and made a mocking bow toward the running bear. Then he turned and moved on. Smiling widely, he was sure he had gotten away with everything. Though he was disappointed he had not found any real treasure, his plan worked, and he was safe from anything dangerous in the forest because he smelled like a dragon. He continued to chuckle at his cleverness as he walked and imagined the crystal vibrating against his chest in shared joy. Placing a hand on the bag, he patted his treasure with satisfaction. He would have food and wealth beyond his imagination, and best of all, he would get a sword and become the warrior he always dreamed of being.

CHAPTER THREE

M orning began to lighten the sky as the black dragon turned and headed back to her lair. Filled with the joy of the flight, she had foraged deep into the mountains for food and was coming back fed by two elks and a bear. The sky was clear, and a huge full moon was setting in the west as the sun began to rise in the east. She was drowsy after her meal and looked forward to a long rest. The food would keep her satisfied for almost a week. Stopping to swoop over a large mountain lake, she landed in the water. Swimming along for a bit after her meal, she washed the dirt and blood off her snout and shook water droplets out of her long black mane. Sparkling like black diamonds with a myriad of colors glinting off her scales in the fading moonlight, she sighed with contentment. Gulping deeply, she satisfied her thirst with lake water. She tucked her wings along her back and arched her neck, resting her head on her chest. Like a large, black spiked swan, she sedately paddled across the surface of the lake, her back legs pushed her slowly forward.

After a while the dragon lifted, spraying water as she rose into the sky. With a graceful spiral upward her wings spread, and she soared swiftly back home. The sun was lighting the plateau in front of her cave as she landed among the burnt remnants of her roaring spray of fire from the night before. She had been in a fine mood that evening and had allowed the expression of joy to bellow forth in white flames. She felt bad about the burned shrubs, and lowering her snout, she inhaled deeply, red chest expanding, and blew out. Dragon breath misted over the charred landscape as her head oscillated back and forth in a half-circle. As she had the night before with fire, she now did with the mist of magical breath. The charred bushes began to sway with the force of her exhale, and soon the blackened sticks began to wave and stretch, growing emerald buds that sprouted into leaves and wildflowers. Now her cave was wreathed in green life once again, and she nodded her great head in satisfaction after healing the land.

The sun glinted off the two black horns that grew back from her forehead, and she shook her heavy black mane. Then she turned and lumbered a few feet away, opened her mouth and made a huge coughing gurgle. She vomited up the bones of the bear she had eaten. After another heave, the elk came up, and they landed in a heap of broken bones, undigested fur, and stomach acid. The dragon turned, scraped some dirt over the mess, and went into her cave, warmed by the rays of the rising sun. Sleepily, she curled her wings around her body and fell into a peaceful sleep.

The dragon slept for most of the day and woke in the early evening, lazily flexed her wings, and rolled her shoulders in a satisfied stretch. One eye peeled open from the bottom to the top, and then the other, and she gave a great yawn, baring sharp white teeth. Lumbering slowly to the small nest she had built, she settled beside it. Safely buried deep in the long hair she had pulled from her neck was her beautiful egg. The dragon mother shook with gleeful anticipation and gave a deep purr.

Dragon eggs incubate for as long as they felt needed, and she was growing impatient. It had been a hundred years since she had last laid an egg, and it was about time for this one to hatch. She felt the joyful anticipation of motherhood course through her dragon blood. If a dragon could smile, she did at the thought. This egg would mean the continuation of dragon-kind.

She caught the stench of her dung inside the nest and decided to clean the lair after she checked on her egg. Reaching out, she extended one long talon and delicately began to drag it through the mass of hair protecting her egg. Turning her head slightly, looking closely with her large amber eye, she could not seem to find the egg.

Clawing carefully, then a little more frantically, she raked her front claws through the nest but could not find it. In a panic, the dragon mother drew a great breath and blew as hard as she could. The shorn hair of the nest blew up and swirled all around. As it settled, whirling her large body in circles, the dragon mother searched and searched.

It must have hatched when she was away hunting. Tilting her head back, throat rippling, the dragon mother emitted chirps that would call her baby. Afraid for the first time in her long life, her mother's heart thundered wildly. There was no answering chirp, no small dragonling scrambling toward her from the back of the cave with its mouth open like a hungry baby chick. The dragon mother scrambled over the rocks and detritus on the ground looking further into the depths of the cave.

After a long time searching, she roared in fury. Her huge head swung back and forth in denial. She banged her head on the cave walls and bellowed, calling more frantically with each passing minute. Her great chest was heaving as she frantically went from wall to wall, scrambling in the dirt, rock, and remnants of her nest. There was no answer, only the stillness as the echoes of her cries died.

While she was away, had her little hatchling wandered lost throughout the cave? There were no shards, no eggshell left lying around. Quieting, she sent more motherly chirps calling right and left. She searched for the better part of the day before she could no longer deny the bitter truth. The egg was truly gone!

The dragon whirled around and stormed out of the cave. She roared, venomous saliva flinging everywhere and scorching the ground and melting rock. She called and called until her throat was sore. When she stopped, breathing hard and heart pounding within her chest, she leaped into the sky. Maybe the dragon hatchling had left the cave, and she should search for it. Search she did, combing the land with keen amber eyes that could spot a small body flying. She crashed through clouds and sped through the skies, then stopped to hover, looking for the sign of a tiny dragon flying high above the mountainous earth. Her strong wings punished the air currents, and the beauty of her flight was lost on the cold, empty sky. Nothing but terrified birds met her sharp gaze.

Finally, she admitted defeat and returned to the cave after hours of hunting. She had to calm herself and concentrate to try and understand what could have happened to her hatchling. Entering the cave again, she stilled, then dropped her nose to the cave floor. Her large nostrils flared, sniffing along the ground, searching for something out of the ordinary. Moving slowly, she pushed her snout among the rocks and nest debris. All she could smell was the scent of her own dragon dung, her hair, and pine boughs of the nest. Her eye slits narrowed. A thin membrane lifted from her eye and focused. She used her night vision in the dark cave and saw small piles of dried dung tracked into the cave. It made no sense to her at first until she realized the tracks so small, so precise, could be from only one thing.

A human.

She lifted her head once again and spat fire with renewed fury! Her home had been violated by a trespasser.

Following the tracks with her nose, she moved deeper into the cave, directly toward the nest. Delicately lifting a clump of her hair, she tilted her head and studied the edges with intensity. Shorn! The nest hair had been cut! Her dragon egg had been *severed* from the security of the nest and taken. The dragon mother thrashed against the cave walls. Rocks and boulders tumbled down around her. In her rage, she beat her wings and roared, and large dragon tears streamed down her scaly cheeks. When she had spent her ire, she plopped to the cave floor once again. Her sides heaved from the exertions.

It was clear, a human had been there and had stolen her egg! Resting her big head on her front, clawed arms, she began to think and plan how to find the thief. Preparing herself, the dragon mother was determined to do whatever was necessary to reclaim her egg.

After a fitful rest, the terrified dragon mother again sped through the skies, screaming her sorrow. Swooping right and left, she cried out in anguish for hours, calling for her hatchling. In a fear-filled rage, she torched the forest surrounding her mountain while she scoured the land and sky. The scattered forest fires smoldered hot but did not spread too far. Still, nothing could be found of the thief's burnt corpse or her precious egg. Returning to her cave on the side of the tallest mountain, she again searched for a sign or smell of the intruder. Slowly, creeping through the cave, out onto the plateau, combing every inch, she just could not figure out how the wretched thief had gotten up there? How had he hidden from her, and where did he disappear to? Placing her nose on the ground, she followed what she thought were footprints. They were misshapen and faint but were uniformly placed. She delicately put one clawed foot in front of the other and sniffed. There was also a very faint trail of dung that led her to one mound that appeared as if it had been burrowed into. She sniffed around it and then followed another underlying scent leading toward the cliff. Winding around in a haphazard path, she began to understand how the thief had reached her lair. She found a certain tree and was careful not to disturb anything while surveying the site where she guessed the thief had stood waiting for her to go hunting. Her nostrils flared as she sniffed, detecting a faint trail.

Suddenly, she saw it. Her vision homed in on the one thing that would put her on a definite path to finding the foul, thieving human. Dried blood was splattered on a rock in a small, irregular circle. It wasn't much, but it was enough. It had to be. The dragon mother's mouth opened, and her long, thin tongue slithered out. She touched the rock and licked the dried blood clean. Then, for good measure, she swallowed the whole rock. A dragon's memory is long, and she knew she would never forget it. From that small splatter of his blood, she had his essence inside her. It was a part of her now, and she would find him if it was the last thing she ever did.

Continuing her search, she crept toward the cliff face and detected the faintest traces of her quarry's blood and sweat on the rocks. Piecing it together, the dragon mother understood. Whoever it was had made the death-defying climb up the towering escarpment, had stood by the tree waiting for her to leave, dripped blood on the ground from some small wound, and then had fallen into a mound of dung in the dark. The thief then went into her home after she left to feed and stole her precious egg. With a growling cough of disgust, the dragon pounded back to the cave.

The hidden place where she kept her treasure was undisturbed, and she dug into the hard, rocky ground. Making huge gouges in the earth with her sharp claws and throwing dirt everywhere, she uncovered a bag made from the fur of many grizzly bears. It was too large for a human to carry off and was undisturbed, but the dragon mother knew she would trade all the gold she had, every ingot, jewel, and coin, to have her egg back.

Dragon mother crouched over her large treasure, resting her heavy head on the bulk. She began to think. Her skin rippled, taking on the brownish-gray color of the dirt and rocks where she lay, blending in with natural camouflage. Tapping a single long talon on the rocky ground, her mind swirled with an idea. It might take her a while, but she would find the human thief.

She regurgitated the rock and ran it along her teeth with her tongue. The blood scent was on her breath as she swirled the tangy metallic taste around, mixing it with her saliva, absorbing it. The thief's blood was in her, coursing through her veins to combine with her flesh and blood until it was an integral part of her, and she knew it. Clutching the treasure hoard to her chest, she planned, slept, and dreamed of the day she would find the thief!

CHAPTER FOUR

T he boy was staggering with exhaustion, thirst, and hunger. He kept tripping and falling, and it was almost impossible to get back up each time. His precious crystal grew unbearably heavy. Finally, by mid-afternoon, he judged that he was far enough from the dragon's cave so that he could risk a short rest. Looking around, he spotted a rotting log. It was embedded deeply in the dirt and loam of the forest ground. Grabbing a stick, he dug under the crumbling wood and pulled out handfuls of dirt, creating a hole to crawl into. Though he hated small places, he decided it was necessary as sleeping out in the open was a bad idea.

It was awkward to dig and move about, with a crystal almost the size of his torso bound to his chest, but it gave him a strange kind of comfort. He was not about to take it off and set it aside after all he had been through to get it.

Once he was far enough underneath the log, he pulled the loose dirt, leaves, and sticks back in to cover himself up and hide in his new resting place. Head pillowed on his arm and one hand resting lightly on the large crystal where it rested against his body, he shivered with the cold but drifted to unconsciousness almost immediately. The boy slept deeper than usual out of exhaustion but also with a strange sense that he was safe. That was a feeling he had not had in a very long time. He smiled in his sleep and dreamed of glorious battles.

The sun warmed the forest where the boy hid. He was almost comfortable under his log shelter. He was filthy, hungry, thirsty, and lost, but his dreams had been pleasant. Now he woke and peered out into the forest streaked with rays of golden sunlight. Birds chirped in the trees and a squirrel ran up a tree.

Suddenly, a distant roar split the peace of the afternoon. Faint vibrations echoed through the ground coming from the direction of the dragon's mountain. The very air shook. The boy stayed huddled in his hiding place as overhead the dragon streaked across the sky. Roaring, it made a sound almost like a terrified woman screaming. The trees bent with the force of a terrible wind as the huge beast flew right above. Faintly, the smell of fire began to permeate the air as the dragon streamed sulfurous breath over the earth, intent on scorching everything in the vicinity.

Mud flaked from the boy's brow as it wrinkled, wondering what the dragon was all fired up about. He had not taken anything of value from the beast, and besides, it had plenty of hair and teeth. The cave must be loaded with more crystals. So, why was the beast so angry? Perhaps it was because he had trespassed into its territory, and he was found out. The boy remained hidden under the log, wrapped in the dragon's hair, crusted with dried dragon dung, and he began to plan in earnest.

What felt like hours passed before he decided it was safe to leave the hole. It had been a while since he heard the dragon overhead or seen its shadow passing over. His legs and back were cramped, and he was so hungry and thirsty his belly and throat ached painfully. It was a risk leaving, but he needed to move on, and besides, he had to pee very badly.

Crawling from the hole, he shook off the leaves and dirt. He looked like a very dirty, hairy creature. His clothing and face were covered in black, crusty dragon dung, his fingers were caked with dirt and dried blood from his climb and from digging. His hair was matted and stuck out in some places. Leaves, sticks, and even a few bugs crawled on him. Still, he managed to open his worn trousers. With a satisfied sigh of relief, he created a small puddle where he urinated for what felt like several minutes. When he was done and put back to rights, he decided he needed to find water and food.

He stopped and listened until he thought he heard the distant trickle of water. Racing swiftly in the direction he assumed was correct, he came to a stream. He went to his knees and awkwardly bent down over his burdensome treasure and shoved his face into the water. Gulping as much down as he could and as quickly as he could, he quenched his thirst. When he lifted his head the mud and dung were running into his eyes, and he wiped his face with a filthy shirt sleeve. His next move was to find food.

Having been on his own, for what he judged was well over a year now, the boy was forced to become a survivor. In his early years, he had learned to hunt, fish, start a fire, and build shelter. At the ripe age of ten, he was quite proficient at caring for himself out of necessity. In addition to having learned survival skills, the boy became a bit cocky and arrogant, but he was not stupid or careless, *never* careless. That would get you killed.

He made his way along the stream following it downhill to get far away from the dragon's mountain. It had been hours since he heard the beast raging across the sky, and he hoped that was the last he would see of the thing. When he reached a place deeper in the forest where the thick trees blocked the sky overhead, he found a large rock cluster hidden by trees that hung over the stream which suited him well. Gathering dry wood, he quickly started a fire with the flint he always carried. The smoke was feeble and dissipated quickly into the roof of the forest, and so the boy hoped it would not be visible from the air. He needed warmth, food, water, and a bath *very badly.*

Untying the dragon's hair from around him, he lifted the bag from around his neck. He immediately missed the weight of the large crystal on his chest, but he needed to find food. Shoving the bag deeply under the rock, he hid it with strands of the dragon's hair, loose dirt, and small stones. Then he went fishing but only a few steps from his treasure. He sharpened a stick with one of the dragon's teeth, using it like a knife, and waded into the stream. He went as deep as he dared and stood very still, waiting for dinner to swim by.

Soon enough, the boy skewered a large trout and roasted it over his fire. Stomach growling loudly and aching painfully, he busied himself. While the fish cooked, in his clothes, boots, and all, he went back into the stream and immersed himself entirely. The black and brown dragon dung washed off with the current and drifted downstream. The boy had never truly been happy when he was dirty, and it felt good to be clean again, but his clothes were wet, and he was freezing, so he returned to his little fire and warmed himself as best he could. Taking off his boots, he held his blistered feet to the fire and let the warmth fill him. Eating the fish, he pulled out tiny bones from among the white flesh, finishing every bit but the hard head, bony spine, and charred skin.

He avoided looking at his treasure until he could no longer stand it and felt a craving to see the beauty of the crystal once again. It was evening now, and by the light of the fire, he dragged the bag forward and tugged the crystal out.

The milky white stone glittered with deep iridescent colors and multiple sharp facets. The boy marveled at its beauty. He had once seen a moonstone the size of a chicken egg, but this was something else. It was almost as big as his entire torso but was not nearly as heavy as it should be for a crystal of this size. Still, it looked like a priceless gem, and he decided it would bring him untold riches and make his dreams come true. Preening with self-satisfaction, he held the big crystal up to the firelight and peered into its depths to see if he could see through it.

What he saw, though, was not the veins and facets of a precious stone, but the round outline of a coiled *creature* inside.

The boy stared in shock at what looked like tiny, folded wings and a tail. Disbelieving, he stared for a long time until suddenly the thing inside *moved!* Its tiny head snapped up almost like the thing inside was looking at him with its eye pressed against the inside wall. The boy gasped and cried out. Dropping the crystal to the hard ground, it cracked loudly as he scrambled back and stared at the thing lying on its side. He was horrified! Long shards had broken off when it fell, and underneath the crystal was revealed as a smooth, round egg. He had stolen a dragon's egg!

It rolled a little toward the fire, and now the heat of the flames warmed it. The tiny dragon inside began to thrash, and then a crack in the eggshell widened and grew. Violently, it began to move inside, pecking and rocking the egg. The boy's eyes grew wide as he watched in shocked horror as a tiny dragon's head began to push out of the thick crystalline shell.

The hatchling pushed, struggling to force its way out of the thick shell. It plunked onto the dirty ground, thin and depleted. Dirt clung to its freshly hatched skin as it stretched its neck and flapped tiny, depleted wings. Like a butterfly just hatched from a cocoon, it fluttered, pulsing fluid into its wings until they filled and grew, taking shape. It peeped, looking around until it spotted the boy. With its first stumbling steps, it hopped toward him on translucent feet, tiny claws scrambling in the dirt, scattering shell remnants in a panicked rush to reach him.

The boy tried to scoot away, but the rock face was behind him, and he had nowhere to go. The dragon baby was now about the size of a kitten, and it jumped onto the boy's lap, sniffed him, and cooed like a dove. Then the little dragon nuzzled its head against his chest, snuggling as if it were looking for warmth or comfort.

In complete shock, the boy sat frozen with no idea what to do, holding his arms away from the dragon baby for fear of touching it. Finally, he relaxed and reached out to steady the little creature curled in his lap. He slowly slid toward the fire where they could gather warmth, and he looked closely at the thing. It was white like the egg, with almost a moonstone translucence to its tiny scales. Its small wings were practically transparent with blue and violet veins streaking through fine membranes. Atop its head and down its spine, the little dragon had a pale blue scruff of bristly hair down its spine. Its belly had a purplish hue to it, and the boy ran one finger down its back, delicately stroking. The dragon began to make a sound like a purring kitten, and the boy gasped but kept petting it.

"I have a pet dragon!" He whispered reverently and sat in stunned shock as the little dragon lifted its head and looked up at him with large emerald eyes. Then, the boy looked up to the skies with unfocused vision and began to swear under his breath, spouting words a man much older than himself would use. Realization hit him hard that he had just stolen the *last dragon's egg* from its mother, and now he had her *baby* sitting in his lap!

As the momentousness of what he had done struck him like a lightning bolt, the boy tilted his head back and cursed loudly.

"Damn it! I stole a dragon's egg! Damn! Damn! *Damn!* No wonder she's so angry!" Then he repeated a stream of fouler words he had once heard a man in a tavern use.

The tiny dragon's head struck out and bit his thumb drawing blood.

"Ouch!" he yelped. "Either you're hungry or you don't like swearing." The boy mumbled as droplets of blood formed on his thumb. The baby dragon eagerly licked at the spot until there was no more blood oozing out. He shivered with strange feelings swimming through him and then they both settled.

After a few moments, he carefully leaned forward. The boy picked up the fish skin, tore a small piece off, and tried to feed it to the baby dragon. It seemed to like it and when all the fish skin was eaten, it curled up, closed its eyes, and went to sleep nestled against the boy's chest.

The boy scooted back against the rock, went very still so he did not disturb the baby, and began to think about what the heck he was going to do now.

CHAPTER FIVE

T he boy fell asleep with the dragon baby curled against his chest. He kept it warm, and it gave him fanciful dreams. Dreams of riches and swords, fighting in wars, of glory and fame, and of riding on the back of a huge white dragon with amethyst wings. Her scales glistened iridescent in the sun's rays, and on her back, he sat like a tall, strong warrior, unbeatable and noble.

In the morning, blurry-eyed and clumsy, he reached for the dragon baby but found it was gone and startled awake! Scrambling to his feet, he looked around frantically. The fire was smoking feebly, and all that he found were the shattered remnants of the dragon's egg. He vaulted over the ring of stones where the fire flickered and looked up and down the stream for a sign of the baby.

Breathing hard and panicked, he did not see it upstream, but downstream, he thought he saw something very strange. It was hard to see, but the baby dragon's shape was there. It had turned muddy green overnight. Its feet were the gray of the stone it was standing on. It held still, wings spread, balancing, as it darted its mouth into the water and came up with a wriggling fish. Tilting its head back, the dragon baby ate the fish in a few gulps. When it saw the boy, it chirruped happily and then plunged in again. It brought up another, larger fish and then flew back to where the boy was standing and proudly dropped the catch onto his feet. The boy stared in astonishment. When the dragon hit the muddy brown dirt, it flushed rich brown, its emerald eyes stared at the boy with obvious pride in its fishing abilities. It burped and regurgitated fish bones, then looked up once again as its tail lashed happily.

Overnight, the dragon had grown from the size of a kitten to the size of a large hawk. It seemed very pleased with itself and crooned, making a purring sound almost like it was speaking to the boy. As the boy picked the fish up, he patted the dragon on the head and praised it. Turning his back on the dragon, he went to collect wood for the fire.

Turning moonstone white again, the dragon gave a little peep and leaped onto the boy's back, scrambling up. Its sharp claws dug in as it wrapped its thin tail around his neck. It appeared as if it did not want to be separated from him, so the boy went along gathering firewood with a baby dragon on his shoulder.

As he prepared his meager breakfast, he crouched down and began to think about his next move. The dragon flew to a nearby rock and watched him intently. It sat regally, moonstone white and almost glowing in the slim rays of the sun. The little wings pulsed and with every stretch and strain its scales glistened. Its head dipped and followed the boy's movements, jerking back when he pointed a finger at the dragon baby.

"I didn't plan on you." He spoke aloud, frowning. "I suppose I'd better take you back to your mother."

The dragon baby instantly turned fiery red, crouched down, and growled, tossing its head back and forth as if responding angrily to what the boy said!

"Do you understand me?" The boy squeaked in astonishment.

The dragon bobbed its head once, prancing on its rock, or at least the boy thought it did. It was still as red as hot coal.

"Look," he said, "I never meant to steal a *baby*. I was only looking for treasure. Your egg looked like a big crystal which is what I thought it was. I got nothing, and I need a lot more to survive. I wanted treasure! I can't sell *you* and seeing how your mother is searching the skies for you and torching the place for miles, I *must* take you back."

The dragon continued to growl, crouching as if it was about to leap, and scratched its claws across the rock. The boy sat back and frowned deeper.

"What? You don't want to go back? To your mother? She's looking for you! *She's your mother!*"

The little dragon sat up and turned moonstone white again. Its long nose bobbed side to side as if saying *'no'*, then turned upward as if refusing to look at him while it slowly faded to a stubborn yellow and flicked its tail.

"I *have* to take you back! I can't keep you. There aren't many dragons left. It was a mistake taking you in the first place! I didn't mean to!" He cried out angrily, "I don't know how to take care of a baby!"

The dragon blinked at him with slanted eyes large and staring. Spreading its mouth open and showing him tiny teeth while hissing menacingly.

The boy chewed on his bottom lip, thinking hard while the dragon baby waited with its tail lashing back and forth. Finally, he seemed to reach a decision.

"Well, I have heard dragons eat their young. Maybe I did a good thing saving you from her?" The boy shrugged, trying to sound convincing, then his voice turned ominous. "Maybe you were her next meal?"

The dragon purred and crooned almost happily while its scales returned to iridescent white.

"Maybe you're an orphan like me?"

As quick as lightning, the dragon darted forward and bit him on the hand.

"Ouch! Hey, what was that for? All I said was that I was an orphan."

It bit him again, drawing a spot of red. Sucking the blood from his hand, the boy stared with wide eyes at the dragon and finally confessed.

"Alright, so I'm not an orphan. I am not afraid to admit it! I ran away! You would have too if you'd have seen where I came from. I was the youngest of eight children!" He emphasized louder. *"Eight children!*

"Every day, I rose at dawn with my Da and worked until sunset! There was never enough to eat, I slept in a small bed with three smelly brothers who used to kick me all night. My oldest sister was fond of smacking me on the head whenever I walked by, and my Ma was always too tired to pay much attention to me, except to yell at me to do chores or get out of the way. The future there held nothing for me but hard work on the farm until my arms and legs fell off, and then I'd die young."

He stabbed a thumb in his chest and puffed up.

"I'm meant for better things. So, I left to seek my fortune elsewhere. I don't believe they even noticed I was gone, except that there was one less mouth to feed. You might say I did them a favor. I'm better off on my own, and they are better off without me!"

With a pout on his lips, the boy sat back, going silent. He took a thin green branch, broke it in half, and scrubbed absently at his teeth with the rough end. The dragon seemed to ripple with pleasure that the boy had confided his story or was finally telling the truth. It peeped and nodded, so the boy continued to talk after a while.

"Maybe, *if* you're going to stay with me, I should name you? Are you a boy dragon or a girl dragon? A boy, I hope, I don't have no use for girls." He wrinkled his nose in distaste.

The dragon sat up and seemed to puff its chest out, then turned its head away as if insulted. The blueish tuft of hair on its head stood up bristling, and the boy suddenly knew with unspoken clarity. It *was* a girl!

"Oh, *damn* it all! Don't tell me you're a *girl* dragon!" The boy jumped to his feet, waving his arms.

Spreading its wings, the dragon streaked toward him and buffeted the boy with *her* wings, pecking sharply at his head. He ducked, covering his face with his arms as the small dragon wings beat him until he finally shouted.

"Alright! Alright! So, you're a girl dragon. I get it!"

The dragon backed off and flew a short distance to her rock perch. She began to preen and, with a long pink tongue, groomed one of her sharp claws just like a cat and then she began to purr loudly.

"Suppose I'll have to give you a girl's name." He said begrudgingly, "I don't know many girl names except for my sister's and my Ma's. Don't suppose you have one in mind?" The dragon continued to groom herself, giving a curt nod.

"My name is Kieran if you're interested, and I'll call you...Sharp Claw!" He grinned triumphantly, jumping to his feet again and dancing in a circle while stomping and shouting. "Swift Wing! Dagger Tooth! Death Flyer!"

The dragon turned a deeper red with each suggested name and shook her head as if rejecting all the boy's choices. Kieran finally sat down and stared for a long time at the dragon.

"Well, my Ma's name was Moyra. I am not calling you that!" He sat back against a rock and considered what to do in silence.

The dragon watched while slowly blinking her large emerald eyes. He held her gaze and couldn't seem to look away. As they stared at each other, Kieran grew lightheaded, and the dragon seemed to waver blurrily before him. Eyes drooping, her color fluctuated in misty vision and then went back to moonstone white, seeming to glimmer. In the shadows of the trees, she glowed brightly, and suddenly, Kieran heard a small whisper inside his head.

"Uuuuunnnnnaaaaaa," he exhaled the word as if it were a sudden, bright discovery. "Your name is Una!" Kieran seemed to come out of a trance, and he put a hand to his head, blinking away the fog.

"Hey! How did you do that? Put that name in my head?"

Una the dragon hopped into his lap and nuzzled the warm side of his neck with her head. She rubbed her body against him like a happy, energetic puppy, licking his face, chirping and purring.

Kieran and his dragon, Una, became inseparable friends.

CHAPTER SIX

The mother dragon woke from a deep slumber brought on by her sorrow. She had been exhausted after her rage across the sky and had not eaten since the last hunt. Upon waking, she remembered that her egg had been stolen, and grief hit her anew like a buffeting storm. A thief had crept into her sanctuary while she was away and had made off with her young. Retracing the steps the thief had taken to violate her home, she crept out of the cave and carefully walked back toward the cliff. She found his scent again, though it had faded since that fateful day, but she did not worry about that. Pointing her nose over the edge of the cliff, she sniffed and found the tiniest spots of blood from some kind of wound, but it was his. She slithered over the side. Heading downward, her long talons digging into the rocks and causing a slight rockslide, she licked each dried blood spot clean and followed the trail. Her claws dug deep into the face of the cliff as she scrambled downward until finally, she reached the ground. She felt a moment of triumph as she pictured him standing at the bottom of the ravine where the towering cliff disappeared high into the clouds. For a moment, she also felt a bit of respect for her thief. It took a great deal of strength and courage to climb that steep escarpment and then to go down again. The dragon mother could not see any marks from ropes. Perhaps when he made his escape, he took them, so he did not leave any trace of his having been there.

Turning toward the deep forest, the dragon mother sniffed the forest floor of dirt, leaves, pine needles, and loam. She tracked like a wolf on the hunt for prey. His faded scent was gone. She searched for hours, heading in different directions, looking for his footprints or a sign of his passing, but found nothing more.

Dragon mother wanted to rage and spit white dragon fire at everything in her path, but she knew that would not do any good, and the forest should not suffer further for his crime and her fury. So, she silently lifted off the ground and flew back to her cave. Swooping in, she landed next to her large bag of treasure and flopped down on her belly in defeat. Turning charcoal grey she blended in with the shadows and contemplated what to do.

Laying another egg was *not* a possibility. It meant finding the male dragon again and mating. Dragons had been hunted almost to extinction. It had taken years for her to find the last one and she was the last remaining dragon in this land that she knew. The father of her dragonling had been a magnificent, pure white dragon with golden horns and deep emerald eyes. They spent a few months together, mating and assuring the dragon mother had conceived. He was an ancient dragon and the knowledge and magic he possessed would be passed to their youngling. It had been a privilege to mate with an elder dragon of his stature, but his whereabouts now were a mystery.

Mating had been a desperate attempt at survival of their race as dragons were disappearing from the face of the world. Once she had laid her egg, the white dragon rose into the cloudy sky one day and disappeared, heading west. Such was the fickleness of male dragons that they did not stay around but left, which contributed to the slow demise of dragon-kind. She wasn't sure she would find him again. For all she knew he'd flown to other lands in search of other female dragons or, he flew away to die. To her shame, how could she explain that she managed to lose the egg to a common thief?

Snorting, the dragon mother blew a puff of white fire from her nostrils and tapped a sharp talon on the cave floor. Her mind whirled with thoughts about how to go about finding the thief. A heavy lethargy took over her consciousness, and memories surfaced of ancient days and forgotten magic. She had a waking dream of walking on human feet and a memory of once living among humans, a creature of legend and mystery.

From the taste of the thief's blood and the scent of his sweat on the cliff face, she could tell he was young, but not exactly how young. He must have been strong to make the climb up the escarpment. Her next thought was about how vast the world was, stretching beyond her lair. She would have to search north, south, east, and west, but she was determined to do it, no matter how long it took. How hard could it be to find a man with a dragon egg? If she knew anything about humans, it was that they boasted of their exploits. The young man might even try to sell the egg and gain fame and wealth with her precious egg. The dragon mother blinked with irritation, or was it tears?

One thing dragons were was patient beyond human under-standing, and the dragon mother knew she would prevail in the end with patience and perseverance. She had not lived this long by being rash and careless. Slowly, she sat up as the ancient memories tickled at the edge of her mind and a plan formed. Old magic stirred and awakened in her, and she recalled how it must be done. It had been hundreds of years since she called upon this forgotten magic, but she knew she could do it again. It would take her a while to put everything in place, but she would make the humans help and was certain she would find what she needed to begin the search.

Night had fallen, and rising from her nest on the floor of her cave, she shook her great mane of midnight hair and flexed her wings. Moving toward the cave entrance, she turned to look back one last time and surveyed her home. Before she went out into the waning moonlight, she gave a few mournful chirps as if calling one last time for the youngling, but there was no answer on the gentle breeze.

Angry fire filled her chest. Stomping to the edge of the cliff, the dragon mother reared back on her hind legs standing huge and magnificent. Stretching her beautiful ruby wings, arching her neck with the bright moon behind, she roared. Her sorrow and heartsickness echoed across the mountain range as her cries rose into the night sky. The dragon mother roared and moaned, spit white fire into the clouds and shook the air with her pain and loss until she crumbled exhausted to the cliff edge. Waiting for morning, she slept.

She dreamt and recalled an old bit of dragon lore that foretold the power to be gained by eating a great foe's heart. When she found this young thief, her greatest enemy, his strength and courage would be hers. She would rip his heart from his chest and swallow it whole, still beating. Thus, taken into her body, he would never escape her wrath. In the legends, there was even a mention of youth and revitalization to be gained, but that was hard to decipher. With the magic gained from this great thief, she could take her vengeance upon the whole race of men! She could picture resurrecting the entire race of dragon-kind. Best of all, the soul contained in his heart, would be hers to torment for eternity. There was much at stake here and the continuation of dragon-kind was of the utmost importance.

The dragon mother vowed she would not stop until the thief's broken body was clutched within her claws and his heart rested within her belly. The desire for what was needed thrilled her to the bone as the magic and knowledge rose to the surface of her mind, coursed through her veins and rippled like lightning across her scales. Waking at dawn, turning her sight to the future, she lifted off the cliff and headed west. The hunt for the thief began.

CHAPTER SEVEN

K ieran and his dragon Una sat by the fire that night and heard the distant cries of the mother dragon. He shook with terror over what he had done and thought again that maybe he should return Una to her mother. He tried to talk Una into going back, but she pecked him on the hand and arms until she drew blood. Then she flew off, always ahead of him, out of reach, dodging his hands and avoiding any attempt to grab her. Finally, he grew exhausted and stopped talking about it and stopped chasing her. He decided he would take good care of the dragon baby as a way of making amends and that would just have to be enough. He had to live with the consequences of what he had done.

Besides, he thought dragons were lone creatures who surely would not have any care what happened to their young, or she would just eat her. So, Kieran convinced himself that he had done right in not taking Una back to the mother dragon. He completely ignored the fact that he did not truly want to. At the end of his contemplation, he decided what was done was done, and they would just have to make the best of it. In the meantime, he would run away as far as possible.

Una was endlessly hungry, and she ate many fish, and bugs she caught, then moved on to small rodents, and eventually rabbits. Her hunting skills were miraculous, and Kieran wondered just how she knew what to do. For the most part, he sat back and let Una bring him his meals as she was the better hunter.

Days later, they had still not moved on and Kieran felt it was time as he was well-fed and restless. He had to think and form a plan that set him on the path to making his dreams come true. Shining swords, victorious battles, and gold rewards were his future, and it was time he set out on that journey.

Una sat next to him, grooming her wings and short fur, like a bird would preen its feathers. Kieran could sit still for hours thinking and making decisions. Now, as he watched the little dragon, those dreams of glory danced closer in his imagination.

On the ground, the shards of the dragon egg glistened in the firelight and caught Kieran's eye. He realized they might be worth something, and began to carefully gather the crystals and pieces of eggshell. Holding them up to the dying light, he looked at the moonstone shards and grinned. He had his treasure after all and decided that selling the pieces was the best idea. A village would be a great place to sell the shards and make him some money. Then he would get new boots and new clothes and eat pie until he burst. Best of all, he would buy a sword and become a mighty warrior! Fame and fortune were within his grasp.

The next thing Kieran thought about was the long strands of the mother dragon's hair he had shorn from the nest. He spent the following day carefully laying them out in long, neat lengths and untangling them. Una kept trying to snuggle in the rows he laid out, and it became a game to keep her from messing up his hard work. Finally, Kieran had to swear at her to get her to stop. Una pecked at him like she always did when she disapproved of what he said or did, and then she flew off to hunt.

Kieran laid the strands out and began to weave them together into a long, continuous braid. After many hours of work and cramping hands, Kieran had a good length of thick black rope. It turned out to be very sturdy and was even a bit stretchy. Kieran smiled with pleasure at his handiwork and cleverness.

The mother dragon had been quiet for days while Kieran hid in the dense forest with Una. Once or twice, he again started to head back to the dragon cave to return the baby dragon, but Una flew off in the opposite direction, and he could not catch her or convince her to go back.

He finally gave up trying and decided it was time to move on. With Una perched on his shoulder, he packed his few possessions and headed downstream toward the nearest village. It had taken a lot of time trying to recall what he knew about the Kingdom of Lyndesea, the land where he was born. Kieran decided that a village that was large enough to have a swordsmith would best suit his needs. He also needed to get far, far away from the mother dragon's mountain. Now that Una was helping him hunt, his belly was full enough of meat and fish, and wild berries satisfied his sweet tooth, but he longed for cheese, bread, freshly churned butter, pie, and would even try an ale!

There was, he vaguely recalled, a village called Appleaid many miles north of where he was hiding. While he feared he was still too close to the dragon's cave, he had to risk going there to sell his crystal shards and buy new boots and clothing. Thoughts of the sword he would buy kept his imaginative mind occupied for the hours he trudged through the forest.

Kieran kept up a string of conversation with the dragon on his shoulder. After so much time alone, it was nice to have someone to talk to. Una seemed to listen to his stories, pecked him when he cursed or lied, otherwise, they got along companionably. During the nights when they rested, Kieran discussed his plans with Una and talked to her as if she were answering back, as she flushed between moonstone white and pale lavender. Her scales often rippled with iridescent colors and flashes of violet, blue, and green. Kieran loved to watch her change and began to think that he could sense her moods by the colors she displayed. When defiant, she changed and blended in with her surroundings until she was almost invisible. When angry, she was fire-red. Nights on his own were no longer lonely now that he had Una, and he loved her more each day. Their bond grew and his imagination called it magical.

CHAPTER EIGHT

T he Village of Appleaid was nestled at the edge of the Ten Thousand Mile Forest and was much further away than Kieran first thought. Traveling steadily northeast, it took him many weeks to finally reach it. What he had initially judged was ten miles turned out to be more like fifty or sixty and felt like hundreds. Kieran finally had to admit that he had no idea how far he had traveled, he just knew it was far away in the opposite direction of the dragon's cave.

Appleaid inhabited a long mountain valley by the shores of a calm inlet that led to the ocean. A massive river ran through the village and numerous sturdy bridges were built across it connecting the many houses, shops, and buildings where the inhabitants lived in abundance. Groves of mountain apple trees grew tall on rolling hills and were heavily laden with fruit in long carefully planted rows. Apples were only one of the things the town was known for. Shaggy mountain cattle grazed on nearby farms along with sheep, goats, and horses. The rich fertile soil in the valley supported acres of wheat, corn, and other vegetables. There was also a thriving fishing trade though it was secondary to the produce of the land. Best of all, the Village of Appleaid had a blacksmith who was well known for his skills.

It was approaching sunset as Kieran crouched next to an apple tree high on the mountain slopes above Appleaid. He munched on a fallen apple thinking hard. Holding it out, Una took a delicate bite off the juicy fruit, and then Kieran took it back for another bite. As they shared multiple apples, he watched the village below and carefully considered their next move. The warm golden glow in the windows of the homes and the distant call of voices caused a lonely uncomfortable feeling in his chest. Wisps of smoke rose from the chimneys of the houses and each building. Watching the families, Kieran had to concentrate on something else rather than a secret longing he would not admit he felt.

"You're the problem." Kieran muttered, not unkindly to Una, but without taking his eyes off the village.

Una ducked her head in shame and made a soft crooning noise as if apologizing.

"What am I supposed to do with you while I go down there to get my sword, huh? I can't just walk into the village with a dragon following me."

Una had grown considerably over the last few weeks and now was as big as Kieran. The span of her translucent wings was almost twice the length of his body. Kieran was silent and continued to think. Una leaned forward and plucked the rest of the apple from his hand, tilted her head back, and gulped it down in a snap of her jaws.

"I have to get new boots. My toes are sticking out of these. My pants are too small and tight. I have to take the crystals into the village and sell them. But I can't leave you Una, you're just a baby. Who will take care of you? What if someone finds you and takes you from me, eh? Or what if they hurt you or worse, kill you!"

Una turned as black as a burnt coal and hopped in front of Kieran showing her fangs. This was her menacing look and Kieran smirked at her.

"You wouldn't let anybody catch you or hurt you, would you? You'd be too fast! You'd fly off and then you'd find me wherever I was, wouldn't you?"

Kieran gave her a vulnerable look as if he couldn't stand the thought of losing his best friend, the dragon. Reaching out he patted her on the head and ran his fingers through the short, mane that rippled along her neck. Una nuzzled his hand and turned white again. Her mane was growing longer, and it glistened a beautiful lavender.

"Una, I have to go down to the village in the morning." He spoke gently and pleadingly, "I can't take you. I'll hide you somewhere and after I've gotten some supplies, I'll come back for you. You'll stay where I tell you to, won't you?"

Una stared at him with glowing green eyes. That dizzy feeling he sometimes got when holding her gaze, hit him as if she were imparting her will to him. Then she spread her wings and sprang into the air. She alighted high upon a sturdy tree branch above him. Suddenly, she shimmered, and her color changed, and she disappeared to greens, browns, and grays, disguised in the shadows of the apple tree. Kieran could still make out the outline of her, but otherwise, she blended in completely with the leaves and branches.

If he closed his eyes, he thought he could sense her. Una showed him how she could hide, and he felt a little better but feared it was not enough.

"I understand Una, you can blend in really good with your surroundings, but I can't risk someone seeing you. If I must, I'll tie you up somewhere safe, but I can't take you with me into the village."

Una's scales burned red in anger, and she flew straight at Kieran. She began to flap her wings and snap at him. Kieran ducked and covered his head with his arms shouting for her to stop. After she batted him for a few minutes she finally flew back up to the tree branches. Staying angry red, she turned her back to him, with her long tail lashing back and forth.

"You squawk like a chicken and you're making too much noise!" Una ignored him. "My mum always said, *'Pouting will get you nowhere.'* You'll have to do as I say because I'm the man and what I decide is the law! I can't risk you getting seen or captured or killed, so you'll hide up here as I said. I'll go into the village, sell one of the crystals, and get what I need. Then I'll come back for you. I promise!"

The two sat in stubborn silence for a while. Kieran leaned against the tree and crossed his arms over his chest, angry at Una's continued defiance. Darkness was falling and staring back down at the warm homes below, for the first time in a very long time, he badly wished he had a roof over his head and a bed to sleep in.

Una's angry red faded into gray and then black as night came and soon both were in the dark. Kieran didn't risk a fire, so he tucked his hands under his armpits, wound the long rope of the dragon mother's hair around him, and drifted to sleep.

When Kieran woke up the next morning and feasted on a few apples picked up off the ground. He tried hard not to notice that Una was nowhere in sight and had to give up on his idea of tying her up. Bundling his few possessions and waiting until he saw some early morning activity beginning in the village below, he readied himself to head down.

"Una?" he spoke to the quiet air. He felt a puff of warm dragon's breath on the back of his neck, and he whirled around sensing she was just behind him, but he could not see her. "Fine, don't say goodbye. Stay here and I'll be back soon. If I get enough gold for my crystal and you're really good, I'll bring you a treat to eat."

Kieran stared through the depths of the apple tree grove and looked around trying to spot his tempestuous dragon. Failing to find her, he turned back in the direction of the village and started to walk down the mountain. A gust of wind buffeted him as Una took off and flew over his head. He could make out a flicker in the air as she coasted above him. Then he began to swear under his breath, knowing that she hated it when he cursed. He walked purposefully down the hill, his toes stubbing on rocks and twigs poked at him as they worked into the holes in his boots. Staring upward, he realized exactly what Una was doing. She was following him down to the village, albeit high enough in the clouds so she couldn't be seen. He was still afraid she would be spotted. He thought he could sense exactly where she flew, but she was completely invisible to the eye in pale blue and white, so no one in the village should be able to see her either.

"Dragon magic." Kieran muttered and shook his head.

As he came out of the trees, he found a worn footpath and followed it into the village. Covertly, he cast a watchful eye into the clouds where he *felt* Una above, still invisible, circling among the clouds overhead. Determined to sell his treasure, buy his supplies, and get out of there, Kieran set his sights on finding the blacksmith.

Entering the village, he was immediately assaulted by several delicious smells, sounds, and sights. The distant roar of a large river was oddly comforting. It had been months since he set eyes on another living being that wasn't a dragon, and seeing the people beginning their day almost brought tears to his eyes. He felt more alone than he ever had since running away from home. Unconsciously, he sent out a thought to Una, searching for her with his mind so that he could feel the comfort of her presence return to him like a distant beacon. He pictured her coasting in the upper air currents watching him with keen sharp vision better than a hawk.

A lone boy walking through the village did not even cause a raised eyebrow. Women dumped the night's chamber pots in between the buildings. Other boys or girls carried buckets of water and slop to feed animals. A couple of men rode horses to whatever destination they had in mind. A shopkeeper threw open some doors and smiled at the bright crisp morning. Chickens chased each other across the street and in the distance a dog began barking. In a pig pen behind one building, a man poured food scraps into a trough, and squealing piglets wrestled each other to get at their breakfast.

Wood smoke coiled through the air as the cold hearths were brought to life and the morning mist rose into the air, disappearing as the sun began to warm the day. Kieran stopped between two buildings, looking up and down the street trying to figure out where to go first. He discovered he had entered the village at the end nearest to where the river followed the shore and emptied into the great loch. At the end of town, a couple streets from where the edge of the forest met the river, along a winding road and across a bridge, there was a wooden sign painted with a symbol for the blacksmith. Visions of hot metal glowing red with fire, beaten into the shape of a hero's sword, ignited Kieran's imagination. He went straight to it drawn by visions of racks of silvery swords just waiting for him to choose one for his own and set him on the path to his destiny.

CHAPTER NINE

W hen Kieran reached the blacksmith's homestead, he saw a large building on one side where a forge smoked as the fire matured. Three horses walked lazily around a nearby corral. A small house by the forge had two stories to it, flowers swayed in window boxes and windchimes made a slow rich *"bong"* as the morning breeze gently blew them to-and-fro. Next to the forge was a large barn with huge open doors on the second floor and two lower doors that were closed. Another large corral held two more horses who dozed lazily in the morning sun. Their tails flicked slowly at a fly or two and occasionally they stamped a hoof. Chickens were loose in the yard and a goat or two lazily grazed on tufts of grass.

The smell of frying bacon and baking bread made Kieran dizzy with hunger. Though he had snacked on apples for his breakfast, he was still famished. There was a tall oak tree by the road entering the forge and Kieran set his back to it and waited for his nausea to pass. He watched for anyone moving around in the house or the barn, but it seemed no one was out this early. The forge fire smoked lazily causing a smoky mist. He waited, anticipating the beautiful sword he would buy.

Sliding down into what he called his thinking position, Kieran crouched, and the worn cloth of his trousers ripped exposing his bony kneecap underneath. Swearing, he watched as the air above the barn rippled, and he knew Una was perched on the edge of the roof. Seeing her invisible outline with wings spread and tail flicking, he shook his head. The horses began to neigh and bolted to the farthest end of the corral by the fence, rearing and snorting with nervousness, and kicking out. Kieran guessed it was because they could smell the dragon who had a definite scent to her.

Suddenly, the front door of the house opened, and a huge man stepped out pulling suspenders up over his shoulders and looking around. He walked toward the corral, searching for what had spooked the horses but could not see Una perched upon the top of the barn.

A plump young woman with a baby perched on her hip came out of the house as well and watched as the big man stood looking for signs of trouble. Moments later he disappeared into the barn and came out with a pitchfork full of hay. Throwing it into a feed trough for the horses, he whistled and spoke gently to them until they calmed. Walking back to the house he said something to the woman, kissed her on the cheek, ruffled the fuzzy head of the baby, and turned back toward the forge building.

That is when the man spotted Kieran crouched next to the tree. He stopped and the two stared at each other for a full minute before the man walked across the yard to Kieran.

"Is it you spookin them horses?" The man crossed his arms over his broad chest and frowned down at Kieran. "Ain't tryin to steal one, are ya?"

Kieran slowly stood and tilted his head up to look the man in the eyes.

The man took a big sniff and wrinkled his nose.

"Boy, you stink! It must have been your foul stench that upset the horses. When was the last time you had a proper bath?" He looked the boy up and down, taking in his ripped, dirty clothing, dirty face and messy hair, waving his hand in front of his face.

Kieran frowned and looked at the man head to toe then mimicked his stance. He was tall, had broad, massive shoulders and thick, muscular arms, probably from wielding a hammer and making swords. He was completely bald but looked as if the hair on his head slid down and took root on his chin. His black beard was almost down to his chest and had two small silver clasps holding the ends together.

"Cat got your tongue, boy? Or you too afraid of me to talk?" the man grumbled.

"I am not afraid of anything." Straightening his shoulders, Kieran sneered and then went on, realizing he had to be polite to the man he intended on buying a sword from. "I just took a bath in a river three weeks ago."

"Hmm," The big man scratched his chin and continued to look Kieran over. "Well, it is time you find another river, dive in clothes and all, though it looks like the dirt is the only thing keeping them rags held together. Where're your folks boy?"

"Look, Sir, I didn't come here to exchange polite talk, I came here to buy a sword. If you're the Blacksmith of Appleaid then I would like to conduct some business with you, if you're not him, please direct me to the man I am seeking." Kieran puffed his chest out and nodded business like.

The big man threw his head back and laughed loudly. It was a rumbly guffaw from deep in his chest and Kieran liked the sound but remained serious because the man was clearly laughing at him. Kieran crossed his arms over his chest, stared stubbornly at the man and frowned, letting him know he was completely serious. Finally, the man stopped laughing.

"You want to buy a sword from me, do ya?" Before Kieran could answer, the man bent a little at the waist placing his hands on his knees, and now that he was at eye level with Kieran, he looked into the man's warm brown eyes and saw concern there along with humor.

"I'll tell you what, I've been up since dawn working. The ghastly smell of you spooked my horses and interrupted my breakfast. You look like you could do with a little food yourself. How about you come to the house with me and while I finish my breakfast, you can have a bite and we'll talk about what brings you to my forge, eh?"

Kieran couldn't help it, his mouth began to water, and he swallowed a loud stomach growl. He swayed a little on his feet and the man reached out his large hand to steady him.

"Come on boy, before you drop dead of hunger."

With a firm hand on his shoulder, the man led Kieran toward the house, and he had no choice but to go. The savory smells coming through the windows made Kieran want to cry but he bit his bottom lip until the pain stopped the tears. A long log stripped of its bark and worn smooth by the weather, and many people's bottoms, was outside the house for a seat. The big man pushed Kieran down to sit on the log, and he went inside. Kieran's stomach growled and his vision began to swim a little. Very quickly the man came out with a bowl and horn cup. He sat next to Kieran and handed him a hunk of bread slathered with warm butter and strawberry jam.

Experience taught Kieran that he should not gobble his food hastily when he had gone so long without proper nourishment and so he ate the bread slowly. Closing his eyes, he savored the warm flavor and the buttery goodness. The jam was sweet and most likely the best thing he had ever eaten. The man beside him held a full plate and after Kieran ate the bread, offered him a sausage. This Kieran did stuff greedily into his mouth while grease ran down his chin. The hot meat made his mouth water, and he finished it in two bites, chewing rather loudly. Next, the man handed Kieran the cup and he gulped cool, fresh milk. Kieran's shrunken stomach could not hold anything more, though he looked longingly at the eggs and another sausage left on the plate. Swallowing the last of his milk he sighed with the relief of having a full stomach.

"What's your name, boy?" The man asked in a calm, soothing voice meant to ease Kieran's fears.

"Thank you for the food, Sir. I do appreciate it. I haven't had bread since..." Kieran's voice trailed away as he strained his memory.

"There's more where that came from. Tell you what, I'll start. My name is Tartan MacLaren. I'm the Blacksmith of Appleaid and this is my home and forge. That lovely lady peeking out the window at you is my wife, Sara. We have a boy, Tarren. He's ten months old and loves to holler all night and sleep all day. Now, I've given you food and told you my name, now you'll tell me yours." Tartan looked at him expectantly as if it were a command and not a request.

"My name is Kieran, and I want to buy a sword from you. I can pay you." Kieran looked at Tartan with piercing blue eyes and a stubborn set to his chin that dared Tartan to defy him.

"Kieran, where is your family and what do you want with a sword? I'll be honest with you, by the looks of the rags you're wearing and the holes in your boots your toes are sticking out of, well you don't look like you have any money."

"My folks are long gone." Kieran did not lie; they were long gone and far away he just did not specify which kind of long gone. "Truthfully, I do need new clothes and boots because I'm growing so fast. I have something to sell. I was hoping to get money for what I need and to buy a sword, then I'll be on my way." Kieran covertly reached for the other sausage on the plate and slowly chewed it savoring the flavor.

"You didn't steal it, whatever it is you've got to sell?" Tartan's bushy eyebrows drew into a frown. "I don't deal in stolen goods. You can just take yourself on your way if you're a thief."

In answer, Kieran pulled his bag of possessions off his shoulder, reached in, and took out one of the moonstone shards from Una's egg. He held it up in the sun. It glinted beautifully, casting prisms as the light caught on the crystal facets. Then he triumphantly told the truth, mostly.

"I found this in the mountains. I am thinking it is worth a gold coin or two." He proudly revealed.

Tartan whistled and his eyes grew big looking at the crystal. It was longer than the boy's dirty hand.

"Well! That is something possibly valuable, but you still have not answered my question. What do you want with a sword? I won't do any business with you unless I know that your intentions are honorable." Tartan looked a little relieved that the boy had found something in nature and was not stolen.

"I want to be a warrior, and a warrior must have a sword. With this, I can buy a sword from you. With the gold that is left over, I intend to buy clothes and boots, and I'll be on my way to seek fame and fortune." Kieran grinned.

"And I suppose you know how to use a sword?" Tartan looked doubtful.

"Ah, yes of course," Kieran scoffed, jumped to his feet, and held his arm out waving the long crystal in his hand as if it were an imaginary sword, "you just wave it around and hit things. I saw a man once throw his sword in the air and catch it behind his back, then he held it above his head and swallowed it! I will be a great warrior like that once I have my own sword."

"Boy," Tartan leaned forward and looked him in the eye, "fools wave swords to do fancy tricks. Men *fight* with swords, but a true warrior fights with honor. He defends king, country and family with his blood, his sweat and his sword. There is a lot more to wielding a weapon than just waving it around and hitting things. The problem is, most of the time if a man has a sword there is always another man who wants to fight him. It takes a great deal of practice and skill to be good at wielding a sword so that you *don't get killed.*"

The last words were punctuated roughly to make Tartan's point. He took a breath and went on.

"Sword fighting is deadly and if you're not more skilled than your foe, then his sword strikes and you're *dead!* That's the easy part!"

Tartan's voice quieted a little more, turning cold and ominous.

"The hard part is taking another man's life, even if he is trying to kill *you*. Warriors fight wars and the bards tell fanciful stories, putting fire in young men's bellies and desire in their hearts. They sell dreams of victory and renown, but the truth is... war is ugly, bloody, and terrible. War is pain and sorrow and the only ones who profit from it are kings who send good men to die for their greed. But it's the women who pay the biggest price because they have to go on living, grieving their husbands, brothers, and sons."

Kieran paled as Tartan's every word rang in his head. Looking up at the sky he thought about Una and what would happen to her if he died. Kieran slowly sat back down next to Tartan again and sat thinking. After a while, he turned a stubborn look back on Tartan.

"Will you sell me a sword or not? I will buy it with this and go out into the world and learn how to use it. I will become a great warrior someday!" Kieran held out the crystal to Tartan who took it.

Hefting the crystal in his large hand, Tartan felt the weight of it and held it up to the sunlight to look into the clear, unbroken depths of the priceless jewel. He considered it for many minutes while Kieran tried to be patient.

"It takes a long time to become strong enough to wield a sword and become skilled enough not to get yourself killed, boy." Tartan looked sad and distant as he spoke. He seemed filled with hidden grief as if looking back at a painful past. Then he nodded and said very quietly, "I know."

Kieran thought he understood and remained quiet. Sometimes grown-ups reveal things you wanted to hear if you were just quiet enough.

"Tell you what I'm willing to do, Kieran. You strike me as an unexpected blessing." Tartan pointed at him. "My apprentice left me six months ago and I haven't found a replacement for him. I will give you three meals a day, clothing, new boots, and a roof over your head if you come to work as my apprentice. It'll be hard work hauling wood and keeping the fire lit. You'll help around the forge, and I'll teach you how to make your own sword and..." Tartan hesitated for a long minute while Kieran held his breath waiting to hear what was on the other side of the 'and' "I will teach you how to use the sword, but you need to put some muscle on those bones first. Do we have a deal?"

Tartan held his hand out to Kieran expecting him to jump at the chance to have a home, food in his belly, and a permanent place to stay, but the boy hesitated. Kieran stood and walked a few paces away to think about the offer, then he looked toward the sky. His eyes searched for the rippling air that gave away Una's hiding place. He could not find her and the calm horses in the pen indicated she was no longer nearby. He began to sweat, his throat drying and nausea churning his stomach.

Tartan's offer was very appealing and if he were ever to be a warrior, he would have to learn to use a sword properly. He squatted down into his thinking position and chewed his bottom lip considering all his options. Finally, he knew there was no decision to make, he could not leave Una. He stood and looked at Tartan and was torn between his choices.

"I," he swallowed hard, "can't say I've ever had a better offer, Sir, but I can't stay here, I..." Kieran closed his eyes that filled with tears. They streaked down the dirt on his cheeks. His shoulders hunched as he fought the flood of emotions overwhelming him. Then he brightened and swiped his face as he got an idea. "But I can come back every day and work as your apprentice, but I have got to... how long will it take to be good at sword fighting?"

Tartan rose, towering over him and Kieran suspected the man already knew he was only agreeing to this apprenticeship to learn how to sword fight, and that Kieran was also hiding something.

"It'll take about ten years to properly teach you how to work the forge and use a sword, so you don't get yourself killed. By that time, my boy Tarren will be of age to start as an apprentice and if you decide to leave, he can take your place."

"Ten years!" Kieran interrupted loudly, his eyes going wide with disbelief.

"Ten years! And I warn you, I'll expect you to be reliable and work hard every day except Sundays when you can have a day of rest. But you must do as I say, don't talk sass to me or my wife, and whatever you do, don't steal from me. I expect hard work, complete honesty, and fairness, and that is what I give back. Do you agree to those terms?"

Again, Tartan held his hand out to Kieran who slowly took it, and they sealed the deal with a handshake.

"Good! First, we start by giving you a bath, some new clothes and boots. I expect you could handle some more food as well. I've got to put some muscle on you boy. You're skin and bones and won't be much good to me being so scrawny. Now, wait here while I inform the wife I have a new apprentice, and I'll see if the last one left some clothing and boots that'll fit you."

Kieran stood alone by the log in front of the blacksmith's house and stared in shock at the sky. What had he just done? He had promised the next ten years of his life in an apprenticeship with the blacksmith. He would have regular food and most importantly, he'd be learning how to use and *make* a sword of his own.

The magnitude of what he had just agreed to overwhelmed him and he stared down at the crystal still in his hand. How was he going to explain this to Una? Would she leave him if he was gone from her for so long? What would she do all day without him? Kieran had not often cried but large tears tracked their way down his cheeks. Wiping his face and nose with his ragged sleeve, he took a long deep, gulping breath. Climbing the towering cliff to the dragon's cave and stealing the dragon's egg was far easier than what he had just agreed to.

CHAPTER TEN

The dragon mother flew toward the edge of the western mountains where men built their castles and villages and plowed their farms. Hidden by the night sky she circled, looking for what she needed. She spotted a massive stone structure on the top of a hill and, flew straight toward it. She landed upon the topmost tower and lowered her head to sniff the air. Moss and vines grew thick over the stone walls and trees grew in clumps overtaking an untraveled road. Men lived there once, but now it was deserted, crumbling in disrepair. That suited her purposes well. Hefting the large bag of treasure in her front claws and clutching it to her chest, she swooped down to a large courtyard surrounded by tall stone walls. Shuddering with revulsion at what she had to do next, she took a deep breath and prepared to work dragon magic.

Calming her thundering heart and the revulsion she felt was critical because the magic would not come easily if it were not truly what she desired. Ancient magic always came easy when the intent was reconciled in heart and mind. She did want to find her egg, and she desperately wanted to kill the thief who took it. She wanted to crush his beating heart in her jaws, taste his blood dripping down her fangs, and swallow his essence. The magic was useless to find someone she did not know and so she would need cunning and perseverance to find her stolen egg. Picturing ripping the heart of the thief out, swallowing his body whole and regurgitating his bones, she knew that she would always keep his remains with her, and she would be reunited with her egg. She would have revenge and his power. To a dragon that meant little, but to the mother of a stolen child, it meant everything.

Reaching out, she raked her long black talons over the ground and created a pit. Then she made many trips to the surrounding forests, gathering fallen trees, and broken limbs. Stacking them in the pit until they towered in a huge pile, she surveyed her handiwork. Rearing back on her flanks, she took a deep breath. Spreading her wings, her massive chest expanding, and glowing red hot, she lunged forward and blew a stream of white fire onto the logs she'd gathered. She blew until the wood caught and glowed hot and white, consumed with flames that reached high into the sky, lighting the entire courtyard with white, dragon fire. She fanned the flames with her wings until a massive inferno raged and then she began to croon. The strange eerie language rang from her throat, and the dragon mother wove ancient magic that, until now, had been lost to the world of men.

It had been centuries since the last time she had performed this magic and although a dragon never forgets, deep down, she would not admit to the repulsion she felt. Any sacrifice must be made to find her egg and so she wove the skeins of the spell into an intricate web.

Her wings flapped, her tail lashed, and her long black mane rippled in the breeze she created. For almost an hour, the dragon chanted rasps, growls and sounds that went from animalistic to more humanlike speech with the passing minutes. The sparks from the crackling fire rose into the air, falling upon the dragon's fireproof back. Her scales prickled and stung and began to glow, flatten and smooth out.

Dragon mother began to shrink and soon her large body was a fraction of the size she had been, then her tail flicked and shortened into her until it was gone completely. Her legs formed into two arms and two legs. Last, her wings gave defiant flutters, blurring and shrinking until they vanished completely into the smooth curves of a woman's back.

Now standing in front of the raging white fire was not a dragon, but a tall, beautiful woman. Long, silky black hair flowed behind her and stretched across the ground which more than equaled the full length of her body. The dragon mother, now transformed into a human female, was the picture of perfection. She ran her hands over her face and down her long neck. She smoothed them over firm breasts and continued down until she reached her slim waist and touched her flat belly. She reached over her shoulders in a moment's panic and then closing her eyes threw her head back suddenly and gave a long mournful scream as she grieved the loss of her wings and the blessing of flight. Because of the thief, she lost her egg and her identity, and now she was cursed, confined to the ground. The last thing to be changed by her spell was her dragon's voice as it softened and cried away in strangled sadness.

In the darkness of the surrounding mountains, birds took to the skies in fear and the animals of the forest crouched low, scurrying to find hiding places as the dragon mother's cries filled the night air. As soon as her human throat grew hoarse, she fell silent. The wind blew, chilling her as she gasped in cold night air. The woman turned as she gave up her grieving and grabbed the thick mass of her hair. Striking out with talon-like nails she severed the locks just below her knees. Then she gathered the shorn black strands and began to whisper another spell. The fine black hair moved of its own accord, spun and weaved as if by unseen hands, and as her enchantment progressed, a fine black gown took shape. Stepping into the glorious garment she pulled it up her long arms and covered her white shoulders. The delicate material flowed over her lush curves without seam or binding. Behind her, the white dragon fire continued to burn casting a brilliant glow high into the night sky where it could be seen for miles.

Next, the new lady of the crumbling manor went to her massive bag of treasure. She grabbed it with one hand and with inhuman strength, dragged it into the dark castle. Descending to the depths of the dungeons she traversed long corridors of old stone; her bare feet stepped confidently in the dark until she came to a chamber large enough to hold her entire hoard. Once all the treasure was deposited into the room, with a puff of her breath, she lit an old torch set in the wall. The room lit up, and she turned. Bursting the bag with one swipe of her sharp nails, the gold, jewels, and treasure spilled across the floor in a glistening flow. Closing the door behind her, the lady entered. Laying down among her wealth, she curled up and finally rested, exhausted after her magical transformation. Dreams of the day she would be reunited with her stolen egg soothed her frantic heart.

In the early morning hours, the dragon mother stirred and rolled over in the pile of her gold and treasure. Pawing through the spilled mass, she searched for what she knew was there and pulled out an empty black leather scabbard. It was artfully wrapped in thin gold wiring, and she chuckled thinking of the imbecilic knight who thought she, as a dragon, could be slain by such a puny weapon.

As she searched through the pile, she pulled out the long steel blade, admiring the silver and gold hilt. It had ruby inlay and a carved crescent moon with three stars. The stars represented the head of the dragon constellation in the northern hemisphere of the sky. She had drained the blade of its magic years ago and now it was nothing but a sharp piece of metal which she could still use. Resuming the search, she found a heavy circlet of gold and rubies and placed the crown on her head. Still not satisfied, she found a matching necklace, earrings, and even some golden gauntlets encrusted with rubies. She just needed a bag and as she gathered gold coins, and stuffed them into a large pouch, she pricked her finger on something sharp.

Scowling, she found what had injured her. Holding it up to the torchlight she turned it and examined it carefully. It was a silver and gold dragon pin with its wings spread wide. It was wrapped around a large round ruby. Smiling, she wound the sides of her hair away from her face and stuck the pin in the back holding her black locks in place. She could feel the wings embrace the back of her head and she was pleased. Looking down she saw a tear of blood welling from her finger, and she stuck it in her mouth. Remembering the taste of her thief's blood she smiled and her determination to find him flared within her breast. Locking the door and sealing it with a powerful spell, she went to explore her new castle.

Garrion Swagger, the leader of a band of fifty outlaws, stood looking out into the night sky toward a white glow deep in the heart of his mountain territory. The breeze carried the faint sound of a woman screaming in agony or sorrow. Even his cold heart quivered at the strange, mournful cry. His flesh crawled and the hair on the back of his neck stood up. Staring at the glowing anomaly, he considered what it meant. Surely, the glow had to be a forest fire, likely caused by a lightning strike on that distant mountain. The quiet, cloudless sky seemed to negate that idea. Garrion caressed his black beard thinking about who or what could make such an agonized, inhuman cry? As the night progressed and the light never lessened, he grew more and more curious. Finding his bedroll, he decided it was worth checking out in the morning. If someone had taken up residence in his territory, there would be a battle. One he would very much enjoy.

The next morning, Garrion Swagger and his men rode in the direction they had seen the white fire glowing the previous night. He had slept poorly and was in a foul mood. He promised retribution against whoever had dared to take up residence in his territory. Perhaps there was loot to be taken and that lifted his spirits a little. As they rode closer Garrion felt that any minute, they would come across those he sought. All he found was an ancient castle in the distance that he had forgotten was there. The horses galloped up the road overgrown with weeds and grass and headed toward crumbing walls and towers. They didn't even have to dismount but rode straight into the courtyard through fallen gates and found what they sought. The horses began to neigh and reared up, balking at entering for some unfathomable reason. It could have been the large, unnatural white fire burning in a large pit at the center of the courtyard. The walls had been scorched from the heat of the fire the previous night and ash speckled the air with blackened snowflakes blowing heavily in the breeze. The taint of magic was in the air.

Fighting to calm his horse, Garrion nudged him toward the castle. Drawing his sword, he looked around warily and assessed the towering walls and fortifications. His eyes landed on the massive weather-beaten doors of the main keep. Garrion was surprised as they parted as if by unseen hands. His horse reared violently almost unseating him and he clamped down hard on the horse's sides and wrestled with the reins to keep his seat. Out into the daylight walked a beautiful woman dressed in a long flowing black dress.

Sunlight glinted off a gold and ruby crown she wore, and it seemed to shimmer. Her long black hair floated behind her in the wind and Garrion was mesmerized by her beauty. She gracefully descended the stairs and glided toward him. All the horses were whinnying loudly and dancing, their eyes rolling white with fear.

"Stop!" the woman raised her hand and commanded.

Instantly, the horses calmed, the courtyard went still and silent. Garrion dismounted and stared in amazement at his now docile mount. Turning toward the woman, he walked forward, climbed the steps in front of her, and bowed reverently.

"My Lady," He began but stopped as he was overwhelmed by her beauty and sumptuous form, not to mention the priceless jewels that adorned her.

The woman's luscious red lips parted, and she took a deep breath. Her brow wrinkled just slightly, and her large amber eyes narrowed in thought. Then she spoke with a strange accent.

"Long has it been since I have spoken your language."

Garrion's black eyebrows rose in appreciation. His eyes slid over her slender figure hugged tightly in the luxurious black gown, the likes of which he had never seen before. His gaze lingered on the swell of her breasts and rose to appraise the gold and ruby diadem in her crown and the jewels around her throat. She was the most incredibly beautiful woman he had ever met. He had to tear his eyes away from her to disguise his growing lust. Looking around, the courtyard indicated the ancient castle was deserted; no one else appeared. Garrion was most intrigued, and his imagination began to flourish, though the taint of magic in the air had him proceeding with caution. This was clearly a sorceress.

"Come," she beckoned to him, "let us speak inside."

Then she turned and walked back through the great doors, disappearing into the shadows. Garrion saw the pale flash of her bare feet. Intrigued, Garrion motioned to his men to stand down. He commanded men to take up guard positions and then he followed the woman's swaying hips inside.

Torches in every corner brightly lit the large room and Garrion could see the leaf-strewn floors and dust covering a long table in the middle of the room. A broken chair was in the corner. The state of the place confirmed it had indeed sat empty for many years. A white fire similar to that in the courtyard was lit in the massive stone hearth. The lady sat calmly in a tall, intricately carved chair. Her hands lightly rested on the arms, and she surveyed the man who stood before her.

"I am Lady Rhiannah Dragahn." She began. Her voice was rich and velvety, making the hair on the back of his neck stand up and other parts of his body harden.

"My Lady Dragahn," Garrion bowed with a flourish, "I am Garrion Swagger, at your service."

"Are you truly at my service, Garrion Swagger?"

Garrion was momentarily stunned by her question. He was caught off guard but recovered quickly.

"Lady Dragahn, you sound as if you are not from these parts and so you may not understand the polite niceties of our language and etiquette. Let me rephrase. I am pleased to meet you."

"Ah," she nodded her head as if enlightened.

Garrion grew slightly uncomfortable with the strange conversation and the woman's amber eyes peering at him with deep scrutiny. So, he got right to the point.

"Are you alone in this castle, my lady? It appears to be deserted. How is it you come to be here? You are dressed like the queen of this crumbling ruin, yet you appear to have no retainers, no ladies in waiting, no servants, and no soldiers. Tell me, my lady, what are you doing here?"

"So many questions." She tilted her head as if considering which to answer. She spoke very slowly as if trying to remember the appropriate words. "I have recently come here. Yes, I am searching for someone who has stolen something very valuable from me, and I can use a man like *you* to help me."

"Lady Dragahn I am not for hire. To be honest, my men and I are outlaws. I run this territory which you are, I might point out, trespassing upon. I am curious to know what business you have here?"

"I told you I am searching for a thief. *You* will help me find him."

Garrion approached closer, a menacing smile dancing on his lips and his eyes trained on the gold and rubies gracing the beautiful lady's delicate throat. The riches were very appealing to him and his eyes glittered greedily. Still, he did not like being ordered around, especially by a woman, and anger simmered in his chest.

"Ah! Lady Dragahn, despite how lovely you are, I don't take orders from anyone, let alone a *woman*. I give the orders. If that is not clear enough, let me explain further. I don't know how you got here, but you are obviously alone with no retainers and no soldiers for protection. This castle presently resides in my territory and therefore it is my domain. You are bedecked in gold and jewels, and I am particularly fond of gold and jewels. What is to stop me from stealing everything you have, taking my pleasure from your body and leaving you for dead?" He gave her a wicked grin that said he was not above following through with his threats.

The lady smiled very slowly, and a dangerous light flickered in her amber-colored eyes. Perhaps it was the torchlight, but Garrion thought he saw a flicker of flames reflected there. His mouth went dry, and he swallowed taking a step back as she slowly rose to her feet.

"You are a thief?" Lady Dragahn's voice was low and angry as she approached him.

"As I said," Garrion tried not to sound irritated, "I am an outlaw, and yes, theft is one of my many sins."

She stopped in front of Garrion so close that he could smell the odd scent she wore. It reminded him of the wind and heavy rain. She licked her lips and gazed at his mouth, giving him an enticing look. Everything about her manner was slow, sensual, and intense. She moved to stand so close to him that he could feel the heat radiating off her body in the thin gown. Her lips were within inches of his and Garrion was tempted to lean forward and taste her. The lady was no doubt trying to seduce him.

"I am looking for a thief, a particular thief. Are you him?"

"I think I might like to be *your* thief, my lady. Pray tell, what do you have in mind?"

"I need men, lots of men to help find the one thief I am looking for, but I also have to make sure you are not him."

Lady Dragahn leaned forward, and her lips met his in a tentative kiss and Garrion reached out, grabbed her arms, and crushed her to him. Very quickly, she bit his lip and drew blood. Garrion was not opposed to rough embraces and felt he had the upper hand but when she sucked his bottom lip swallowing his blood, he suddenly felt very strange. She released his mouth and shoved him away looking very disappointed and almost angry.

"You are not him!" She hissed and abruptly turned away, strolling back to her seat. Sitting down once again like a queen upon her throne, she addressed him in a strong voice.

"From now on, you will serve me, Garrion Swagger. I require your assistance to find my thief and recover what was stolen. You will move into this castle and serve me as your queen. I require your complete loyalty and unfailing devotion to my cause."

Garrion wiped his lips with his fingers and stared down at the red blood glistening there. He staggered back against the table feeling dizzy and disoriented. Then he looked up at Lady Dragahn, his vision blurring slightly then changing into sharp focus. He recalled the smell and feel of magic in the air, and this gave him great pause, but the lady was speaking.

"Move your men into the castle immediately. Have a few of them clear the filth from this hall. I will give you gold for furnishings, food, servants, obtain general supplies and I think I remember I like wine. Get some of that as well. First, I must test each of your men to make sure none of them is the thief I seek. Bring them in immediately and line them up."

Garrion turned as if it were his greatest wish to do her bidding and, within a few minutes, all his men were lined up, awaiting their orders.

Lady Dragahn rose to her feet and stopped at the first man in the line. Slowly, she drew the gold and silver dragon pin from her hair and as fast as a snake strike, lashed out and pricked the man's neck with a shallow stab. The tip of the pin came away wet with a tiny drop of the man's blood. Licking the red drop, she tasted his blood and frowned in disappointment. She moved to the next man. Repeating the test on each outlaw, Lady Dragahn tasted every one of them. None turned out to be the thief she sought.

Returning to her tall chair, Lady Dragahn sat slowly and regarded Garrion Swagger with her amber eyes.

"Garrion, you and your men will be rewarded for your service. For now, dismiss them to their new duties and then...bring me a map!"

CHAPTER ELEVEN

K ieran had never been dressed so finely, nor had he been so
well fed. He had trousers that fit, a soft linen shirt with bone
buttons, a forest green coat, and soft woolen stockings. Best of
all were the new boots that fit his growing feet. He should have
been overjoyed but he was not. Returning to the forest outside
of Appleaid to the same spot where he left Una, he turned in
circles looking for her and calling as loudly as he dared. Suddenly,
she materialized in front of him, rippling with brilliant colors and
crooning, happy to see him. Kieran ran to her and threw his arms

around her neck. Burying his face in the soft lavender mane growing down her neck he hid the tears that filled his eyes. The dragon sighed with affection and rested her head on his back. He held on for as long as she would allow.

When he had collected his emotions, Kieran pulled away and went to sit with his back to a tree, in his thinking position. Una crouched down in front of him and seemed to admire his new boots and clothes with an inquisitiveness that was almost human.

Kieran was quiet for a long time and then he began to explain what happened at the forge. First, he repeated his heart's dream of learning to wield a sword and becoming a warrior. Then he spoke of the blacksmith's offer to take him on as an apprentice. Una sat up and looked at him with her large emerald eyes, attentively searching his face.

Sitting majestically, she gleamed blue and gold, blending with the scant sunlight. Her scales rippled and her long snout twitched with motion as if she were deep in thought. Looking in the direction of the village, her head tilted right and left with understanding. The long tail that wrapped around her feet thumped the ground in an impatient rhythm.

"I swear Una, I will return to you every night and I can spend the whole day with you on Sundays, but this is something I *have* to do. I want to be a mighty warrior. The blacksmith will teach me, and I can make my own sword. You must stay out of sight and out of trouble. Do you understand?"

Una tilted her head at him and blinked then she nodded as if she understood every word he said. Kieran sighed with relief and settled back against the tree. Reaching into the bag he always carried, he produced a half loaf of bread that Sara the smith's wife had given him. Tearing it in half, he gave part to Una. She sniffed it and then devoured it in one bite.

Kieran gathered stones and put them in a circle with some small sticks. Before he could take out his flint to start the fire, Una inhaled, her chest scales glowed blueish as she gently puffed out a breath of white fire, igniting the sticks. Gazing in wonder, Kieran wrapped an arm around his dragon, ate his bread, and was asleep almost instantly.

The first day of Kieran's apprenticeship dawned and he rose, stamped out the smoldering coals of his fire and threw dirt over them. He said goodbye to Una. He instructed his best friend to stay out of sight and not to get into any trouble, not to eat any of the cattle or livestock belonging to the villagers or let herself be seen. Then he headed back to the blacksmith's forge. Overhead, Una followed in the sky, changing her color to mirror the morning blue and the white clouds, until she was completely invisible. As always, Kieran sensed where she flew above him. As he walked, he contemplated the strange connection he had with the dragon. Sometimes he felt as if she were speaking to him and that they understood each other. Sometimes, he feared he was just being a fanciful child and knew as of today, he had to grow up.

When he reached the forge, the sun was coming up over the mountaintops and starting to warm the valley. He watched as Una once again landed on top of the large barn. The horses bolted to the other side of the corral and Kieran motioned for Una to fly off, but she rested her head on her front claws and closed her eyes as if she were going to take a nap, before disappearing completely, blending in with the red and gray wood of the building.

"Ah, so you've come!" Tartan MacLaren stepped out of the cottage. "Have you eaten?"

Kieran was startled by Tartan's sudden voice calling to him. Recovering quickly, he just shook his head slowly.

"Alright, come in and break your fast, Boy. It is going to be a long day, and you need to build your strength."

Eating his fill of Sara's magnificent cooking, Kieran avoided answering Tartan's questions about where he slept at night while politely refusing a bed in their extra room where the former apprentice had stayed. They quickly finished and headed to the forge. The rest of the day was spent with Tartan teaching, Kieran learning, and listening to instructions of all kinds. He endlessly gathered wood for the forge, fetched water from a nearby stream, and shoveled charcoal. Those were just a few of his chores. Kieran fed the horses, who didn't like his smell, and he took care of other animals on the small homestead. There was a goat, a pig, and more chickens than he could keep track of.

As the day went on, Kieran constantly watched for Una on the top of the buildings or flying overhead. Tartan caught him staring up and asked him what he was daydreaming about with his head constantly in the clouds.

"I was just judging the time of day, Sir." Kieran thought fast.

"Well, keep your eyes on your work boy. The day will end when the work is done."

Kieran worked harder than he ever had in his life, even from before when he was on the farm with his family. His back hurt and he had bruises all over his arms and shins, and blisters on his hands from shoveling coal for the fire. Before his first day as an apprentice blacksmith was done, he thought seriously about quitting. Foraging for food in the mountains, playing with Una all day, and being on his own with no one to boss him around was far easier and much less work. The hearty lunch and dinner Sara prepared for them convinced him to stay a little while longer and he had given his word. Kieran may be a thief, a runaway and curse like a grown man, but he tried to be as honorable as possible. Though always on his mind and in his heart was the beautiful dragon he must keep secret.

Another great disappointment occurred when Kieran learned Tartan mostly made horseshoes, metal bands for barrels, nails, and various farming tools. To his dismay, Kieran saw no swords glowing in the hot coals or hanging finished on the walls and let his dissatisfaction show. At the end of the day when the sun was going down, Tartan called him over to the back of the building where the forge fire was now only dying coals. He opened a small, locked room in the back and waved Kieran over where a large black, wooden chest sat in the shadows. Lighting a lamp, Tartan unlocked the chest and opened it. Reaching in, he pulled out a heavy dark cloth and unwound a long, shining object.

It was the most glorious sword Kieran had ever seen. The long, straight, steel blade glittered in the lamplight. A smooth channel ran down the middle and the double-edged blade looked sharp enough to penetrate the toughest armor. Tartan displayed the black wood handle which he called a grip. Kieran reached out a finger to touch the decorative carving in the silver cross guard but when he saw how filthy his hand was, he pulled it back swiftly. The pommel was plain and silver with more carvings to match the hilt. Awed and impressed, Kieran could only stare with wide-eyed amazement.

"It's beautiful!" Kieran gasped and watched as Tartan wrapped the sword back up and put it back in the chest. He locked it with a large metal lock.

"It's deadly!" Tartan said, pointing a finger at him. "Never forget that, boy."

"Is it yours? Were you a warrior? Did you fight in wars? How come you're only a blacksmith now? Why is the sword in the trunk? Does it have a name?" Kieran's questions streamed out one after the other. "What..."

"Hold your questions boy!" Tartan interrupted calmly. "That sword has never seen war. It is virgin steel, unbloodied. It is an unnamed sword. No, I wasn't a warrior, but I trained to become one when I was a young lad. I'll tell you my story someday. For now, I only wanted you to see what can come from learning the craft. Eventually, you'll be able to make your sword as I promised, and I hope you never have to use it. Today was hard and there are many more, harder days ahead, but for now, you see what can be learned and accomplished."

Kieran stared at the closed trunk where the glorious sword lay hidden again.

"Next week, we will start lessons learning to be skilled with a sword. You did well today, and you'll be hurtin' for it tomorrow, but it will get easier as your body gets used to the labor. Now, head home to your bed."

Sighing with awe as he left the forge, Kieran dreaded the long walk back to the apple grove. As tired as he was, he began to despair over returning so far away every night to be with Una, but his fear of leaving her alone for so long was worse. As he turned to walk out into the night, a flicker of two small white flames in the trees behind Tartan's house caught his eye. He thought he heard his name whispered. Stopping, he stared into the blackness thinking his tired mind and eyes were playing tricks on him and was startled as he saw it again. Una was the only one who could make white fire and so he followed what he hoped was a signal that she awaited him there. He reached the forest and followed the flickers of flames up the gently sloping hill along an overgrown path. Suddenly, a shadowy shape loomed in a small clearing. Una's nostrils flared with twin white flames briefly outlining a small overgrown glade in light, and Kieran realized it was an abandoned cabin. Walking closer, he peered through a door sagging on broken hinges. The place was almost empty with a dirt floor, a broken chair and something that looked like it had once been a box bed with a few broken slats and no mattress. There was a very small fireplace that was blackened from many fires in better days.

Kieran dropped his small pack just inside the door and realized that Una had found him a place to stay that was close by the forge. The easy walk up the hill had taken him less than a quarter of an hour, he judged. It would be the perfect place for him to stay and have a roof over his head, which was something he had not hoped for until now.

"Una!" Kieran gulped, "How did you find this place? It is wonderful! We can stay here! It's close to the forge and close to you! While I'm gone during the day, you can protect the cabin for us. I'll come to you at night, and this will be our home!"

Una nudged him inside with her nose and Kieran began to gather some of the sticks and leaves that littered the floor. He set to making a fire in the fireplace and once it was blazing with a puff of dragon breath, they had light and warmth. The place felt like home!

"From now on I'll come here after my day working at the forge. You'll be safe here and there will be less of a chance anyone will see you. You can hunt deeper in the forest without alerting the village, there is a dragon around. We'll both be well-fed, safe, and happy! Then when I'm an expert at using a sword, you and I will go out into the world and seek adventure, riches and fame!"

Kieran went to Una and threw his arms around her neck and hugged her. Half of her body could only fit through the small door and her tail trailed outside, but they curled up on the floor and Kieran was immediately asleep. Una watched the flickering flames and listened to Kieran's deep breathing as he slept tucked against her side. Spreading a wing over him she finally closed her eyes, then boy and dragon sought adventure and glory in the boy's dreams.

CHAPTER TWELVE

L ady Rhiannah Dragahn and Garrion Swagger stood beside a large table staring down at the map spread upon it. Nestled within the Ten Thousand Mile Forest was the newly named 'Dragon's Reach,' the castle acquired by Lady Rhiannah. It was marked in fresh black ink like the announcement of a new regime. The cities and villages were also clearly marked from one end of Lyndesea to the other. Numerous red flags marked the areas where Lady Dragahn had sent her men out to search for her missing egg.

"This is taking far too long!" She shouted while pacing across the floor. It had taken the better part of a year to repair and furnish the castle, set up the men and get everything situated. Though none of that was her priority, there always seemed to be some delay, and the hunt had only just begun.

Her hands curled and clawed the air in frustration as she raged about delays. Her footfalls were muffled by thick carpets spread upon the stone floor. Heavily carved furniture littered the room and new leaded windows let in colored light. The wealth spent on equipping the castle was apparent in every corner and alcove. The outlaws now lived like kings thanks to the lady's patronage.

"My Lady, we are doing everything we can. I assure you; I will find the thief eventually."

"Scour every town to the west. Question anyone who has a sudden display of wealth. Anyone bragging about a great adventure, or a large haul, or claiming to have something magnificent and rare for sale, or a secret treasure, should be questioned."

"Lady Rhiannah, my men will search across the entire western area of the continent, I assure you. We have informants, we've offered bribes and a reward. They will gather information of treasure, but you've said nothing specific about what you are seeking. Perhaps our thief has left the western lands, and we should also head south."

"No! I am sure he went west! His trail led west..." she stabbed a long-nailed finger on the map.

Lady Rhiannah recalled the bottom of the towering escarpment where the fading tracks of the thief and the trail leading away went toward the west. His scent was fresh in her nostrils as she remembered nosing through leaves, twigs, dirt. As a dragon she found each place his foot fell and every place his hand touched, while she followed the path until it was too faded to detect. The pain of losing her egg rose fresh within her breast and the fate of the dying dragon race weighed heavily upon her heart.

"Rhiannah, my love," Garrion interrupted her reminiscences as he moved forward and snaked his arms around her from behind. Smoothing her long black hair to the side, he trailed kisses down her neck. "Why don't you give up this fruitless search? A treasure such as you've described will surely turn up one day. With your sorceress powers and wealth, we can take over the entire country. Let us leave this tiresome castle for more opulent places. We'll attack the main city where the King of Lyndesea resides, and you and I can take over and rule the entire country. I'll make you queen. We'll live abundantly as the new rulers of the entire land."

"Garrion, I will not give up my search for all the treasure or kingdoms in the world! I must find my...what was stolen from me. Finish in the west. Leave no place unsearched, no bit of information is too small to consider. Find the thief who has a mystical, one-of-a-kind treasure, someone will brag about stealing something so wonderful and rare it should be obvious. A thief has it and will display great wealth or even power, which is where we must go to find what was stolen. One thing is certain, he is strong and cunning to have evaded me thus far, but he will be found."

"It would help if you would tell me *exactly* what you are searching for? You've only given me a vague idea, a one-of-a-kind, mystical treasure is not much to go on. Is it a magic sword or a talisman? Is it a book, or a magical crown, perhaps it is enchanted armor? I've brought you some of these things and you scoff at me and rage because none of them are what you are looking for. It is pointless not to be more specific. If I am to be successful, then you must reveal *exactly* what it is you seek?"

Garrion waited and a prickle of anxious excitement crept up his spine. Lady Rhiannah had turned back to the table and stood stone still, looking at the map. Then she turned slowly and stared at him with her strange amber eyes. They flickered in the light and made him uneasy as looking at her directly always did. Her blood red lips parted, and she finally told him what he wanted desperately to know.

"I search for the thief who took my egg, my *dragon* egg. It is possible that it has hatched by now and so you should also listen for tales of a dragon being seen. The thief will be someone powerful who has been able to keep such a valuable secret as this."

"A dragon?" Mouth going dry, Garrion realized that Lady Rhiannah was completely serious. "Dragons have not been seen in Lyndesea for hundreds if not thousands of years. They are only creatures of myth and legend."

She did not offer anything further. Staring at her, his mind began to whirl with the implications. A dragon egg had never been seen or owned by men before, at least not any remaining alive to boast about it. Dragons had all but been hunted to extinction in the distant past and only mentioned in tales told by bards in taverns and old men around campfires. They were creatures from fairy tales and folklore. Foremost in Garrion's mind was how this could benefit *him*. Smiling, he took her hand in his and bowed over it, kissing the back of her fingers. Flushed with excitement he gave a seductive purr.

"Now, was that so hard? We will finish searching the west and then head south to please you, my lady." He pulled her into his arms trailing kisses across her cheek, searching for her mouth.

As he kissed her, his mind whirled and greed filled him with ways to use this new information. The wealth and power a dragon's egg could bring him was staggering to contemplate overwhelming Garrion Swagger with anticipation, and he held the key to having it all in his arms.

CHAPTER
THIRTEEN

Two and a half years passed since Kieran began as Tartan MacLaren's apprentice. The work had been hard, but he was learning valuable skills. He was almost thirteen years old as his next birthday was only two months away. His heart despaired that he had more than seven and a half years of apprenticeship left to go. Over seven years before he would have his own sword and be able to leave and go find adventure and glory with Una by his side. His lessons in learning the sword skill were progressing slowly, and he had, as of yet, not even touched a real sword. They practiced only with blunt wooden sticks. Sadly, he had multiple bruises attesting to his lack of competence, but he was doggedly persistent. Worst of all, he had yet to see Tartan forge a single sword or weapon of any kind beyond eating utensils.

Working as an apprentice to a blacksmith had other benefits. Kieran's body changed because of his hard work and regular hearty meals. He grew tall for his age and was putting on muscle. His hands and feet were large, and he grew skilled at wielding a hammer and axe. Though he was learning to work with metal, he was proving to have a knack for carving wood as well. Often in the rare moments he had to himself, he carved dragons out of thick blocks of wood and on the few pieces of furniture he had in his very small cabin. He even carved a small wooden dragon for Tarren, Tartan's two-year-old son.

He often missed the old days when he was free to wander the forest with Una. Now, with Tartan, Sara, Tarren, and their new baby boy named Soren, he had a family but would never admit to missing that connection.

Up in his tiny cabin, Kieran worked to repair holes in the roof and walls. He acquired a straw mattress, repaired the slats of the long bed, replaced the broken leg on the chair and it was comfortable. Tartan's wife Sara had given him a few things like a couple of thick blankets, an iron pot, a cup, a plate and a wooden spoon. He earned a small wage as the apprentice blacksmith and purchased a few other things he needed.

Una had grown considerably and could no longer fit inside the cabin. As if by magic, she bent the young trees next to it and created a woven hut in the shape of a cave just outside. Over time the leaves grew thick, and it made a living shelter for her as well. She blew dragon breath over the surrounding woods and soon they had a thickly sheltered hideaway. During winter months it was enough to keep the dragon covered and dry. Kieran was happy that she was content.

Kieran did not know how big a dragon could get when fully grown. He guessed she was about as big as she was going to get, or so he hoped, as she now towered over him considerably. She had also changed. Her wings were amethyst color, huge and membranous, the thicker iridescent white scales on her body were outlined with dark violet and blue. A thick mane of dark violet hair flowed over her long neck and partially down her back. On her head were twisted white horns. Her clawed feet, black talons, and sharp white teeth were impressive, but her most beautiful feature were the large emerald eyes that flashed with mischief and often unwavering stubbornness.

Kieran and Una had a deeply bonded friendship. It was more than that, he loved her with his whole heart and was devoted to her in a way that he did not understand. The way they communicated was nothing short of magical, though it felt completely natural. Kieran spoke out loud to her and, though Una could not speak words, she had a way of making herself clearly understood as if she put thoughts into his mind. Kieran's earliest dreams of riding a magical dragon were permanently squashed as he felt riding his best friend like a horse was somehow demeaning to her. Though Una often put the image in his mind, he could not bring himself to climb upon her broad back and take to the skies as she wanted. It was a constant argument between them. At night, his dreams were plagued by the thrill of flight and fighting glorious battles mounted on his dragon.

When Kieran was away during the day at the forge, Una stayed hidden in the mountains. Her ability to camouflage and hide led them to believe that no one in the village knew that a dragon lived close by. Una was never pleased to be parted from Kieran, and he often had to reprimand her for following him to the forge where she risked being seen. Many days she lounged invisible behind the forge building and Kieran tried not to admit that he felt better with her nearby. Often, he stopped to watch her fly overhead and Tartan frequently yelled at him to stop daydreaming and keep his mind on the work.

Tartan's horses no longer reared in terror when she was in the vicinity as they got used to the dragon smell that was part of who Kieran was. Their life together moved in a rhythm of hard work and, when time allowed, they hunted and played in the forest as they had their first days together. Kieran had never been happier, but soon their happiness and security were threatened.

One day as Kieran worked inside the forge barn, he heard a wagon entering the yard. This was nothing out of the ordinary, but he felt an extreme sense of foreboding. Looking out the doors, he quickly jumped back out of sight. Kieran's throat went dry, and his heart thundered in his chest.

Three men riding in a wagon rolled into the blacksmith's farm, and headed toward the barn where the forge smoked, and Kieran hid. Two men sat on the front bench and a younger one lounged in the back which was piled with supplies and a squat barrel for water. Driving the wagon was none other than his *father* and with him were his two older brothers. Though it had been over three years since he last saw them, he knew who they were.

Tartan was striding across the yard and approached the wagon just as it drew near to the building where Kieran hid a few feet away in the shadows. Too frozen to move, he was terrified of discovery and placed his back against the worn wooden wall, hoping he was hidden enough. Sweat ran down his face, and his breathing was heavy. He gulped his fear down and his belly turned sour. As he listened intently to what was happening outside, he heard Tartan call out to the men.

"Good day sirs, do you need some metal work done today?" Tartan wiped his hands on a cloth and greeted them in his usual friendly manner.

"Nope," the older man spoke sharply and looked around the large yard as if searching for something. "I'm not here on business. I'm looking for someone. My youngest boy dun ran away from home a couple years back. Glenn's his name and he'd be about, oh, I dunno, ten or twelve. We been searching hard for him ever since he went missin'."

Tartan looked surprised and searched the faces of the men in the wagon. The older man speaking, had a wrinkled face worn by years of working in the sun. A tattered sweat-stained hat shaded dark, angry eyes. He had a crooked mouth with an underbite that stuck out to the side and gave him a mean, suspicious look. The two younger men with him took after their father in looks, but in stature, they were thicker as if years of physical labor had not yet bent them to its hard will. The younger looking one of them had a shock of blonde hair like Kieran's and dirty locks hung into the same blue eyes. His nose was crooked, and his face held a blank, unemotional look. The other man had the father's darker brown hair and the same mean arrogant bearing. They all reeked of ale, sweat and road dust. Tartan could tell they must have been drinking heavily for him to be able to smell it on them at this distance.

"This is your son you're looking for." Tartan repeated very casually.

"That's what I said! Me'names' Beck Dunn. I come from Buttermilk Town south of here, about two weeks' travel. Been lookin' for my boy on and off for nearly two years now, and when I find him, I'm gonna drag him back home where there be work to do on the farm. Then I'll make sure he never even thinks about runnin' away again. He put me to a lotta trouble."

Beck Dunn appeared meaner than a shaken hornet's nest and as vicious as a hungry bear. Smacking one fist in the palm of his other hand, his face turned red with anger. The two boys with him grinned almost in anticipation of a beating to come.

Kieran knew Tartan was no fool. He'd have realized right away he was the boy they were looking for, and he knew exactly what he had waiting for him should his father get ahold of him.

"So, what's it to me?" Tartan asked impatiently. "Why come here looking for the boy?"

Inside the forge barn, Kieran tried hard not to breathe, move, or flee in terror. His father had a loud booming voice, and he heard every word that passed between him and Tartan. He silently willed Tartan not to give him away. Then all his thoughts rushed to Una. What would happen to her if his father took Kieran away?

Una! Una! Una! Kieran squeezed his eyes and shivered with trepidation and need. His mind sent out a call to her and his fanciful imagination wished she could truly hear him calling from this far away. Kieran longed for her with all his might and wanted her close by so that he could just fly away before Tartan gave him up to his father, as he surely must.

His father's voice rose again, snagging his attention. More sweat dripped down the side of Kieran's face.

"At the pub in town, they say you have a young apprentice working for ya. Said he appeared outta nowhere and only been here a year or two. Now, I'm thinkin' you'd better call that young apprentice out here so that I can have a look at him. If he is my youngest boy, I'll be takin' him home to face what he got comin' for runnin' away."

"It is true. I have a boy working for me. He might be about the age of the boy you're looking for, maybe a year or two older. His name isn't Glenn though. So, he can't be the boy you're seeking."

"Oh, can't he? My boy's a clever one, could have lied about his name. Bring him out!" Beck Dunn scowled a challenge at Tartan. His black eyes stared from under his hat, and he leaned forward as if watching for a lie. He shivered with anticipation that finally his search was over.

"Sorry, my apprentice is not here today. He lives in the mountains with his younger sister who has fallen ill. They are very close, and he stayed home to help tend her. So, you see, he can't be the boy you're looking for as he has a sister. Unless you've also a daughter who ran away with him? Now, I've work to do, so I'll kindly ask you to be on your way."

Beck cursed and clenched his teeth in frustration and glared like he wanted to argue with Tartan. The boys with him also scowled angrily as if they were looking for a fight. The air was full of tension as tight as a bow string.

"When will he be back? I think I should just meet this apprentice of yours and judge for meself that it ain't him."

"I can't be sure. As I said, his sister is very bad off. I've two young sons and can't risk any sickness spreading here, so I told my apprentice to stay away until the girl is completely well again. It could be a few days, or it could be weeks or a month before he returns. Who knows?"

Tartan shrugged his broad shoulders and stared down the men in the wagon. His feet were placed wide as if readying for a fight.

"Sorry to say it, but your son is probably dead if you haven't found him by now. It stands to reason that a young boy alone in the wild mountains would not be able to survive for long, especially with the winters as bad as they are here."

"Eh, he better be dead because when I get my hands on him, he might not be alive for much longer."

"Mr. Dunn, I'm asking you to be on your way now. You're keeping me from my work." Tartan sounded as if he was losing patience.

Kieran waited for his father to argue further, but just then, he felt a familiar presence. There was a strange quietness and the horses in the corral stirred as they did sometimes when Una was nearby. *'Oh, no!'* Kieran thought and stared out the back door of the barn. The air stirred as if Una was there. She was invisible, but Kieran sensed a strong call in his mind. Her cry was frantic, and Kieran feared she would show herself or do something rash if he didn't get to her quickly.

Then everything seemed to happen at once. A wind devil came up and whirled around the yard creating a dusty vortex. Sara came out of the house carrying the baby who was wailing up a storm with Tarren following. Kieran's father was loudly cursing his bad luck while his horses reared, and dirt pelted them. Tartan was insisting Dunn leave his property, loudly proclaiming that he was upsetting his farm.

Una's call was frantic in Kieran's mind. His skin itched and his body tried to suppress the urge to bolt. He pushed down the fear that had frozen him to the spot and unpeeled himself from the shadowy wall. Running quietly out the back door of the forge barn he headed toward Una. As soon as he hit the sunlight, he saw the invisible outline of Una's form. He ran to her. When he was within reach, she struck out and with a snap of her jaws grabbed him by the shirt and flung him onto her back. Kieran tingled. His mind screamed in sheer terror before feeling himself engulfed in Una's magic, watching in horror as his body disappeared. It was as if he were immersed in water covered in Una's mystic camouflage. With a flap of her giant wings the dragon rose. Kieran's hands dug in, and he clung to her dragon mane. They lifted into the air and flew toward the mountains. Kieran risked a look back and saw that his father had his back to him, had turned the wagon and was leaving the yard. He had escaped and it was unlikely neither he nor Una was seen in the mayhem. All that they most likely knew was that the wind had picked up and buffeted them, frightening the horses.

Kieran just escaped being discovered by his father and finally, he was flying on a dragon, *his dragon!* His heart skipped and he was terrified of the heights they reached at first, but as he learned the shifting and movements of Una's body, he relaxed. He held on and soon his heart was soaring with the thrill of flight. Una sent him her impressions of how happy she was. She purred and her scales rippled iridescent white under his hands, and then she let out a chirping roar. Kieran knew that she had wanted this for a very long time. He sensed her gratitude that he was finally with her, completely in her world. It was as if magic began to tingle in the air around them and Kieran felt Una's joy. His heart was pounding with the thrill of flight and feelings he could not name. He could feel her great heart beating beneath his legs where he clasped her. It thrummed and when their hearts beat strong in rhythm together, they were as one soaring above the clouds. As if their spirits united completely. Kieran felt strong and invincible.

After hours of flying together, Kieran asked Una to head back to the cabin. He had avoided his father and was elated. The dreams of flying they had shared since Una first hatched were all reality now and were even better than he imagined. Una was happier than he had ever felt her being before. Something changed between them as they flew and the bond of love swelled between dragon and rider, and Kieran would never be the same. Neither would Una.

CHAPTER FOURTEEN

K ieran hid with Una in his mountain cabin for the next few days. He struggled with guilt and fear. Not only was he missing work at the forge, but Tartan had lied for him when his father appeared. Tartan hated lying and dishonesty of any kind. It was a doozy of a lie too, making up an ailing sister for Kieran, but it was clear that Tartan understood what was going on. Not sure of when it would be safe to go back to the forge, Kieran crouched inside the door of his hut in his usual thinking position. It never occurred to him that his father would come looking for him, or that he would try to take him back to the farm. That was one place he refused to go ever again, especially because he knew a beating, or worse, awaited him. Once he had his sword and was a skilled warrior, no one could make him do anything he didn't want to do.

His thoughts turned back to flying on Una's back. He wrapped his hands in her long mane, using it like the reins of a horse. His boots rested against the thick scales of her sides and his knees clamped tightly to her shoulders as he leaned forward along her back. It was not as frightening as he envisioned, and they rose into the sky streaming toward the towering mountains surrounding the Village of Appleaid. Time flew away with them as they soared through blue skies, wispy clouds, and chased flocks of birds.

There was a musical quality in the air as the wind streamed across his ears and buffeted his face, whipping his hair back. Kieran's other senses heightened, and his muscles bunched as he held on tightly. As soon as Una's speed slowed, her body coasted smoothly like a boat on water. Her wings, held out straight to the side and they glided with the air currents making slight adjustments to turn or maintain their heading. Kieran heard or rather felt her in his mind, telling him to let go and be at ease. Trust filled his heart, and he slowly let go and lifted his arms. A sense of freedom overwhelmed him. The coolness of the mountain air, the warmth of her body under him, and the vastness of the world stretching below, made Kieran feel like the king of the skies. It was as if his body had become one with hers. He saw and felt what she felt, and he became one with a fierce dragon pumping strong wings and roaring with the joy of flight. For just a moment he felt as if his destiny were assured and his dreams would come true. Together, nothing could stand in their way.

Una took him on an adventure greater than even his fanciful mind could imagine. The air was thin and the speed they gained was exhilarating. She took him to a place high in the mountains where towering, jagged peaks stabbed the sky. The wind had eroded holes in the soft stone and a deep melodious tune played around them like massive flutes accompanied by hollow echoes, airy trills and high shrills. They flew until the sun began to set on the distant horizon and Kieran's stomach began to growl.

The following morning at the cabin, he looked across the small clearing where they lived and stared at the spot where Una lay basking in the elation of their flight the previous day. The top scales on her back were gilded in light and her back turned gold as if she were soaking up the sun's rays. Her long violet colored mane rippled in the slight breeze and turned burnished gold while her legs and belly took on the green of the forest floor. Her eyes were closed as if she were sleeping, but Kieran knew she was awake.

"Una," he called her from the doorway of the cabin. "We should talk about what happened back at the forge."

Una opened her eyes and blinked at him. Nodding, she agreed.

"I told you long ago, I'd run away from home. That was my father and brothers who came looking for me. When he showed up and I was scared...well, what I want to know is did you hear me calling you? I mean, you must have. I was thinking how badly I needed you and how afraid I was, then...you appeared. Did you *hear* me?"

Large emerald eyes held Kieran in a mesmerizing stare, then Una nodded her head slowly. She opened her mouth and made a little chittering sound.

"I knew you could understand me, but you heard from that far away?"

She nodded again and then Kieran went on, realizing he could no longer account for their communication as fanciful dreaming. This was the undefined moment when Kieran grew from a boy to a man as he considered the implications of magic in his life and his bond with the dragon. His dragon was magic!

"You can understand everything I say, and you'll always come when I call?"

Una rose and sat on her haunches. She nodded once again.

"I always thought it was my imagination all this time and I was talking to myself. I didn't want to believe it was true. I just thought you were an ordinary animal."

Crouching down like a cat who was about to pounce, Una bared her teeth and growled at Kieran. Waves of impressions came to him that she did not like being called an animal. Then another thought hit him, imparting to him that he should have known she could understand him because, of course, she was magical.

"Ok, ok, I get it you're not an animal and yes, you're right, I should have known you were magic. I mean, I knew! You are wonderful Una." Kieran dropped his eyes, and his heart swelled with emotion. "I think you know how I feel about you."

Una calmed a little and nodded once, then she held his gaze, and Kieran got the next wave of impressions. Una was telling him she had great magic and that he had yet to see the extent of her powers. He had no idea what she was talking about. Kieran acknowledged she was hinting that there was more. He finally stood and looked down at his feet guiltily.

"I'm sorry I had to ride you. I liked it but it just seems wrong somehow." Kieran was smitten with another wave of Una's anger. Her scales flushed deep red, and he felt that his words and the sentiment behind them hurt her somehow.

"You *want* me to ride you?" he said incredulously, not wanting to admit that it had been something he had always dreamed about.

Flickering to white again, Una nodded again and then crouched low and turned sideways toward him as if she wanted him to mount. Her wings folded against her sides, and she waited. Kieran walked toward her and ran his hand down her wing then over her side as she sent him an impression of him climbing up her leg to reach her back. Kieran did, placing his boot on her bent leg, climbing up he slung his leg over her back between low spikes. Once he was settled, Una's great wings pulsed, he felt her body bunching underneath him and she lifted off. Wrapping his hands in the long violet colored hair cascading along her neck, Kieran hung on. He had ridden horses bareback since he was able to walk, and he clamped his legs on her sides to keep his seat.

They lifted into the air and climbed higher above white puffy clouds. Una headed toward the mountains away from Appleaid where no one could spot them.

This was the best of all, Una had him in her element, flying too high for even birds to climb. Her wings pumped and glittered amethyst and sapphire blue in the sunlight as they reached heights above a cloud bank, and Kieran could see for miles and miles. His skin rippled with gooseflesh, and his hair flew back with the force of the wind. The warmth of Una's body kept him from freezing and her joy was infectious. He whooped loudly and the sound echoed among the clouds. They were one in the sky!

Una showed him more of her favorite places to fly over, the best places to perch in the sun which were high upon the mountain tops. They looked down over vast, deep valleys and sharp jagged peaks. Like a queen surveying her kingdom, Una preened majestically on the highest peaks which Kieran named "the Dragon Mountains." All these places were unreachable by man, except for Kieran who stood beside his dragon, treading where no man had ever trod before, like the king of all he surveyed. His heart, tethered to hers, understood what it was like to be a *dragon*. They were one in heart and mind!

When they landed at their cabin home it was evening, Kieran dismounted and then stood leaning against Una feeling the expansion and contraction of her ribs as she breathed. He did not want to leave her. Their hearts, that had beat with the same cadence while flying, were still in tune. Kieran's body hummed, he felt taller, stronger and in many ways wiser. It was as if Una had imparted her wisdom to him as they flew in the skies. He hated leaving contact with her and as he pulled away from the warmth of her body, Una seemed to sigh with sadness. A feeling of loss smote him. Una's scales rippled and turned dull gray with the shadows. Kieran ran his hand down the side of her neck. He staggered under the weight of her frustration and sadness to be parted from him. His brow wrinkled, and he could not understand.

"We will fly together again soon, Una. Don't be sad." Then Kieran went into his cabin experiencing his own pain. He missed the days when they curled up together, but she was far too large now. Una had followed but only stuck her nose inside. Once he placed logs in the fireplace, she sent a slim stream of white fire into the wood and the cabin glowed brightly with its light.

Images flooded Kieran's mind; Tartan and the forge, the silver sword Tartan showed him the first day Kieran began his apprenticeship, Sara and the two little boys, the forge flickering with golden fire and Una waiting in the forest alone, just beyond the forge. A question seemed to hang between them.

"Yes, I'm going back to Tartan and Sara. I have to tell them the truth about running away. Wait for me here. If they make me leave, we'll just go. I don't want to disappoint Tartan, but I can't stay if they're going to be mad and I don't want to be kicked out of the apprenticeship. We've made our own way before, right? We can do it again."

The words he had not spoken echoed in his heart. He had not become a skilled swordsman, nor had he forged his own sword yet and so leaving would mean his dreams might be lost or delayed. Una agreed with Kieran's decision and curled up outside the hut to sleep. Kieran ate apples, bread, and cheese he had in the cabin, washed it down with cool water and went to bed. The rough planks of the ceiling glowed with the reflection of light from the fire. He could feel his heartbeat slowing in sync with Una's as they drifted off to sleep and slipped into dreams, where they flew once again.

CHAPTER FIFTEEN

Hidden in the brush and trees, Kieran watched Tartan's little farm from the shelter of the forest shadows. Una lay on her belly beside him. All was calm. The chimney lazily sent smoke swirls from the morning's fire rising into the air. The horses dozed in the pen, and the chickens were slowly pecking their way across the yard. As usual, Tartan had been up before dawn and lit the forge fire, and the doors were thrown open.

It had been two days since his father had shown up looking for him and he felt ashamed now that his great secret was revealed. Slowly, he approached the house with his hands in his pockets, his head cast down. Kieran had never been so conflicted in his life. He wanted to be back at his cabin with Una, he wanted to go back to being Tartan's apprentice and more than ever he wanted to be a skilled swordsman so that he never had to be ashamed or afraid again. The biggest fear he had, now Tartan knew the truth about Kieran, was that things would never be the same. He had been found out, proven dishonest and that was not who he wanted to be.

Skipping the morning meal with the family, he went straight to the forge barn and began to lay out the tools, pumped fresh water into a bucket, piled up wood, and stirred the fire into charcoal. After a while Tartan came striding through the door.

"Morning Kieran." He called as he always had since the first day.

"Morning, Sir." Kieran replied, a little sheepishly.

"Sir?" Tartan looked surprised. "What in blazes are you calling me 'Sir' for?"

"Well, I just...I missed a couple days of work. I hoped...you're not angry at me, are ya?" Kieran looked down at his boots and noticed how his trousers didn't reach the top of his boots anymore, and he had the poorly timed thought that he was growing very fast.

"No, not angry. Though, I do wish you would have told me the truth about where you came from." Tartan righted a wide stump and sat down on it. He crossed his arms over his chest and looked like he was patiently waiting for Kieran to reveal everything he previously left out. He shook his head and marveled that the boy seemed to have grown at least two inches in the few days he was gone.

"It's true. That man was my Da and with him two of my brothers. I ran away when I was ten years old. You see, there were eight of us children. There was never enough to eat and always too much work to be done. My Ma was always exhausted, taking care of us all and she never had a kind word for anyone. My Da never seemed to notice me unless it was to criticize me for work not done well enough. My oldest sister used to smack me every time I was in arms reach and my brothers, who I had to share a bed with, used to beat on me when Da wasn't around. It was miserable, and cold. I was always hungry and tired. I saw my future ending like Da; old, mean, with too many mouths to feed and I couldn't stand the thought of it. So, I ran away thinking they'd not even notice I'd gone."

Kieran sat heavily on a stump and rubbed his hands through his hair.

"And your name is actually, Glenn?" Tartan asked.

"NO!" Kieran protested. "Well, not anymore. I guess it was once, but that name never fit me, like boots too small and pinching, rubbing sores into me every time I was called it. I left it behind with that old life."

Tartan waited patiently for him to go on with his story and though he was frowning, his eyes were sympathetic.

"I left seeking adventure and to make my dreams come true. I wanted more than working on that farm until my hands bled. I traveled to different towns for a while and listened at the doors of taverns. That's when I heard tales of wars and the glory of being a warrior. One day, I was begging in a village and heard a bard telling an ancient tale of a man who did great deeds and was the best swordsman who ever lived. His name was Sir Kieran Cray. He was the King's Champion. When I heard that name, I felt like I'd woken up, and been branded, renamed. As if I'd finally found myself, and I was truly alive at last. From that day on I was Kieran, on a quest to become a great warrior. I told you I saw a man who could twirl his sword, throw it in the air and catch it, even swallow it without being hurt. He did all kinds of tricks, and I wanted to be just like him. Kieran Dunn, the mighty warrior. Except, not Dunn, never like that mean old man. You're the only one who's been kind to me, and I was wondering if I could be called Kieran MacLaren?"

Kieran didn't know why but his eyes teared up and he shook with the passion of his story and the conviction that he was on the right path for his life. An overwhelming desire to see his dreams fulfilled possessed him until he felt feverish. He spoke with conviction.

"I felt it was my destiny to become a warrior. When I *found* the crystals in the forest, I knew they were very valuable, I saw a way to buy a sword of my own as you know. Everything seemed to be going my way when I met you and you promised to teach me how to fight with a sword...well, you know the rest." He paused and said more quietly, "I'm sorry I lied to you, and I'm sorry you had to lie for me...about the sick sister."

Tartan stared at him for a while and Kieran had to look away at the intense look he was giving him.

"*Kieran,* I didn't lie. I know you have a girl you hide in the forest. I know that is why you won't stay at the house with Sara and me. You slip up sometimes and it's like you're talking to her. I've heard you call her sometimes when you think I'm not around."

Kieran's face grew more shocked as he listened to what Tartan revealed.

"Why don't you bring her here to meet us and stop keeping her secret? I can't figure it out, but I know you have your reasons and will in your own good time come clean. I may have fabricated a little story based on a few guesses for that man who came looking for you. I didn't want to lose a good apprentice, but also, I didn't trust the man as soon as I saw him and understood who he was."

Tartan looked almost hurt as he went on and revealed the rest.

"I had hoped in time, you and the girl you are hiding would come to trust me and you'd bring her to meet us. I know you're taking care of her and whatever your story is, I'll help where I can. You're only twelve years old, but you seem to have a good head on your shoulders and you're a hard worker."

"I'm thirteen! Well, next month I will be." Kieran grumbled.

It was as if cold water had been thrown in his face when he found out that Tartan knew about Una or at least thought he knew. It was all due to Kieran's carelessness. He never knew that Tartan overheard him talking to Una sometimes throughout the day even if it was a slip of the tongue or speaking his thoughts aloud. It was a terrible shock that Tartan knew but also it was an absolute impossibility to bring Una to meet Tartan anyway. Schooling his features as if he wasn't terrified, Kieran swallowed.

"She's not...um..." he was stymied and had no idea what to say next.

"Never you mind, boy. When you're ready, you bring your girl here to meet us. She would be welcome. Sara would love to have another female around the house, but only when you're both ready, though I worry about her alone in the forest. Now, about your father. You keep hiding inside the forge for a few days and I'll do some asking around to make sure he's left Appleaid. Hide in the back room if you see them coming back again and if you've no wish to go back to your family, then I'll respect that. Besides, you've promised to apprentice with me for ten years. You've got about seven remaining. I'm not about to let you out of our bargain." Tartan winked at him, rose to his feet and turned to his forge. "Now, *Kieran MacLaren*, let's get to work."

Kieran's heart soared as Tartan acknowledged his chosen name and as much as made him his son, then he scratched his head. He'd never met anyone as kind as Tartan and Sara. He was overjoyed to be staying on as apprentice and not just because he was learning to fight with a sword, but he was also beginning to look at Tartan as the father he always wished for but never had.

CHAPTER SIXTEEN

B eck Dunn didn't want to give up the search for his youngest son. Initially, he'd waited a good six months to see if the boy would get hungry and come home on his own, but he never returned. Then Beck had to wait through the harvest season before he could start looking for the boy. Winter hit and delayed his search further, but after the next planting season, Beck left his oldest son in charge and set out to find the youngest boy and teach him a lesson.

The visit to the blacksmith left him with an itchy feeling that his search was over but that had turned sour. Now that itch writhed under his skin and continued to crawl over his spine. Stubbornly, he could not ignore the suspicion that the blacksmith was lying. He also knew he could not keep searching for much longer. Leaving his farm so long was costing him dearly. He had to find that runaway boy and get back soon. He grumbled viciously that the boy would pay for the trouble he caused. If he weren't already dead, he just might be after Beck got his hands on him.

After leaving the blacksmith's yard, he drove his wagon to the local tavern where he could quench his thirst and ask more about the mysterious apprentice and his so-called sister. The smith's story was too shady for Beck. It could be as the smith said that a young boy couldn't survive alone in the mountainous wilderness and was dead. Beck knew that his youngest boy was the cleverest of the lot of them and would more than likely be able to do well enough on his own.

That day the tavern was abuzz with talk of an outlaw army terrorizing the lands far in the south. The outlaw leader was said to be a mysterious woman of great beauty, cunning, and cruelty. They were rampaging across the countryside, stealing everything they could carry, killing those who fought back and taking hostages. Talk of preparing for an invasion if they should come to Appleaid, was tainted with fear and anger. The risk was of the magnitude the town had never seen.

Beck was impatient to change the subject and, after downing a few ales, began to ask the same questions he had asked earlier that morning, about a boy showing up in town within the last couple of years. The other patrons seemed incapable of speaking of anything else other than the impending outlaw force possibly coming their way and bringing war. The town of Buttermilk was far beyond Appleaid, and Beck did not care what happened after he left and so resumed his questioning.

Only now, the tavern keeper seemed less open to giving more information than he had before. Except he did say that he had not heard that the apprentice had a sister. He said the boy's name was *'Kieran'* and confirmed he was sandy haired, clever, friendly, hardworking, and was well-liked in the town.

Those revelations really had Beck's hackles up as that meant that it probably was his boy living under a false name, and that he was working hard for someone else rather than back on the family farm. He decided he was going to have to use a bit of cunning to get the truth out in the open. After begrudgingly paying for the ale, he and his sons drank, they loaded into the wagon and left town. They did not go far though, only enough distance away to turn and head deeper into the forest to camp in the area somewhere within a few miles of the blacksmith's farm.

Deciding that a little spying was in order, he and his other two sons put their heads together and came up with a plan. They would watch the farm for the apprentice to return and see for himself if it was his youngest son.

Taking care not to be seen, the two brothers hid but were lazy and mostly slept the day away when they were supposed to be keeping watch. Beck himself kept an eye on the house, mostly dividing his attention between looking for the boy and watching the blacksmith's plump wife at her chores. That night when they returned to their camp, they ate stringy rabbit they'd poached and planned their next move.

It was after a long two days of spying, a tall, slim lad strode out of the forest toward the blacksmith's forge. Beck perked up and watched, his eyes narrowing and looking long and hard at the boy walking right out in the open. He was lean and had broad shoulders built stronger from working at the forge. His sandy blonde hair swept his shoulders and when he turned to look over the homestead, Beck could see the long nose that was a predominant trait in the Dunn family.

Grinding his teeth until they cracked, he realized he had been lied to. Now, he needed to decide what he wanted to do about it. The blacksmith was a large man with massive arms and broad shoulders. He would be strong and looked like a fierce fighter. Beck realized that he had to be smart about this. So, he hunkered down and just watched his son working the day away for someone else while he had cows at home that needed to be milked. Smoke rose from the forge building and the boy chopped wood, fed the livestock, carried buckets of water and the sharp ring of a hammer striking metal rang throughout the day.

Beck waited patiently, planning the best way to grab his son and drag him back to the farm where he had years of missed work to make up for. Red in the face and sweating with a kind of anger that made his stomach sour, he moved quickly and gathered the other two. Shaking them awake where they were supposed to be paying attention to the blacksmith's farm. He silently beckoned and drew them back to their camp.

The best place to covertly grab Kieran, Beck reckoned, was up the hill in the direction where he'd come from in the forest that morning. It couldn't be done too close to the blacksmith's farm in case the boy put up a fight. Knowing that any noise would bring the blacksmith running to defend his apprentice, Beck figured that it was best to follow him into the forest and get him then. That way, they would only have the boy to deal with and would not cause a ruckus. The blacksmith would never know that the boy's father had dragged him back to the farm where he belonged.

CHAPTER SEVENTEEN

T he fire was banked for the night, the wood piled high for the next morning, and all the tools hung neatly in their respective places. Kieran shared a sumptuous dinner with Tartan and his family as usual. After that, as the sun began to set behind the mountains, he bid them all a good night and headed home, anxious to see Una.

He walked up the familiar trail toward his small cabin home. The forest was eerily tense as if it held its breath. A prickle of wariness crept up the notches of Kieran's spine. He sent a questioning call.

"Una? Is that you?" An impression came back to him of Una perched upon her favorite high peak a few miles away.

The evening light was bright enough for him to see the trail ahead but there was no indication anything was wrong. Kieran stopped just outside the clearing where his small cabin was nestled comfortably in the trees and peered through the thick branches. He watched for whatever had spooked him. Not seeing any reason to be wary, Kieran slowly proceeded home.

It was a terrifying surprise when his father stepped out of the cabin Kieran had called home for the past blissful years. To his right and left, each one of his brothers also stepped out of the trees at the same time.

Swallowing hard, his heart beating painfully in his chest, Kieran's blood turned cold as he stood face to face with the man who had the power to drag him back to his old life.

"Cozy little place you have here, Glenn, or should I be calling you *Kieran* now?" His father's voice was surprisingly calm, which did not bode well. The sound of Kieran's old name felt flat and unfamiliar to his ears. He stayed silent.

"What? The name your mother gave you ain't good enough? You gotta make up another and pretend you've no family, and no responsibilities? You think you can just disappear?" Beck's voice grew dangerously accusing and rose in volume.

Beck Dunn was holding two bags in his dirty hand. One was small and clinked a little as he gestured when speaking. That was the bag that held Kieran's wages earned from working with Tartan at the forge. It was the other bag that had Kieran's nerves tingling with outrage. That one held the remnants of Una's egg. Beck pocketed the bag of coins as if it were his right to help himself. With his other hand he reached into the bigger bag and pulled out a long glittering shard of crystal. A look of astonishment froze Beck's face. His mouth hung open as he held the precious fragment up. It glittered in the evening sunlight that streamed in thick bars of bright gold through the trees. He gave a low whistle of appreciation.

"What have we here?" Surprised, Beck appraised the precious crystal. "You steal this boy?" He sounded impressed and angry at the same time.

This bag also held the dragon's teeth which would raise more questions than Kieran wanted to answer. He stood frozen in his spot shivering with fear, eyes wide and mouth going too dry to speak. The fact that his greedy, abusive father was holding Kieran's most precious possession, something that was part of Una, made him want to attack the man. Though his heart wanted to be brave, he balled his fists and stood helpless to do anything against the three of them.

"Thought you could run away and have a grand adventure, did ya?" Beck's voice was tinged with disgust as he reached in and pulled out another crystal shard. "Your mother won't quit nagging me to go find you. I'm almost glad I did." He paused, looking into the bag at the other things left inside. "You know what I do with boys who steal, shirk their duty to family and run away? There's wood to chop and water to haul, there's crops to plant and reap, cows to milk, and here you are, living the fine life, doing just as you please. You're lazy and good for nothing except forcing your sisters and brothers to do *your* share of the work!"

Kieran almost felt like crying, but he realized he was not the boy he used to be. He was learning a trade, and he learned how to fight with a sword. Despite being only thirteen, he knew he was big and stronger now and could defend himself. His mind was reeling with danger and growing rebellion.

Returning the crystal shards to the bag, Beck looped it through his belt. Then he drew out a long knife from its sheath at his side. Holding the gleaming blade up in front of Kieran's face, he turned it slowly so that Kieran could appreciate the weapon.

"After your brothers beat the stubbornness out of you, I've got a plan to keep you from runnin' off again. You see, if'n you cut the muscles in the back of the leg, just above the ankles," Beck brandished the blade meaningfully, "it can lame a man. He can still work, but he won't be doin' any more running. You get my meaning, boy? Don't worry though, by the time I get you home it'll be healed enough for you to get back to your chores right away. You'll be lame, but you'll still be able to work hard as you should! I'll teach you to run away from home!"

The threat of crippling and a beating was terrifying. His father had not said anything about his mother or sisters being worried about his safety. None of them wanted him back for anything other than being a slave to the farm and doing the work they all wanted to avoid. None of them missed him for him. His mind went wild and all he could think of was Una. He kept his eyes trained on the bag holding her egg's crystal shards and then there was the big knife Kieran was sure his father wouldn't hesitate to use on a beautiful dragon.

"Una! Una! Stay away! It's too dangerous at the cabin! My father's found me! Don't come home!"

Terror had his legs shaking. How could he go back to his father's farm and still become a warrior who rode a dragon into glorious battles? It was at that moment that he realized his dreams were childish and that standing glaring at him was reality. He was nothing more than a farm boy who ran away from home to avoid a long life of back-breaking work. All he had to look forward to was permanent crippling, and frequent beatings. He would be dragged back to the farm, worked to death, starved, and his dreams would be cut short forever, and what would happen to Una?

"Ain't runnin' no more, boy!" Beck's fury at his youngest son unleashed with a maniacal laugh.

While Beck chastised him and confiscated his hard-earned wages and most precious possessions, his brothers had been moving stealthily around to flank him. Both grinned and started toward him. Butch, the oldest, cracked his knuckles and Dodd pounded his fists together, looking forward to the beating they were about to hand out.

Kieran's muscles flexed and he thought about the sword training he had been through with Tartan. Comparing his size to theirs, he was a little shorter, but broader in the shoulders, lean and fast. He might be able to hold his own against one of them, but two attacks at once was questionable. Wood would be practically useless against a long knife. Kieran realized he had few choices. He could beg his father for forgiveness and promise to go with them and return home. If he made a deal never to run away again, maybe Beck would not cut his ankles, he could be spared laming and a lot of pain. He knew the surrounding woods like the back of his hand and could disappear again. Or he could fight back and give as good as he got before the three of them overpowered him and cut him. It was all a matter of how badly Kieran wanted to resist and keep the life he had built away from his family. Then there was Una, he would fight to the death to remain with her.

As his brother's advanced, he backed up a few paces and glanced down out of the corner of his eye, he spotted a stick. It was long enough to emulate the wooden practice swords he was used to. He bent down carefully and picked up the make-shift weapon.

"What're you going to do with that? You puny little cow shit!" Butch mocked while Dodd just grinned. His broken teeth flashing with excitement.

Before the fight could break out, Kieran's father's laughter choked, and his face turned sickly green. Staggering back, his eyes travelled up above Kieran's head and grew so big they almost popped out of his head. Butch gave a strangled scream and tripped backward. Dodd stopped in his tracks shaking, as a wet stain began to grow down the inside of his leg.

A hot puff of air ruffled Kieran's hair and he turned to look up, knowing what he would find. Una stood behind him defensively, sheltering him between her front legs. Her thick mane and scales glistened blood red, her claws and horns gleamed violently black. Her green eyes narrowed menacingly while her lips curled in a snarl, showing sharp, white fangs. She loomed possessively over Kieran and lowered her head to meet the eyes of the three men threatening him. Her body shook with a deep growl as her wings spread protectively.

A strange feeling came over Kieran and he felt as if he were encompassed in the dragon's magic. It was as if they were once again, flying in the sky. He felt her red anger and strength bursting from her chest, and the desire to spit fire and incinerate their enemies.

The low growl continued to rise from deep in her chest and Kieran felt the reverberation in his very bones. The forest clearing shook with the force of it. Butch doubled over, slammed to his knees and heaved up the contents of his stomach. Una let out a slim stream of white fire that just reached the men. The flame licked their faces, so close that their eyebrows were singed. Dodd's shirt began to smolder, and he patted it frantically while squealing with terror.

Kieran reached up and placed a hand on Una's long neck. Proving the dragon behind him was a friend and that he at least was safe. Part of him was terrified, as he sensed Una was on the verge of snapping up his father and brothers with her great jaws. As much as he disliked them, he didn't want them dead.

"My friend here doesn't take kindly to thieves. I'll just be taking my things back." Kieran did his best to sound confident, as if he were in charge. He pointed with the wooden stick he still held, "Carefully, set the bags on the ground and back away."

His father was too afraid of the dragon not to do as Kieran instructed, and he pulled the bag of crystals out of his belt and slowly set them on the ground. Dodd continued to make a squealing sound as if he were too terrified to speak. Butch recovered from his sick and was shivering with fear.

"G-G-Glenn, what is that thing?" Beck pointed a shaking finger. Then his glare fixed on Kieran's face, and he screeched, "Your eyes! They're glowing green!"

"Glenn is dead. You'd better forget about him. My friend here is *always* by my side," Kieran spoke loudly to drive his point home.

He felt the power consuming him, transforming him into an extension of Una! As one, their connection flared, and it was as though he could not see with his eyes, but hers! His vision was sharper, homed in on the cowering men as if he were in two places at once. Their fear stirred loathing inside the pit of his stomach, and he had no familial feelings for any of them. They were just thieves and bullies!

"If you want to avoid being scorched into charcoal, you'd better leave *now* and don't come back. If I hear you've told a single tale about my friend, well, I know where you live, and we'll pay a visit to shut you up!"

Kieran did not boast, he merely spoke the truth of what he was willing to do. Una was sending him waves of anger and images of snapping the three men with her jaws and crunching their bones into mince. He foresaw the blood and broken bones of his father and brothers and felt her fury. The feelings she sent him took him over and he wanted to rend and tear them up as well. Pointing behind them with the stick he had intended to defend himself with, he warned in a deeper, raspy tone, as if he and Una spoke with one voice. He felt his skin burning red.

"We'll give you one chance to leave with the skin on your bones. Go back to your farm while you can!"

The stumbling panic of his father and brothers gave a kind of satisfaction that bordered on pride. Moving in unison, Kieran's head turned mimicking Una's above him and together they listened with the dragon's keen ears as they ran. Still, they each wanted to tear through the forest and burn and bite those who threatened them. They stood as one for a long time and Kieran felt Una's rippling scales, wind-combed hair and flexing claws. He marveled at this feeling of connection and allowed it to consume him as their hearts beat as one.

After they could no longer hear his father and brothers, he turned and climbed up Una's side. He straddled her and felt the magic that made them blend with the forest. They leaped into the sky, and he felt everything she felt, everything that she was and that they were together. Kieran wanted to shout with joy, as he bent forward and clutched her flowing mane, he melded with her mind further, laying safely tucked against her back. The wind streamed past them as she allowed her vision to flow into him, and he rejoiced in the motion of her wings. Pulling magic from the skies, completely in-tune with each other, they soared into the dusky night where they roared their joy with one voice.

Kieran slept, but his mind did not rest feeling Una's presence more keenly each night. Ever since the day they scared his father and brothers away, their bond had strengthened and the connection they had in heart and mind was unbreakable. He had long since realized he would never be a normal human again and often it seemed difficult to tell himself apart from Una, as if he were the dragon and she human. Especially when they were flying, he could not distinguish his body and mind from hers. Thus, he sensed a growing impatience and frustration within her. For what, he could not guess.

This night, he knew she was just outside the door of his cabin sheltered in her cave of trees, but he missed her terribly. He thought he would dream of being a dragon, on this night after he and Una had been one in the sky for the entire day, but he did not. Instead, it was as if he stood outside his own body watching his human self, sleeping peacefully. The scent of magic permeated his dream. His mind whirled and his dream took a strange turn as suddenly an imaginary girl stood at his bedside watching him. Kieran had an impression that it was Una dreaming she was a real girl and that they were sharing the same dream. She was slight of build, maybe a few inches shorter than him. Her hair was violet like Una's mane. She was lovely with sparkling green eyes that caught the firelight and reflected it back, a flickering green flame in large almond shaped eyes with long black lashes. Kieran instantly loved the beautiful young girl who stood beside his bed like the specter of someone he had never met but knew heart and soul. He felt as if it was Una's dream creating the girl she wished to be. It made an odd sort of sense to him in that he felt like a dragon when they flew and now, she dreamed of being a girl as he slept.

He was a dragon with her flying, and she was a human with him on the earth in their minds. She slipped into bed beside him and rested her head on his chest. Caught in their shared dream, hearts beating as one, Kieran wrapped his arms around her and kissed her forehead. They clung together the whole night through.

When Kieran woke in the morning, he was alone, as he expected. The dream of the human Una was just that, a dream, a product of his overactive imagination and maybe his dragon's as well. It was often hard to separate the dragon from the man he was becoming. He was struck with a strange sort of guilt. He rolled out of bed and placed his bare feet on the floor. Immediately he felt conflicted over his dreams and before he even put his boots on, he ran to the window of the cabin. Outside he saw Una's large body sleeping curled up just outside under the shelter of her tree bower. Her scales had taken on a rich green, blending in with the colors of the forest. Her violet head was facing away from him, and he saw the giant swell of her back, and her magnificent, folded wings. The rise and fall of her sides showed she was still sleeping.

Kieran went to a bucket and splashed cold water on his face. He took a clean shirt off the peg and dressed quickly. Sitting back down on the bed, his mind whirled and he wondered if he should hide last night's dream from Una. So, he flooded his thoughts with what the day might bring and practiced sword training in his imagination. Clinging to his desire to become a great warrior was easier than admitting the desires of his dreams.

Grabbing a hunk of cheese, he walked out the door and went to her. He remembered the day they had been flying as if it had happened only minutes ago and sent that wonderful memory to her of them together in the clouds.

Una sighed, slowly opened an emerald eye, and watched as Kieran walked into the forest. Her knowledgeable eyes saw him head downhill toward the forge ready to face the day and if a dragon could smile, she did.

CHAPTER
EIGHTEEN

As Kieran approached eighteen, he had grown almost as tall as
Tartan. His shoulders were broad, and his arms were gaining thick muscles as he swung a hammer regularly. His hands were
strong and his legs powerful. He had been Tartan's apprentice for
going on eight years and the hard work was having a positive effect
on his growing body. He learned not only to make horseshoes,
fix wagon wheels, build barrels and make various farm tools, but

he was becoming a master at crafting wooden handles. He carved animal figures for Soren, the new baby. Tarren was old enough that he could take over some of the farm chores and the young boy looked up to Kieran like an older brother. They never spoke about Una again since that first time many years back when Tartan lied to Beck Dunn. Kieran was grateful for that and never mentioned his father confronting him or them meeting Una. Luckily, they never saw that man again. The boy, Glenn, whom Kieran had once been as a young runaway, was well and truly gone.

Sometimes, Kieran caught Tartan looking at him with strange contemplation on his face. Once or twice over the years he even broached the subject, but after a while, he stopped asking about Una.

The lessons in sword fighting continued and Kieran became very proficient if not highly skilled with the weapon. By the force of his will, he learned and challenged Tartan to teach him more. He could also throw an axe with great accuracy and a knife as well.

Kieran began to feel a little restless as the days went by and when things were slow at the forge he asked for an extra day off to spend more time flying with Una. She was a huge, fully grown dragon and they spent every free minute together. They flew in blue sunny skies, in rain and even through falling snow. In mind, heart, and soul, they were one being in the air, but after almost falling off one or two times, Kieran fashioned a saddle of sorts. It was much like a horse's saddle, but the stirrups were more secure so that he could slip his boots in and not fall off should Una flip over. He also fashioned a strap out of the dragon mother's hair that tied him on. Their joy in being together was complete.

As a man, Kieran started to feel strange. Each night he dreamt of flying on Una's back, but he also dreamt of forging a long, deadly silver sword and fighting in glorious battles. Also, each night the same dream girl slipped into his bed, where they curled up in an embrace. Always, Kieran would wake feeling bereft, wishing she was real. He never discussed his desires with Una.

Thoughts of females frequently intruded on Kieran's conscience as his body began to change in ways he couldn't discuss with anyone. He became fondly known around the Village of Appleaid as the blacksmith's *'handsome'* apprentice. Whenever he walked through the town, the girls would call his name and praise his attractive face, shoulder-length golden hair, and muscular build. As he grew into a young man, they would giggle and bat their eyes at him. Some flirted openly with him, coming by the forge or stopping him on trips to the local tavern when he visited with Tartan. It was on his eighteenth birthday that a girl tried to kiss him. The second their lips touched, Kieran felt a flaming fire in his head. Despite her willingness and his hunger for more, he felt Una knew what he was up to. Feelings of jealousy overwhelmed him and because she was always part of him, watching him, her anger within his head roared like an inferno. Kieran had pulled away from the baffled girl, made his excuses and quickly left her.

After that stolen kiss, Una was furious with him and would not speak to him for days. He tried to explain that it was natural for a man to be attracted to woman and that someday Una might have to share him with a human girl. She filled his mind with jealousy and anger, and Kieran had to lay down as he felt like he had a burning fever. Her scales remained crimson for days and nothing would console her. In his dreams they did not fly, but the dream girl came as she had every night for the past few years. The night Kieran kissed the girl in the village, her slanting green eyes were filled with sad tears of betrayal, tracking slowly down her cheeks. Instead of laying down with him, she just stood by his bed staring at him with silent accusations frozen on her pink lips. As Kieran slept, he wanted to talk to her, but it was only a dream and all he could do was watch as she turned and left. After a few nights absent, she returned once again, and they went on as if nothing had happened. Una's scales turned back to her normal iridescent white and she seemed to have forgiven him.

At about the same time, Una stopped being angry, she also began disappearing at night and instead of the girl of his dreams, he dreamed of white fire and mysterious chanting. Kieran would wake up feeling strange as if he drank too much ale and would stare off into the mountains where a white light illuminated the sky in the morning gloom. He was relieved when the human girl returned to his dreams and curled up beside him again in blissful imagination.

There was talk in the town of Appleaid of strange goings-on, impending war heading their way and some whispered quietly about spotting a dragon in the sky. Some had seen a red dragon, some a black dragon and many a glittering white dragon. Whenever Kieran heard someone tell these tales, he brought up the fact that dragons were gone from the world and convinced the person they were wrong. As rumors spread, Kieran warned Una that she was growing careless, allowing herself to be seen. She just lifted her nose petulantly and turned away with a smoky huff.

One morning Kieran woke, wishing the beautiful girl was real with all his heart. There was a strange aching in certain parts of his body. He had to hide these feelings from Una because he knew his dragon would not understand his need for human female companionship. He rolled over and threw the covers off and sat up placing his feet on the dusty floor. Staring down, bothered by the night's dreams and the needs of his changing body, he noticed beside his feet there were two perfect, smaller footprints. Kieran stared at the floor for a moment trying to understand what he was seeing. Picking his feet up he saw his larger bare footprints in the dust and then a smaller, slimmer pair next to it, tracking out the door. He could not understand it. Then suddenly it struck him that the imaginary girl he dreamt of every night would not have left real prints in the dust as she left his bed because she wasn't real. Yet, two sets of prints, one of his and one of...stunned into motion he flew out of bed, grabbed his trousers, and stumbled across the floor pulling them on as he headed toward the door. He had to find Una, his dragon.

Stepping out into the chilly morning air, he did find her. Una was waiting in the clearing outside his door. Her large emerald eyes looked apprehensive and darted away not meeting his directly, as guilty revelations glinted there. Kieran stopped and rubbed the sleep out of his eyes and looked again. After so many years together, their communication was just like when two humans spoke out loud. As a dragon she did not talk in words beyond chirping, purring and growls, but impressions, only their understanding was just like having a conversation after their long time together. Sometimes, when she was angry with him, she would close her mind, and he could not hear her. He often hid his thoughts. Now was one of those times.

"Una...did you see? Listen, ah, I've been dreaming about a human girl. I know it is strange, and I've hid her from you, but she comes into the cabin at night?" The words were clumsy on Kieran's tongue. Recalling the last time he kissed a human girl and Una's jealousy, he knew he needed to tread lightly.

He was embarrassed and a little frightened to know what she thought about his dreams of a human girl, though he realized she had to know a little because of the bond they shared. His dreams were hers, the magnitude of what that meant, stunned him. Suddenly, Una's thoughts flared with so many emotions at once Kieran staggered back grabbing his head in a stabbing pain. His mind was flooded with impressions of sorrow, happiness, fear, apprehension, and above all, longing. Overwhelmed, he raised a hand to desperately push the torrent of her thoughts away. He squeezed his eyes shut to stop the dizziness that overtook him.

When he opened them, he thought he was still not seeing clearly as Una's dragon form began to waver and ripple. Wings spread; she reared up and suddenly began to shrink. Kieran watched wide-eyed as Una, his *dragon*, changed with some kind of unknown magic. When the transformation finished, standing right in front of him in the flesh, was the girl from his dreams. She appeared to be about his age and was completely exposed. Before him, was the green-eyed girl with dark lavender hair, high cheekbones, rosy lips and small round breasts. Mouth hanging open, Kieran couldn't draw breath, as the sight of her human form stunned him into a shocked silence. Staggering and backing up until he hit the wall of the cabin, the rough wood was all that was holding him up. He was in shock and shook with fear!

His heart beat out of his chest, and he flew into action. Ducking back into the cabin and grabbing his extra shirt off the peg, he bolted back out. Closing his eyes, he held the shirt out to the girl waving it frantically. He felt her take the shirt and he waited until he figured she was covered. Peeling his eyes open one at a time, Kieran looked and yes, where Una his dragon was, now stood the human female from his dreams.

CHAPTER NINETEEN

Moving backward, Kieran just blinked and stared at the girl in front of him until he could speak.

"*Una?*" He shouted incredulously, not really believing what he was seeing.

"Yes," she whispered in a sweet voice that was new to him, but at the same time, familiar.

"What have you done? How is this possible?" Kieran's hands waved up and down at her and he slowly shook his head, not understanding. "What in blazes is going on? You're a girl!" he accused. "How? When did this happen! Why didn't you...how long have you been able to...*Una?*" Kieran's mouth went dry, and he kept shaking his head in disbelief then he got angry at her, "Who are you?"

"Don't be angry with me Kieran. I just wanted to be with you. *Human* like you! I made the magic to change. It was easy. When you are away during the day, I stay a dragon, but I wanted so badly to be like you...to speak to you with a voice and...it was my choice."

"You've been sneaking into bed with me for how long? I thought I was dreaming! Why did I never know before now?"

Kieran was shocked. Then he noticed that Una was standing barefoot in the dew-covered grass and was shivering. Grabbing her hand, he pulled her into the cabin and sat her by the fireplace in his only chair. He started a fire and as soon as it was blazing, he turned back to the *girl,* Una.

"Una, how can you be human?" he still could not believe his eyes.

"It happened that day we first flew together. I hated being away from you. I wanted to be human like you and when I wanted it badly enough, the magic came. It is a thing dragons can do...I can explain everything. I'm sorry, I was going to tell you eventually." Her voice grew angry, and her eyes flared, "then that girl kissed you and I nearly..."

"UNA!" Kieran jumped to his feet. Holding his hands out toward her, he stopped her from going on. "Don't say anything more."

He blushed hot red, and began to pace, and tried to think, but his mind would only focus on one thought and that was, he had been sleeping with *her for real*. Well, of course he had been sleeping with her, when she was a dragon and evidently as a real girl. It was all too confusing to make sense of. He turned and looked at Una's beautiful face, sitting in a shirt too big for her, her bare legs showing. His body stirred and he flushed and turned away. Whirling around he had an idea.

"Wait," he said, "can you just stay a dragon? Don't turn into..." he waved his hands in front of her, speechless.

"Don't you think I'm beautiful?" Una's voice dropped and she looked sad.

Yes, I do, that's the problem. Kieran thoughts screamed in his head. He looked up and she was slowly smiling.

"Why is that a problem?" Una asked sheepishly.

"Because I am a man and...like this...well..." He waved at her again, then his hands hung to the side helplessly and he realized he had no idea what he was trying to say. "Wait! I didn't say that out loud. You're in my mind when you shouldn't be!"

"I've always been connected to you since I hatched. I can hear your thoughts, read your emotions as I have always done, and I share mine as well. It is nothing new and has always been thus between us." Una shrugged as if invading a person's thoughts was commonplace.

"Humans don't read each other's minds!" He was shouting again but quickly calmed down because he didn't want to scare her. "Can't you just stay a dragon?"

"I won't." She said stubbornly and stood crossing her arms over her chest.

Taking a step toward him, she looked up and searched his eyes, her own filling with tears. "It is simple. You are mine. I want to be with you as a dragon *and* as a woman."

She placed her hands on his bare chest and gazed at him with wide adoring eyes. Pressing close she repeated, "I want to be with you in *every* way."

The fire was warming the small cabin, and Kieran was staring down at Una. His body surged with heat; his breathing quickened as did his heartbeat. He recalled all the nights they slept side by side and the hardening of key parts of his body revealed the problem with Una becoming a woman.

"How can I explain, Una? When a man and a woman...things happen naturally, they..." his voice softened and faltered. He shrugged bewildered.

"I know. I've watched humans from the shadows...what they do with their bodies...I want that with you Kieran." Her hand slid up his neck and one rested on his chest. Kieran stared down at her. Una, the woman, was sensual and enticing, sweet smelling and irresistible.

All the strange emotions he had when he was around females came frothing to the surface in an unmanageable churning and throbbing need. He wanted to lean down and see what it was like to kiss her, but this was *Una*. He had known her since she hatched, knew her as a dragon, but not as a girl, a woman!

"Una! You *have* to stay a dragon!" the protest ushered from his mouth in a plea.

Denying the desires of his body, Kieran had to move away.

Her hand slid from his chest. Her eyes burned with dragon fire as she shook her head, *"No."*

Turing away he ran his hands through his hair and over his face trying to think. Then he realized what he needed to do. He grabbed his other shirt from where he had tossed it the night before and pulled it over his head. Then he went to a wooden chest where his other clothes were neatly folded. Pulling out an old pair of trousers, woolen socks and boots he grew out of, he turned back to Una.

"Una," he tried to sound as if he were completely in charge. "First, you must put more clothes on. Humans wear clothes. Second, you cannot continue to listen to what I'm thinking. Humans do not read each other's thoughts or speak within their minds. I need a certain amount of privacy. I think it best that you stay here in the cabin when you're in human form and hide as usual when you're in dragon form. I can't leave you here like this...a beautiful girl alone in the woods, or you could be in danger. Third, we can't...sleep together anymore, it's not proper for two people to be so close, unless, well unless they are married…" Kieran's brain stopped, and his thoughts went blank. He could not think one step further.

"I understand, Kieran. It will take a while for you to get used to me in this form. I will do most of what you say. I will honor your wishes by not listening to all your thoughts unless you are in danger, or if you need me, then call and I will hear. I will wear the clothes, but I want to be with you from now on. I want to go to the forge with you in human form and I don't want to be away from you anymore so that girls can kiss you. I get too lonely by myself, day in and day out. Say you'll take me with you?"

"Take you to the forge!" Kieran's voice rose again as he yelled. "Are you mad! No one can know about you. What if someone hurts you or…?" He couldn't even conceive of all the bad things that could happen to a beautiful girl around humans. "What if someone in the town finds out there is a dragon up here? One that can take human form?"

"We've been here for years, and no one suspects a thing."

"That's not true! There has been talk in the town and in the tavern of war coming and monsters seen in the area. Someone mentioned seeing a shadow in the shape of a dragon on the ground and seeing one flying in the clouds! I've heard talk and rumors of you, and we can't just ignore that!"

"I've been watching and learning the human ways. I know how it is done, and I can be careful, Kieran. I just want to be part of your life down there in the village. I'm tired of being alone and away from you. They may suspect a dragon is in the area, but dragons have been gone for years, they will think nothing of a human girl."

Kieran stared in shock and wonder. They would think a lot of a girl who possessed her beauty! He tried to organize his thoughts away from the physical.

"Don't read my thoughts anymore or anyone else's for that matter unless you are in dragon form. I'll speak to Tartan about all this... about you. I don't know how to explain you, but I'll come up with something. Now, I'm late. Tartan will be expecting me. Please put those clothes on."

Kieran wanted her to cover up her lithe, shapely legs and *everything* else. Una picked up the clothes but then stopped and turned back to him.

"I will do everything you say Kieran, but I am coming with you. I'll wear the clothes; I'll try to be more human and keep my dragon secret. I'll do anything you say, but you must do something for me."

"What?" Kieran swallowed, fearing what she would ask next.

"Kiss me. Like you did that girl in town. I want your kiss on my human mouth." Una's luscious mouth was set in a determined line.

Kieran's chest ached in a strange way and his hands itched. His cheeks reddened with embarrassment, but he wasn't sure over what. The fact that Una had seen him kissing another girl or that she wanted him to kiss her was maddening. She was a dragon, but not at this moment. Worst of all he *felt* her desire for the kiss and the need was overpowering, blending with his needs.

"Please." She whispered and stepped closer.

Moving as if in a trance, Kieran slid his hands around her waist, and her slim form was warm and *real*. His shirt was too large for her and hung just below her bare hips. The collar gaped open partially exposing the pale, round breasts underneath. Breathing increasing and blood heating, Kieran swallowed hard and pulled her against him as if in a trance. Kissing her was not a problem, *stopping* kissing her was.

"I can't Una. I need time to deal with these *changes* in you and, well, one thing at a time. Ok? For now, can't you just be happy I'm taking you to the forge?"

Una just stared at him then gave a little smile and nodded. Bending to grab the trousers and socks that she dropped on the floor, the shirt she wore rode up and Kieran saw the curve of her hips and more. His mouth went dry. Turning away to give her privacy was his only choice.

Once Una was dressed and Kieran had his bodily desires under control, they headed down the mountain toward the forge. Beside him Una practically skipped with excitement, and her smile was radiant. A soft breeze blew the lavender and violet strands of her long hair across her lovely face. They frequently stared at each other as they walked and Kieran was not certain how it happened, but her hand was in his. Stopping several times, he tried to convince her to stay a dragon, but she stubbornly refused. The realization hit him that no human had hair the color of pale violets and he stopped before they reached the edge of the forest.

"Una, this isn't going to work." He stopped her and said sadly. "No human has hair this color."

Una stared at him considering and then, just like when she was a dragon, her coloring flickered and changed. Her hair went from the dragon violet to stark black. Kieran was struck by the harshness of the color against the pale peach of her skin and his brow furrowed. This was going to take some time to get used to. Una realized he didn't like the color, and it began to lighten. Her hair flickered through a variety of colors until she sensed she found the one he liked best. Now instead of the violet she stood with hair the same rich golden color as his. Kieran smiled.

"Beautiful!" he whispered entranced, and then cleared his throat and blinked, "I mean that's better."

He was grinning as he swallowed and wiped his face of emotion. He was not sure at all if he was going to ever get used to looking at his dragon in human form. Una went up on her tiptoes and quickly pressed her lips to his then tugged his hand and they walked from the forest hand in hand. Through the trees they had seen Tartan's forge fire smoldering feebly, and the horses mingled around the corral. They approached the house with Kieran taking the lead and Una, in a sudden burst of nerves, clutched his arm and hid behind him. It was a fine summer day, and the window shutters were open. The front door was thrown wide letting in sunshine and fresh air. The thick smell of biscuits, bacon and eggs wafted toward them.

Tartan was still at his breakfast when Kieran suddenly appeared at the door. Instead of entering he stood outside almost as if he were afraid to go in.

"You're not that late, Kieran. No need to worry, come in and break your fast."

"Ah, Tartan, Sir, ah Miss Sara," Kieran hesitated nervously.

Sara looked up and smiled at him as usual. A minute later, both Tartan and Sara's mouths hung open as they watched Kieran turn and speak quietly to someone standing next to him. Then he grabbed that someone's hand and pulled a slim, shy girl to his side. They looked at her from head to toe, taking in everything about her from the long dark gold hair, boy's shirt and pants that hung too big on her, to the old pair of oversized boots she wore.

Tartan slowly stood and pushed his chair away from the table. His eyes were wide and round. The air in the room was still, and baby Soren stopped fussing. They all stared at each other. Even Tarren, who was usually boisterous in the mornings, was silent.

"Ah," Kieran began again, "Tartan, Sir, Miss Sara, this is *Una*."

Una clung to his side and stared at them. Her wide green eyes, slightly tilted and almond shaped, were bordered by thick dark lashes. Her other fine features of fairy-like beauty held their attention.

Tartan was speechless, and so it was up to Sara to break the spell they were all under.

"We were wondering when we'd finally get to meet you, Una." Sara said gently as if she didn't want to scare the girl away, "though Kieran hasn't told us much about you, we're happy he finally decided to bring you down. Please come in. You must be hungry. Tartan, make room for Kieran's Una."

Each time Sara spoke the name *Una,* Kieran gave a shudder of disbelief. The scene felt strange but right, like something that had been missing from his adopted family and was finally falling into place.

They pulled an extra chair to the table and Sara hurried to grab a plate and utensils for her. Kieran had been expected, so his place was already prepared. Tartan was still standing in a daze staring with his mouth open. Sara had to pull him down to sit and elbowed him hard in the ribs to awaken him from shock. She also put voice to the glaring question between them all.

"Kieran, she's lovely! You know we would have welcomed Una with open arms." Sara spoke happily while dishing a good size portion of eggs and sausage, onto a plate and set it before Una with a biscuit. "It don't make no sense that you hid her." She scolded.

"Una's been uh, *away* for a little while." Kieran offered a bit awkwardly. "She's sort of just got here."

Una plucked up the biscuit with a finger and thumb and carefully lifted it to her nose. She took a long slow sniff and smiled before biting into it.

"I knew Kieran would eventually bring you to meet us. It's been long overdue." Tartan finally spoke, his voice was soft but directing his words to Kieran, could not keep the censure out of his voice. "Has something happened? Are you two in trouble?"

Kieran blushed and realized he had not thought this through very well. So, he stuffed a buttered biscuit in his mouth while thinking fast. Not being able to talk with his mouth full, he would not meet Tartan's eyes. Somehow, he had to explain everything to Tartan and Sara without revealing that Una was also a dragon and he had only, just that morning, discovered that she could take human form.

"Kieran?" Tartan prompted a little sharply.

"Una and I, well, she's *special* and I didn't know how to...I was afraid that..."

"Are you Kieran's sister?" Sara asked.

Una shook her head *'no'* and took another bite of the buttered biscuit as Kieran had.

"Out with it, Kieran!" Tartan said rather forcefully.

"Una is not my sister. She is, *more*...and my best friend." Kieran had a flood of images from Una speaking to him as she had when she was a dragon. The images were stronger and coming so quickly he had a hard time separating them to come up with a cohesive story to put into words.

"I didn't want anyone to know of her because we, I was afraid. She's special and..."

"Kieran rescued me many years ago when we were both children." Una recovered for him. Her soft voice cut through his struggle for words, taking over the narrative with confident ease.

"It was a time before we came to Appleaid. I hid because I was afraid to go around people, but I became too lonely in our home and Kieran wanted me to meet you because you are family to him, and he loves you. It was my fault, but I don't want to hide anymore."

"I thought you just said she's been away and just got back?" Tartan looked suspicious.

"It's complicated." Kieran scratched his head and couldn't look at them.

"Well, we are so glad you finally came down from the mountain and hope you're back for good now." Sara was beaming with joy and Una smiled back. "You've nothing to be nervous about around us. We'll just take it slow. I confess I'm a little bit miffed at Kieran. We could have provided proper clothes for you at least. I hope you've had enough to eat all this time. It will be so nice having another woman around. Please don't be shy anymore and come as often as you want. If you'd like, I have an old dress or two we can alter to make a fit for you, and you won't have to wear Kieran's old clothes anymore."

Una grinned happily and nodded her head. Kieran stared down at his plate and did not say anymore on the subject. The rest of the meal went smoothly while they all lingered at the table longer than usual. When everything was eaten, Sara took charge and ordered the men to go work while she and Una cleaned up and Una got some new clothes.

CHAPTER TWENTY

Tartan had never been truly angry with Kieran, but there was a first time for everything. He placed a heavy hand on Kieran's shoulder and steered him out to the forge where he pushed the lad down onto a stump. Facing him with crossed arms, glaring under furrowed brows, he seemed to be trying to calm himself. His breathing sounded as if he was a maddened bull about to charge. Kieran could not meet Tartan's eye and stared down at his hands.

"Kieran," Tartan began. "I knew you had a cabin up in the woods not far from here, and that you had a girl up there that you hid for reasons of your own. I thought she was your sister. I honored your wishes to keep that part of your life private, but this...*she*...changes things. I've a need to know what is going on. Though I can come up with a few guesses, why now?"

Kieran swallowed and his shoulders slumped. He ran his hands through his unruly hair and over his face. He felt the soft stubble of a man's beard beginning to grow and something inside him longed to unburden his heart. Taking a deep breath, he started to tell as much of the truth as he could.

"Una told the truth; I did sort of rescue her. I told you I ran away when I was ten because I wanted adventure, to become a warrior, and to learn how to wield a sword. You met the cruel man who called himself my Da. I told you then, I'd left life on that farm to seek my fortune. I found, *took* Una, and then fate brought us here. She's very special and I..."

"What do you mean you *took* her!" Tartan's eyes flared as he shouted. "All these years you've hidden a child you took!"

"I... thought she was in danger, and I took her from her mother not knowing." Kieran looked desperate, and his voice rose. "I was just a stupid kid and thought Una was unwanted and in danger. I rescued her! She didn't want to go back and...I wanted to take care of her."

A note of panic entered his voice and Kieran began to plead. "I couldn't bring Una down here until today, then things got out of hand, and I couldn't keep her secret anymore."

Tartan's voice lowered suspiciously and said slowly. "What things got out of hand?"

"Una only today revealed to me that..." Kieran realized he could not divulge what truly happened without giving away more of the truth. Tartan would never expect or believe that Una was a dragon in human form, but partial truths could get Kieran's predicament sorted out. "That she is a *woman*." Which was the truth.

His eyes darted to Tartan's and Kieran saw understanding flash in his eyes. He rushed on talking about the first thing on his mind and changing the subject from his real crime, the theft of the dragon's egg and forgotten magic that made a dragon a human.

"We've always slept together and this morning...well, it's the first time I ever saw her as a *woman,* and everything changed. Una said she is lonely, I've always been afraid to bring her here, but didn't know what else to do. It all is jumbled up. I wanted to talk to you about...I need advice from you Tartan...man to man."

They stared at each other in silence. Kieran infused his lies with truths and was too nervous to say more and let the partial knowledge he'd spoken reveal what it would.

"I think you're asking about more than you think you're asking. As I said I've known about the old cabin up the mountainside, I suspect that is where you lived. I've also known you've had someone up there with you. I didn't meddle because I knew you had your reasons. When your father came looking for you a few years back, I thought we'd meet your Una then. I admit I was a little wounded that you didn't seem to trust us with the rest of your secrets, but I didn't push. Now you're a man and she is a very beautiful girl, er, *woman*. You're both growing up and it's time you became a man and take responsibility for Una like you should."

"I don't know what to do with her...as a *woman*. She in no way feels like my sister, I can tell you that much." Kieran's eyes went wild, and he blushed furiously.

"Now you wake up with your tally-wacker all hard and aching and you don't know what goes where, but you just know she's the cause of it?"

Kieran blushed even redder, closed his eyes, and nodded his head once.

"She's...she is *magic*." Kieran revealed the truth, but his voice turned wistful.

"Every woman is magic to the man who loves her." Tartan nodded knowingly, thinking Kieran was saying something else and not talking about real magic.

He had told the truth about Una even though speaking of her change into a woman meant many things. The dreams of sleeping with Una in female form these past couple of years was leaving him frustrated physically and mentally. He kept the conversation going with the two lines of truth sorted in his own head and was glad Tartan's understanding was simple and not about stealing dragon eggs and that dragon suddenly, magically, changing into a desirable female. Kieran was not used to seeing her in that form and he had a lot more to sort out in his mind and body. He was glad when Tartan's face and tone softened.

"I think of you as a son, Kieran, and you have no father to advise you. I think you know taking that child was wrong, even if you were too young to know better and your intentions may have been good at the time. You've no right to pass judgment on the girl's parents, but I suspect there is more to the story. I know you're still lying to me, and I told you long ago I don't like thieves. This is the worst thing you could have ever done. Imagine how the girl's mother and father feel all these years without their daughter! It was your choice to run away from your parents, and I understand why you did. I can't understand why you'd take that girl from her home."

"It wasn't a home!" Kieran yelled in desperation, not able to reveal all the truth but needing to make Tartan understand. "It was an accident...I didn't mean to take her. I tried to take her back, but she wouldn't go. I just know, I need to take care of her! We'll leave if that's what you want."

Kieran panicked inside. His dream of making a sword was vanishing in front of his eyes and he knew he still had far to go to become a skilled warrior. Leaving Tartan and the forge could mean an end to his dreams.

"It's not what I want, Kieran." Tartan's voice rose in frustration.

Kieran couldn't help but sigh with relief, but the look of disappointment on Tartan's face made him hang his head in shame.

They had never argued before and it was impossible for him to judge how mad Tartan truly was.

"Let's just deal with one thing at a time. If you want my opinion, I think you should marry that girl. You're of age to make it proper and legal. You've got a few years of your apprenticeship left here and, to tell the truth, I'd always hoped you'd stay on. Now you'll have a wife and someday children, having a trade to earn a living will be what is best for you both. You don't have to give me an answer now but think on it."

Tartan's face flushed a bit and he cleared his throat before continuing.

"One thing is for sure, and I'll be blunt...you're becoming a man, and Una is a desirable woman who obviously loves you. It's bound to happen with you two together in the same cabin, that you'll...er...well there is a whole *physical* side to consider of your relationship. I suspect that became apparent to you this morning which set everything in motion. My suggestion is that you two get married sooner rather than later. We'll have to think about telling Una's parents she is alive and well, at some point. For now, we've work to get done. There's unrest in the valley and we've been commissioned to make weapons. A war is coming."

With that Tartan turned away and went to build up the fire in the forge which was Kieran's usual job.

Kieran sat on his stump thinking hard. Tartan's advice along with the words, "make weapons" echoed in his mind.

Everything was happening too fast. First, Una's change, and finally, he was about to learn what he desired most! Sure, he trained with a sword all these years, but now, he could make his very own weapon! His heart thundered with the excitement of becoming a warrior but then it faltered. He needed to consider everything Tartan said. What did that mean, a war was coming? That would change everything. Could he finally become the warrior he left home to become? Tartan turned his back to him and shoved a long bar of iron in the coals.

Maybe he would have to marry Una, the woman, if she would consent. What that meant between him and Una the dragon, they would have to work out. Regardless, he was responsible for her. He would do anything for her in either of her forms.

Leaving the forge and walking toward the house Kieran yearned to turn back, go to the forge and watch the coveted sword come to life, but... *Una.*

The next steps between them would be up to her, but...*she was a dragon!* He needed her to stay a dragon. Otherwise, his dreams would be impossible to make reality! Everything would change.

They needed to talk, and he'd tell her Tartan said they should marry, if it was something she wanted. As he approached the house, he saw her step out of the door as if she were expecting him. She wore one of Sara's old dresses, a lilac-colored frock that hung just past her knees. It had not been taken in properly and hung loose, but she looked beautiful and different in feminine clothing. Sara had taken the time to braid Una's hair, and a cream-colored ribbon was weaved throughout the thick golden braid that laid over her shoulder.

Stopping in the middle of the yard to gawk at her, Kieran's blood rushed in his veins. He had not been this afraid since he first saw the crystal crack and her dragon head peep out of the shards of her egg.

Una ran to him and threw her arms around his neck. They were kissing and laughing, overwhelmed by everything that happened to them. Una's transformation, Kieran facing manhood, sword making, the coming war, and their future together, was still very unknown. Between kisses, Kieran asked her to marry him and between gasps and laughter she said, "Yes!"

At least, that is how it went in Kieran's imagination. In reality, they just stood staring at each other in the middle of the yard. His mind was completely closed to her as was his heart. The horses milled around nervously, and the chickens pecked at their food in the pen. Una's face was pale. Her borrowed dress rippled in the wind.

Kieran's voice sounded strained and small. He was going to say how beautiful she looked but stopped himself. Instead, he stated simply, "We need to talk, Una."

She nodded her head and took his hand. She could feel the range of emotions and uncertainty flaring inside him.

From the wide forge doors Tartan tied his leather apron around his middle and watched Kieran and Una standing in the yard. He looked over and saw Sara watching from the doorway of their home. She had a wistful smile on her face. They looked at each other and smiled.

When Kieran and Una turned and walked into the forest toward their mountain cabin, Tartan didn't stop them. He just shook his head and went back to the heat of the forge, letting the two young people go and figure out their future. The iron bar, destined to be beaten into a sword, began to glow red-hot.

CHAPTER TWENTY-ONE

R oaring across the battlefield were the shouts of men and the clacking gears of a trebuchet winding up, the releasing twang and woosh of large boulders shot through the air. Upon Lady Rhiannah Dragahn's command, the men battered the large gates protecting a sprawling castle. She had no idea the name of this place, it was just one of many she had defeated over the past eight years since she had taken human form. Garrion Swagger's searches among gangs of thieves and outlaws, throughout towns and small villages, had been fruitless. Now, she concentrated on wealthy lords within the proximity of her old cave. If the thief was within these walls, she vowed to find him.

Her militia had grown in number to over two thousand men and she was unstoppable. Tirelessly, she brought war to the country and ranged far and wide. With each battle won, every man still alive, old and young, was brought before her. She tasted a droplet of their blood in her endless search for the thief who had stolen her egg. Late at night she could be seen walking among the fallen and tasting or smelling the spilled blood of the dead.

It had been over eight years, and her patience was wearing down. Secretly, she feared how powerful and shrewd the thief was to avoid her for this long but would never let that sentiment pass her lips. In her private moments she let tears of grief and loss fall unguarded. In other moments she paled and feared for the end of all dragon-kind. If anything, the lack of recent news regarding other dragons was alarming as it meant her kind was truly almost gone from the Earth.

Lady Rhiannah sat astride a dancing black stallion and watched the siege. Though she knew the egg she searched for had more than likely hatched by now, her mother's heart would not give up on finding it, or a young dragon. The sorrow she felt could not be adequately described and, as a dragon and a mother, being parted from her young was heavy in both her hearts. It was a wound in her chest that would not heal and a fire in her mind that would not be extinguished. Dragons age differently than humans and her hatchling might now be bigger than the horse she sat upon. Expanding her search to include information about a dragon loose in the land seemed necessary. Her quest to find the thief could not stop and her thirst for vengeance was a red blinding fury. Destroying and hurting men assuaged her pain only slightly, and she vowed she would not stop until she was reunited with her hatchling. Her mouth watered at the thought of conquering the thief, eating his heart, and gaining his power for her own. Perhaps it would mean the beginning of a new age for dragon-kind, her reunion with her young and two dragons raging across the sky bringing destruction to humans in retaliation for hunting dragons to extinction.

The magic that she used to transform into a human allowed her to change back into a dragon at will. She did not return to her natural state very often for fear of being seen and went to extensive lengths to hide it. Many moonless nights were spent flying through the skies endlessly searching the clouds for signs of a young dragon. If it were not for the wind caressing her wings and the feeling of freedom, she would not be able to go on, her sorrow and fear would overwhelm her. Having been robbed of the years watching her young grow and of teaching her hatchling the ways of dragon-kind, she only knew wrenching pain and indwelling rage.

Bringing her thoughts back to the battle before her, the gates of the castle finally splintered and as per her command, no man was killed unless unavoidable. They were brought before her, lined up, questioned, tested, and then let go. The castles and land they conquered were looted by Garrion Swagger and occasionally, in her rage at being continually thwarted, she put the main buildings to the torch. Then they moved on to the next town or noble's keep and it all began again. The name of Lady Rhiannah Dragahn became feared and reviled.

The treasure they took piled up and her soldiers were well-paid, well-fed, and very loyal. Lady Rhiannah cared little about the pillaging or what the men did after she questioned every male they came across. They also stopped at every farm and hovel and accosted the rich and poor with equal ferocity. Her search left no stone unturned, and her reputation spread throughout the land. Word of her search for a mysterious treasure spread. The questions she asked related to thieves and treasure, magic, and mythical creatures, sparking interest in the heart of every warlord, thief, and ruffian. The word *dragon* was whispered in hushed tones and men called her, blood-thirsty, cruel, and insane. Thus, she became known for her collection of curiosities and treasures as well as her viciousness.

Lady Rhiannah was also known for her exotic beauty. Men pursued her for that as well as for her wealth and power. Nothing much interested her but the endless search for the thief, the devouring of his heart and her recovering her young. Her name was known and feared, and terror swept before her with only destruction left in her wake.

Recently, worrying about her lost dragonling had to wait as she had more immediate concerns. Her actions had been noted by the

High King of Lyndesea, and an army was headed her way. They were crossing into the Ten Thousand Mile Forest and would catch her outlaw force soon.

The thought struck her that a peace treaty could be presented to the king, but negotiating may show a weakness her vengeance would not allow. Garrion Swagger frequently suggested that perhaps by showing a bit of leniency to the nobles they defeated, they could usurp their forces into Lady Rhiannah's and increase their numbers. He did not mention working toward making the dream he had of becoming king a reality. Starting with this victory, they would begin to add the support of a powerful noble, his thousand or more men would be added to her numbers. When the King of Lyndesea confronted them, they would have a stronger defense of over two thousand strong. Until they found out how many men the king was bringing against them, any course of action would only be decided based on speculation. The search for Lady Rhiannah's thief would have to wait so she could address the immediate threat. Such was the way of humans, she often lamented. While Garrion continued the search for the dragonling in the north, she grew their defenses to the south.

Bringing her out of strategic thoughts, word was delivered to her of a nobleman approaching. With him were two heavily armored knights and a young standard-bearer carrying the white flag of truce. It was undoubtedly the lord of the castle they had been sieging.

Lady Rhiannah retreated to her opulent tent and changed out of her golden armor. Keeping the castle's lord waiting was a petulant thing to do but further demonstrated her power over him. Clad in a low-cut ruby velvet gown, dripping with gold trimmings and costly jewels encircling her throat, she sat in a high-backed chair. Intent upon greeting him like a queen, she sat straight and waited for him to come to her. The lamps within cast golden light upon the costly furnishings within the tent. After arranging the long train of her dress, she signaled her attendants to bring in her subdued adversary.

The man, whose castle she just conquered, was in the prime of life despite a little gray at his temples and in his beard, and he still had a full head of rich brown hair. Appearing virile and impressive, he was handsome in heavy chainmail, a gold breastplate, white gambeson, and fine brown leather boots. His bearing was strong and he appeared impressively regal standing before her with his helmet tucked under his arm. A flash of memory struck her, and she recalled the white and gold male dragon she mated with to conceive her first egg, the hatchling that had been stolen. A shiver swept across her shoulders, and she bit her lip intrigued.

The problem with taking human form, she discovered, was that human desires often invaded her dragon senses and arose at the most unfortunate times. In another light, it could be argued that possibly this was a most opportune surrender. An intense attraction hit right between her breasts, but to hide all but a spark of interest, she waved an attendant forward to serve her wine.

Fully recovered from her reaction to the handsome noble, and highly intrigued, she gave him a winning smile and sipped her wine. With Garrion away in the north, a plan began to take shape in her mind.

Lord Stephan Arceneaux waited patiently while the woman before him looked him up and down. He could not help but be affected by her beauty and flaring intelligent eyes. It was hard to keep his gaze from straying down her long neck to the swell of her breasts. It was there his eyes wanted to linger as the soft mounds rose and fell with each breath she took. He waited for recognition to fill her amber eyes because he suddenly *knew her*. She seemed to be waiting for him to break the silence and so he cleared his throat, tore his eyes from her low neckline, and swallowed his awakening arousal. A playful smile spread over his lips and his golden eyes sparkled with mischievousness.

"I am Stephan Arceneaux, Lord of Arcenaxe Castle, which you've just seized. I yield to you, my lady. I wish to spare my soldiers and subjects from further harm and avoid the destruction of my home. What would you have from me in exchange for our lives?"

"Lord Arceneaux," Lady Rhiannah spoke in a strange accent with a sweet seductive tone. "Welcome."

She had been watching the man before her as he tried to keep his eyes from her breasts. Smiling with satisfaction, she leaned forward to give him more of a view of all she had to offer. As expected, his eyes wandered from her face to just below her neck and he blushed with appreciation. He stepped closer and the scent of him hit her like buffeting wind. It was animalistic, wind and rain and...her eyes grew as her suspicions flared. She breathed deeply, leaned back and let his aroma soothe her.

At that moment, she knew him as well as she knew herself though it had been a long time since they last met. Now, his men, his wealth, and strength against her enemies were all wrapped around her taloned finger. Rising to her feet she approached him slowly and held her hand out to him. He took it, kissed the back of her fingers and held her gaze. She shivered and felt the heat coming off him and felt the eyes of every man in the tent upon them.

Lord Arceneaux smiled knowingly, stepped close, pulled her into his arms and kissed her with the passionate desperation of long separated lovers.

The knights accompanying him shifted uncomfortably not understanding what was happening. They paid them no mind. The handsome lord holding her had all her attention. Taking his arm, drawing him toward a table to the side of the tent, she gestured for him to sit. Then the reunion began. When she was done with this distracting war, together they would be unstoppable in finding her hatchling and so she began to unfold her story.

CHAPTER TWENTY-TWO

"**A**re you sure you can't stay a dragon?"

Pacing the forest floor, Kieran repeated the question over and over, and each time Una vehemently refused. His dream of riding a dragon into battle and becoming a renowned warrior was quickly fading away and his nerves prickled. Her long shapely legs caught his eye, and he had to turn away because she was highly tempting in human form.

As a human, her colors changed to fiery red, indicating her displeasure, and he knew she was growing angrier with each minute. The accusation and hurt in her eyes broke his heart and finally, he stopped asking her to stay a dragon.

"Una, at least explain this transformation to me so I understand. How did you learn to change from a dragon to a human?"

Una sat on a stump that served as a seat and calmly explained in a patient voice.

"All dragons possess inherited knowledge of magic and dragon lore. As a dragon, I have the abilities of dragon-kind, and I possess the memories of many of the ancients. It is a way to bring prosperity to our race and continue dragons whose numbers have dwindled upon the earth. I know who my mother and father dragons were, though I've never met them. I know dragon history and abilities just as instinctively, I know how to fly. Dragons age faster than humans and live longer. Though I've only lived eight years as a dragon, my growth rate means I appear to be an eighteen-year-old human, like you!"

She paused smiling, but seeing he wasn't smiling back, continued.

"As a human I age as slowly as you. When my desire to be with you overwhelmed me, the magic came to fulfill my desires. So, I went into the mountains and cast the transformation spells and here I am." She smiled like a child trying to please her playmate and waited for him to process this new information.

Yes, there she was. Fresh and beautiful and enticing. Kieran stared at her realizing he had so little experience with women that it was embarrassing. He had years of experience with a dragon and knew her as well as he knew himself, but to think that they had shared a bed for a while now was disconcerting to say the least.

"How long have you been sneaking into my bed at night? How is it that I did not know what you were up to?"

"Kieran, you and I have an unbreakable bond, but I can keep secrets from you. Well, we can keep secrets from each other. We are not just human and dragon friends. There is a mutual relationship that runs deep, you as a rider and me as your dragon. I simply wanted more and dragon lore, *dragon magic*, made it happen. *On the land and in the sky, we are one.*"

Her last words echoed like a creed and Kieran shivered as if recognizing an ancient rallying cry.

"The truth is, you have nobody to blame but yourself. You had a dream one night of a girl and gave me the idea. I called the magic and became her, but I am also Una the dragon when I wish to be."

"You didn't answer my other question. How could I not have known all this time? I slept through each night for however long and never knew! Why have you revealed this to me now?"

"I kept my change a secret until you were ready. There is a spell to make you sleep deeply, so you never knew." She paused and a thunderous look passed over her face. "I told you why I chose *now* to show myself as a human."

Stopping in his tracks, Kieran remembered what he intentionally tried to forget. He kissed a village girl and Una knew. He had been thinking about girls ever since he was sixteen and Tartan explained the changes he was going through as he became a man. When he turned eighteen, women seemed to be everywhere with enticing breasts and long shapely legs, swaying hips and kissable lips. The village girls let him know with certainty they found him attractive, and his ego had swelled as did the possibilities of what could happen between him and one of the girls. It was the natural order of life only now he wouldn't have to convince a human girl not to be afraid of his dragon. Logic told him there was no other woman for him than Una.

Tartan's words echoed in his head. *"Now you wake up with your tally-wacker all hard and aching and you don't know what goes where, but you just know she's the cause of it?"*

Said, *"tally-wacker"* was stirring now with all the talk of girls, and kissing, and sleeping together.

"Una, when a man and a woman, well, when they love each other, they, well...Tartan says we must marry!"

"I know, Kieran. I told you, I've seen humans together and I wanted that. I want that with you! A dragon is full of passion, and it has been done. Well, a thousand years ago humans and dragons mated. Would marrying me be so bad?"

"I want to be a warrior!" Kieran yelled ignoring her last question. "We were going to fly through the skies in search of fame and fortune *together*. You know this! We've worked toward this for years. I am so close! Tartan has been teaching me to use a sword and I'm good at it! My dream of becoming a warrior is at hand. I've only two years left of my apprenticeship. As we speak, he is at the forge making swords, and I'm missing it. I'm supposed to learn but instead I'm up here arguing with a stubborn dragon...ah, *girl*...dragon! I don't know what you are anymore."

Kieran knew he sounded petulant and childish. This was not how he wanted this conversation to go, but he was speaking the truth. As he turned to look at Una, the girl, it struck him that his words hurt her. Tears filled her eyes as she slowly stood and stared at him. He stared back, not knowing what else to say. The desires of his heart and body were at war with what his eyes saw, and his mind knew to be true. Mistrust flared within him, but then remorse replaced that as soon as the first tear slid down her cheek.

Una stepped a few paces backward, then wordlessly turned. As she walked away, her form rippled, grew, and she transformed into Una the dragon. Without a backward glance, she spread her magnificent wings and launched into the sky alone.

The sun glittered on her scales like precious jewels and threw prisms of light at him as she gained altitude in the sky and disappeared. Kieran did not call her back; he had no idea what more to say. Down the mountain, he could hear the ringing of a hammer on metal, and he turned and headed back to the forge. He had a sword to make.

CHAPTER
TWENTY-THREE

R eturning and standing alone outside the bower she made
of trees; Una fought the change from woman to dragon.
As a dragon her thoughts had been instinct driven toward
flying, feeding and protecting the man who was her mate and
rider. Her skin rippled and her mind was feverish with anger
and the drive to go after Kieran was overwhelming.

Growing up together, they had argued and played as children do. As man and woman, they had loved. Though their love encompassed two forms, as dragon and as mates. Her passions ran fiercely in many different directions where Kieran's ran in two. One was simply as a man for a woman, and the other was being a rider of her as a dragon. It was impossible to put into human words how deeply the connection between them ran. It was old magic, the kind that men wrote about in ancient tombs but had long since been forgotten. As the race of dragon-kind dwindled, the relationship between men and dragons had been lost. Dragons deteriorated, becoming more animal than sentient knowledgeable creatures.

Dragon memory was passed down through blood, bone, sinew, and instinct. Una was painfully aware that she was one of the last dragons in the land. If her kind disappeared completely, that would be a tragedy of immense proportion. Though she could recall thousands of years of dragon lore and legend, they meant little to her as the kings of those days were now dust in the ground and those dragons had disappeared from the skies. Dragon-kind passed these stories down through inherited lineage, so that they would not be forgotten, and the wisdom and magic of the species would carry on through those memories and the hope of future generations. It was as if the dragons of the past realized that their kind was going extinct and worked to prevent that. As dragon-kind evolved, they absorbed some of the magic of human mages and shapeshifting became a common thing through survival instinct.

She did not know if other dragons walked the Earth and were hiding among those who had hunted them to extinction in human form. The possibilities seemed endless, would they flourish or fade into time, and their greatness eventually be forgotten by history and only remembered as myth. Una felt sad that the skies held no sign of those magnificent dragons of her past and the future looked bleak.

There was one other dragon Una knew, without a doubt, that still walked the Earth and flew in the skies, and that was her mother. She prodded her feelings about the mother dragon, like a loose tooth. She contemplated seeking her out a thousand times, but something warned her that doing so would be a mistake. Una knew her mother had retreated so deeply into animalistic behavior that she would never allow Kieran to live if they were found together. As he was the one that had taken Una from the nest, the mother's vengeance would be unspeakable. *"On the land and in the sky, we are one."* It would kill her if Kieran was harmed.

Una's skin fluctuated colors taking on the muddy green-brown of the dying leaves beneath her feet. Her hair waved in the wind like willow-the-whisps and blanched the orange of autumn leaves. As always, she let her emotions show and her anxious indecision was apparent in her fluctuating colors, even as a human. Without Kieran here to calm her, she shook with the effort it took to stay in the shape of a girl and not change and go raging after him as a dragon.

The night Kieran had dreamed of Una as a human girl, the memories of the shape-changing magic came flooding into her. She spent hours and then days probing and learning from those memories passed down from her ancient kin. Her blood surged, and her scales flashed with colors of complex emotions and the strongest desire to learn what it was she needed to do and how to do it. When the desire was inescapable, she went into the mountains and created the spell to shapeshift into a human girl. Though walking on two human feet was difficult, she soon mastered shifting back and forth from dragon to human. That was when her drive to be with Kieran overruled many of her fears. She cast a heavy sleeping spell on him so he would not catch her, and slept by his side for years letting him think he was dreaming. The day she felt his physical desire for another female was the day she decided she had enough of the deception, and revealed all that dragon magic could do. If there were any repercussions to her actions she did not know. All she knew was that she needed to be with him as a dragon and now, as a woman.

Pounding glowing hot metal was an excellent way to take out frustrations and Kieran blocked out all thoughts of Una, girls, and dragons. He could still feel her at the back of his mind like he felt the sweat dripping down his face. With a little concentration, he knew in which direction she flew, knew she was angry at him and knew he would have to make it up to her later. Facing her after his day of labor, their small cabin home, her beautiful face and sadness was not something he looked forward to.

Tartan tried to talk to him about Una during a short lunch break and Kieran was tempted to reveal everything. He did not know if he could speak the words, *'Una is really a dragon made human by magic.'* It sounded unreal in his own mind but revealing it to Tartan would be crazy. In some ways, it seemed like a betrayal of his bond with Una and no matter how many times he tried to speak the words, they would not come. So, the secret remained untold.

It was Tartan's last words that day that finally helped make up his mind.

"Kieran, a deep connection between two people involves mutual understanding, respect, and trust. Whatever is on your mind, if you really love someone, it is your heart that matters. What does your *heart* tell you?"

Flashes of memory hit him vividly. Climbing the escarpment to the dragon cave, finding Una's egg and its hatching, her sleeping in his lap, her rippling colors and playfulness, her protection and most of all, the lonely days her presence filled. The dragon in his life made him feel strong, like nothing could ever stand in his way. His path in life seemed clear; he would become the warrior he dreamed of, and nothing would stop him. Once again, he saw the fear in his father's eyes as she protected him and he realized that no matter if she were dragon or human female, he loved her and could never live without her in either form. Then there was the change that came over him when they flew together, he felt like a dragon and his father had exclaimed that day that his eyes glowed during their confrontation in the forest. It could be argued, she made him part dragon when they flew, so it was only right she was part human. A human woman was not for him; he was destined for greater things and Una in dragon form or in human form was part of that destiny.

As the evening drew near, and the skies darkened, Kieran banked the forge fire and turned his steps toward home and Una. She waited for him. A lamp flickered inside the cabin, the chimney smoked lazily, and the small clearing glowed with a homey warmth. The smell of roasting meat permeated the air and Kieran realized she must have dinner waiting for him. Her long hair was loose and flowing in the slight evening breeze. Being away from each other that day had given him time to put things in perspective, and he had come to some decisions. As he approached where she stood as he last saw her, he saw hope flash in her eyes. Reaching forward, he gently took her in his arms.

"Una, I want every part of you, magic, dragon, and woman. We will go on as we started, *together*, no matter what comes. Whatever you want, whatever I can give you, I will do my best. *On the land and in the sky, we are one.*"

Una smiled and pulled him into a kiss. The world dissolved into the scent of him and the taste of her. It was a sweet kiss that quickly became fierce as Kieran gave into the passion he felt for Una. They knew without saying any more that from that day forward there would be no division between them. They were of one mind and one heart.

Now that the question of their marrying was put to rest, Kieran and Una looked forward to the future. They lived together and flew together and paved a way to live in both worlds. Una assured him that they were bringing back the old ways between dragons and riders and their love grew.

In the next few days, the Village of Appleaid Founder's Day Celebration would be held. Since it would also be their wedding day, the young couple brimmed with anticipation and happiness that healed the last vestiges of a rift between them. They found a way to reconcile human and dragon, magic and love. As the days passed, they both became more comfortable with Una in human form. She was accepted by the people of Appleaid with open arms because of her sweetness and beauty. On the occasions Una changed back to a dragon, and they flew through the sky together as if nothing was different and their life together was happy. The future seemed promising.

Tartan explained Una's sudden presence one evening over an ale at the local tavern. Rather than reveal that she had been hidden in the forest all these years by his apprentice, he embellished a little saying she was a distant relative and had come to stay with them. He told how it was an instant love match when Kieran met Una and that everything settled into place with the young couple as it should. Thus, the wedding became a source of added excitement at the upcoming celebration a few days away. The village bustled with activity preparing for the nuptials and Founder's Day party, and despite the fear of war that had overtaken the people of Appleaid, everyone seemed joyful.

One not-so-enjoyable addition to the village was the appearance of mercenaries brought by news of the king's army heading toward Appleaid. The sight of heavily armed men became common, and the fear of war was palpable. Where it had only been a distant rumor over the last year or two, now it was becoming a reality. The village tavern was constantly busy and at times rambunctious drunkards had to be dealt with. Tartan's swords had become a sought-after necessity, and he and Kieran had more business than he could keep up with.

CHAPTER
TWENTY-FOUR

G arrion Swagger and two of his men reached the Village of Appleaid to reconnoiter and gather information as they usually did when they visited a new town. After finding nothing as usual, he had come far north and learned that the King of Lyndesea's soldiers were on their way to the village. The king's army had flanked Lady Dragahn's, and he would have to report that between their forces and searching the northern lands for her dragon egg, was a force of over five thousand men preparing to war against them.

As was always his duty on behalf of Lady Rhiannah, he looked for anyone possessing a mystical treasure, abundant wealth or a dragon egg. Posing as mercenaries, they listened for rumors of dragons and even lied, saying they'd heard tales of a dragon seen in the area in hopes of loosening tongues in the direction of his interest. The man who tended the bar introduced himself as Hertle. He mentioned in a lighthearted tone that it had been a few years since any dragon was spotted in Appleaid and that even those sightings were quickly disregarded by most townspeople as tall tales. His opinion was that there never had been a dragon living among the mountains above Appleaid and that it had been a fabrication told by a man from the small town of Buttermilk in years past. Hertle postulated that the man lied to get folks to buy him ale and that the man had been run out of town years ago as a useless drunk.

Most people they asked considered it good luck to have such a mythical creature as a dragon living nearby as long as the monster left the livestock alone. Hertle added that it had not been seen in recent years.

Having imbibed the town's sweet apple cider, Garrion and his men made to leave. His path to the stable where their horses were, led him through the bustling market toward the end of the village. However, Garrion was a man whose ambition ran as deep as his desires. When a particular maiden in the crowd caught his attention, Garrion couldn't help himself. He covertly watched her lithe form as she flowed through the stalls and was overwhelmed by her innocent beauty. After a few casual questions to one of the locals he got a sense of where she lived and figured out a way to go after her. Looking for a bit of fun, he and his men waited for her on the north bridge, sure she would pass that way.

Today was the first day Una would venture into town on her own. This trip to the market was a great adventure and she exchanged many smiles and greetings with the townspeople who accepted her without hesitation. The sky was perfect blue with no clouds in sight and the excitement she felt burst forward as she headed into town. Her loose hair rippled in the slight breeze, and she shone prettily in a new, flowered dress. She had instructions from Sara on the few things she needed to purchase at the market and had been eager to go about the task.

Under the afternoon sun, as she walked back to the forge farm, Una smiled and hummed a tune. She had been gone longer than expected and was anxious to tell Kieran all she had seen and about the people she met. Una felt as if nothing could dampen her happy spirits as she made her way to the north bridge at the end of the town, until shadows fell across her path.

Three men loitered on the bridge ahead and upon noticing her, they straightened and moved forward to stand shoulder to shoulder, blocking her path. Soldiers and mercenaries were not new to her as she knew the king's army was headed for Appleaid, so she did not worry at first. When she saw the lustful looks on the men's faces her dragon senses flared. A shiver of warning coursed down her spine, and the smile left her face.

She slowed and tried to go around, but they stepped in front of her, and she was forced to stop. Alarm rippled across her skin along with the immediate realization that she was in danger. She could not simply shift into dragon form and vanquish them, or else she would reveal her true nature.

"Good day, my sweet." The black-haired man in the center spoke first and his oily tone had the hair on the back of Una's neck standing up.

"Please let me pass, Sir." Una said. Her voice shook just a little. Looking past them, she realized that the forge farm was further away than she could run to and reach safety. These men would surely catch her even if she managed to make it past them. She gripped her basket of items bought at the market and was determined to act like a normal human girl. Alarm ran through her veins, and she took a step back to turn and run to the safety of the village, instead, she sent a call to Kieran.

"Kieran! Come quick! To the bridge!"

"A fine day to go to market." The man spoke again taking another step towards Una.

"Please let me by, I cannot tarry." Una tried to look as frightened as a human girl would. As a dragon she would have no trouble dealing with these men, but the fact that she was not in dragon form echoed in her head.

"Oh, do stay with us. It has been a long while since we've had the pleasurable company of such a beautiful maiden. Perhaps you'd like to share a cider with us at the local tavern?"

Garrion was anything but lonely and the men with him chuckled. On the right and the left, they moved to try and surround her. Una tried to run through them, but the big dark one in the middle grabbed her.

Wrapping his arms around the girl, Garrion pulled the maiden against him. The breeze chose that moment to rise, and the scent of her hair and sun-warmed skin hit him. Holding tightly, he lowered his nose to her golden head and took a long slow inhalation. A sense of familiarity hit him hard, and a thrill of awareness coursed through him. Threading his hand through her loose locks and burying his face within, he sniffed again, taking in the scent.

"You smell so sweet," Garrion purred as the recognition hit him. Where had he encountered her scent before? He grinned widely. His senses were screaming with a revelation, but he needed to be sure.

"Let me go!" the maiden wriggled and fought against him. Her arms tried to push him away as he tightened his hold.

"Who are you?" Garrion held her tighter, and his voice turned urgent.

"Never you mind, just let me go!" Una continued to fight the unwanted embrace.

Kieran had been hammering a piece of white-hot metal while Tartan stood to the side watching and slowly pumping the bellows. The boy had strength and talent, and the blade came together swiftly. Suddenly, the call from Una rang in Kieran's head louder than the ring of the metal.

"Kieran! Come quick! To the bridge!" Una's call was startling.

His hand pausing in mid-air Kieran stopped, listening. The urgency in Una's voice in his head was alarming, and he turned to stare toward the forge doors. Tartan's voice muffled as Kieran shoved the metal back into the coals, and he dropped the hammer to the anvil. Whirling, he grabbed the first weapon at hand and ran. Tartan called after him not understanding what was happening.

Garrion and his men were laughing, and he was very amused by the girl's struggles as he continued to question her. From behind them at the other end of the bridge, a young man appeared and shouted at them.

"Let her go!"

The lad looked strong but foolish confronting three, heavily armed mercenaries. He was broad across the shoulders and wore a blacksmith's apron. More surprising was the silver-hilted sword the boy carried and threatened them with.

"I said let her go."

"And who might you be, young man?" Garrion asked, then slowly released the girl. She quickly grabbed the basket dropped in the struggle and ran to the sword wielding youth who stepped protectively in front of her.

"You should probably leave Appleaid." The boy warned in a steady voice.

"In good time, boy, but first tell me your name?" Blood thrilling with suspicion and speculation, Garrion itched to know more about this young couple.

"None of your business, get you gone! Now!"

Though large and muscled, the boy looked untried and posed little threat to three more experienced warriors. The sword he held glinted in the sun's light and Garrion was a little impressed with the lad's bravery. He was confidently brandishing an impressive weapon and held it unwavering in a defensive stance. The long blade was etched with the figure of a dragon. A ray of sunshine caught the crystal in the sword's pommel, and it sparked with sun fire.

Garrion smiled as he realized two things at once. Before him there were two very interesting people. The overly brave lad and the beautiful maiden presented him with possible answers he had been seeking. Though they were younger than whom he thought he sought, there was a chance the answer to the mystery he had been trying to solve over the last many years, might be right in front of him. At least one of them was, the other, the girl, was a most intriguing mystery. His men moved to draw their swords and advance toward the two, but Garrion halted them with a gesture.

"Where did you get that fine sword, my boy?" Garrion asked.

"It is my own." Kieran answered with a hint of pride he couldn't contain. "I made it."

"Very impressive. I suppose you know how to use it?"

Kieran must have thought the man was mocking him because he just motioned, taunting the men.

"Why don't you try me and see?" He grinned.

"Ah, young and brave." Garrion shook his head. "There are three of us against just you boy. Do you think to be able to best us all?"

The lad did not have time to answer. A huge bald man with a long black beard approached from down the road. He brandished a wood-chopping axe in one hand and a worn hammer in another.

"Is there a problem here?" The gruff voice of the newcomer boomed as he took a place beside the lad with the sword.

The mercenaries were now confronted by a man who appeared to be the town blacksmith. Garrion had a lot to think about and with a slight bow as if he were giving up rather than fighting, smiled and stepped back with a nod.

"Is this lad your apprentice?" Curiosity overwhelmed Garrion and he knew he had to calm the situation quickly because he needed information more than anything else. "He is either very brave or very stupid."

"He is my apprentice if it is any of your business, and I can vouch he's not stupid." The blacksmith took a position by the boy's side. "I can also vouch he knows how to use that sword he is holding."

They faced off in the air made tense with danger. The beautiful girl watched from behind the men. The breeze blew her hair around her, and she shone like a golden nymph in the sunlight. Her strange eyes flickered with menace and not the fear she portrayed. Garrion thought for a moment that her eyes flickered with green fire, but it may have been a trick of the sunlight because it was there and gone in a flash.

"No harm done, my good fellows. We just wanted the pleasure of the young maiden's company. I can see now that was not the best of ideas." He gave another bow and held his hands wide in surrender. "We want no trouble. We'll be on our way and wish you a good day."

As he turned away, Garrion tingled with excitement and knew he had much to think about. He memorized the location, noticed the wooden sign advertising Appleaid's blacksmith, and memorized the lad. The maiden, he'd never forget. Motioning to his men, they turned and left. He needed to think long and hard on what to report back to Lady Dragahn. His pulse leaped, knowing there had to be a way to use this information to *his* advantage.

CHAPTER
TWENTY-FIVE

A t the edge of the Ten Thousand Mile Forest, the Village of Appleaid bustled with excitement and activity. The long mountain valley glowed golden with lamplight, and campfires, and the echoes of music and laughter rose into the air day and night. The shores of the ocean inlet were filled with revelers coming from ships at anchor on the calm ocean. People came from the mountains, the grasslands, and the sea to participate in the week-long Founder's Day games and celebrations.

Despite the threat of war gathering in the south, the people let go of their cares and honored their ancestors with the fruits of the earth's bounty. The river that ran through the village was cluttered with floating lamps and the bridges crisscrossing the town were decorated with flowers and colorful ribbons danced in the breeze. The groves of mountain apple trees were heavily laden with pink and white blossoms and the green of apples almost ripe and ready for harvest. The savory smell of roasting meat filled the air. Even the fishermen joined in the revelry.

The most boisterous and festive celebration was at the blacksmith's farm. Lamps brightly lit the yard, and flowers decorated every post and fence rail. The sound of a lute, fiddle, pipes, and a squeeze box played song after song accompanied by the singing of talented musicians. Fueled by casks of apple cider fermented to sweet perfection, and frothing ale, the dancing went on late into the night after a joyful wedding ceremony. Kieran, the blacksmith's apprentice was married to the lovely Una.

Tartan, in his best vest, white linen shirt, and polished boots, sporting more silver clasps in his long beard than usual, hosted the event with evident pride. Bolstered by ale, he had awkwardly taken Kieran aside and explained everything he knew about a woman and married life and then he rushed through a brief explanation of what was to happen on the wedding night. Kieran paled dramatically.

Una, crowned in a wreath of apple blossoms and tiny pink roses, looked lovely in a white dress embroidered with flowers. Her green eyes sparkled in the lamplight. Everything was new to her, and she wore an infectious smile. She danced with joyful abandon, her hair flowing freely around her. If anyone noticed it ripple occasionally in lavender shades, it was attributed to a trick of the lights and too much cider.

As the evening grew late, Tartan covertly suggested Kieran and Una slip away to enjoy their wedding night. The jokes and crude innuendos had begun so it was past time they sneaked away before mischief took hold. Kieran, who had a bit too much cider to drink, held his bride's hand and they escaped into the cool summer night running up the mountain to their home. In the early morning hours, as the sounds of music, laughter, and singing chased them into the forest, the two young lovers, now married, went to celebrate alone.

When they reached their little cabin, they slowed to a walk, still holding hands, and their laughter turned into quiet nervousness. There was only one awkward moment where they stared at each other waiting for one of them to make the first move. That lasted until they got in the cabin doorway and spotted the new feather bed that was a wedding gift from Tartan and Sara. The moments that followed were a flurry of clothing removal and boots dropping between passionate kisses, giggling, and heavy breathing. Though they had been sleeping together for quite some time, this was the first night they allowed their desire for each other to unleash. In a tangle of limbs, much laughter and kissing, they consummated their marriage and let their love finally take them to the next level of devotion.

"On the land and in the sky, we are one." They quoted in unison and quickly fell asleep.

Kieran and Una spent the next several days alone together. Now husband and wife, and sometimes dragon and rider, they explored the depths of what that meant. Una showed him the history of dragon-kind working the magic she knew of, through ancestral memories and inherited knowledge. Her blood sang and her eyes sparked as she spoke of the past, then she turned sad as she revealed that dragon-kind was disappearing from the Earth and she was one of the very last. His eyes glazed over with visions of men riding dragons in the long ago past. Magic took over and played before his mind's eye as if he witnessed it as reality. He saw and understood how deep the binding was between dragon and rider, more than ever now. Kieran asked if what his father said was true, had his eyes glowed when they were confronted with danger? Una confirmed that they most likely had and as bonded dragon and human, her magic flowed into him and strengthened when together. Over time, he would become stronger, faster and more cunning than the ordinary man. The changes had begun in him when they bonded after she hatched. Though he would never become a dragon when they flew, they were connected on a dragon level that increased with time. The way it had been in history, when man and dragon became melded together, it was in a way that hadn't been seen or done for hundreds of years. Una couldn't be sure if she was the last dragon or not but knew that the days of dragon-kind were dwindling. The visions she showed him gave him the desire to bring back that way of life, even if it were just between the two of them. Her magic would make it happen.

They fully embraced, joining body and soul and grew in the knowledge that life would never be the same. Kieran was elated and spoke of his dreams for the two of them. In the sky or on land, as human and human or as human and dragon, they were truly one now. His dreams of becoming a legendary warrior were within his reach, as soon as his apprenticeship with Tartan was over, they would...

Kieran couldn't think past leaving the man who was a mentor, teacher, a father, and a friend. At times, he began to question his choices as the ambitions of his youth started to look more and more obtainable.

The morning Kieran returned to the forge; Tartan watched the young man he raised, walk out of the forest and approach the barn. What he saw stunned him. Kieran had visibly changed. Somehow, he was larger, he had been tanned by the sun, his hair was more golden, and the lines of his face sharper. It looked as if his muscles had enlarged over just a few days. The boy he knew was gone and now, stalking toward him was a *man* Tartan barely recognized. When they greeted each other, Tartan stared in shock.

"Good morning, Tartan." His words stumbled a little.

Kieran greeted him cheerfully in a voice Tartan could swear sounded deeper.

"Kieran, you look..." Tartan faltered, staring him up and down, wondering what had happened to him, "marriage looks good on you."

He shook his head and doused the feeling that something unnatural had happened. Following his apprentice into the forge barn, he wondering what was ahead for such a man as this.

In the days that followed the end of Appleaid's Founder's Day celebrations and the marriage of Kieran and Una, he and Tartan worked non-stop forging swords, weapons and armor for the war that was no longer a rumor. The village elders and prominent citizens gathered and relayed a report that the King of Lyndesea was heading toward Appleaid. Scouts had come in advance, conscripting young men into the army to fight for their king. During the next few weeks, they were joined by an entire company of men, and the hillsides were littered with tents and an encampment that no one in Appleaid had ever seen before.

The young men in the village were anxious to leave the sleepy life of apple farming and adventure into the glory of war. For the people of Appleaid there was little difference between the soldiers recruiting their husbands, sons, and brothers, and the mercenaries who had been flocking to the village over the last few months. There was a noisy bustle of activity, and soldiers everywhere. The late summer apple harvest was in, and the army paid in gold for the supplies they needed so there wasn't much grumbling among the inhabitants of the village.

The day that the Commander of the King of Lyndesea's army approached the blacksmith's farm was one that meant the culmination of Kieran's dreams. It was the day Tartan dreaded as he was loath to let him go. The days of his apprenticeship were almost over, and he meant to talk Kieran into staying on permanently. With him having a wife now, Tartan had thought it was almost a guarantee. He drew up plans to enlarge the forge barn since the business was thriving. Tarren was old enough to begin his apprenticeship but there was no one like Kieran. Shadows darkened his mind as he remembered days past when men he knew went off to war and never returned and the devastation that caused.

Commander Rothchild Bodine was a warrior to his core. Some stories hinted he had been born with a weapon in his hand. As they recruited men in the Village of Appleaid, word had reached him of the local blacksmith and the quality of swords he made. The errand that had him seeking out the blacksmith was of great importance as the war ahead would need supplies in the way of swords, knives, spears and armor. This was not one of the tasks a man of his stature typically undertook in person but there were the most interesting rumors of the blacksmith and his apprentice. He was interested in seeing for himself.

He heard reports that the apprentice was a young man of impressive stature and a fierce undaunting nature. To hear the village gossip, his skill with swords and weapons was almost of legendary proportion. They most likely were embellished, but if such a young man existed, he would be very useful. If the stories were not true, having a blacksmith to repair weapons on the long march to war would still come in handy. Hanging over every consideration was that the winter would hit in a few short months, and they were in a race to finish this campaign and outrun harsh weather.

Riding a sleek white horse, he and a few of his officers crossed the northern bridge and headed toward the blacksmith's farm. A cacophony of noise ensued as they rode in. Chickens scattered and geese honked their displeasure at having their sleepy day interrupted. The horses in the corral cantered along the fence watching the newcomers and the pigs squealed having been woken from their afternoon naps.

Tartan heard the noise and emerged from the forge barn. In his hand was a well-used hammer which he gripped in trepidation.

A shiver went across his shoulders, and he knew that the day he always dreaded had come. Kieran would be presented with the opportunity he had worked ten years toward. Tartan could only hope that the boy he raised from a starving waif to an impressive young man, would choose to stay and not go to war. Judging by the looks on these men's faces, Kieran might not have a choice.

"Good day, sirs. Do you need some metal work done today?" Tartan gripped his hammer tightly and greeted the mounted men. The sun was in his eyes and beat down on his bald head. His usual friendly manner was muted. Shading his brow with a big hand he saw soldiers, and he had no welcoming smile for them.

"I am Commander Rothchild Bodine. I've been tasked by the King of Lyndesea himself to recruit men for the war ahead. Our army could use a blacksmith, and I've also heard tell you have a young apprentice who is of fighting age and can wield a sword with some skill."

"Aye, I'm the blacksmith and I've an apprentice, he's my son but only eleven years of age, not old enough to swing a sword in any battle." Tartan knew who the general was referring to but evaded the point anyway.

"Don't assume me a fool, Sir Blacksmith. I've heard of *another* apprentice, an older one. Bring him out so we can have a look at him. We're in need of fighting men for your king's protection and I'm in no mood to be thwarted. If you don't cooperate, I'll have my men search for him and any other men of eligible fighting age."

It did not sound like Tartan was being given any choice.

Kieran had heard the horses enter the yard and as soon as he could safely set aside the sword he was working on, he approached the forge doors. Unlike the last time someone had come looking for him, Kieran was not going to cower in the shadows. He listened as the commander spoke to Tartan. Removing his apron and wiping the sweat from his face, he felt prepared to face the destiny that had come looking for him.

The company of soldiers was loud enough that they also caught the notice of Sara and Una who came from the back of the house carrying baskets. Kieran watched as they set their laundry down and headed toward the ruckus. Tarren carried a bucket of water from a nearby stream. They all converged in front of the forge barn and stood together as a family.

A hush descended over the newcomers as Una stepped to Kieran's side. He placed a possessive arm around her waist and drew her close. Sara likewise drew Tarren to her side with a protective hug. Tarren wrestled to be free from his mother's over protection, but there was no getting out of her grip.

"Commander Bodine, this is my apprentice Kieran and my son Tarren."

Kieran watched Tartan's face as he begrudgingly introduced them. Then his gaze turned, and he noticed Commander Bodine and his men gawking at Una. In a sharp, protective move, he placed her behind him, shielding her with his broad shoulders. She would not be hidden though and instantly stepped out, staring fearlessly at the soldiers.

"I am Kieran." His tone was cooperative, but beneath the surface, his excitement pounded like a hammer on an anvil.

Kieran, the blacksmith's apprentice, was an impressive young man, tall with broad shoulders, large biceps, and powerful legs. Sandy blonde hair hung to his shoulders, and a leather strap pulled the front away from strong handsome features and blue-green eyes. The lad was impressive and looked like the personification of the legendary Sir Kieran Cray, the King's Champion of old whom the lad was obviously named after. Such a waste a man like this was in a mere village forge.

"I am Commander Rothchild Bodine. We are gathering men for the king's army." He dismounted his horse and walked toward Kieran and Una. Despite his usual discipline, he could not divert his eyes from the beautiful girl.

"I can sell you weapons and armor, but we've no wish to fight in any war." The blacksmith was speaking again clearly in an attempt to gain the commander's attention away from Kieran and Una. "We can be of more use to the king here where the forge and tools are. I need my apprentice with me, not away somewhere getting killed in a war."

The blacksmith stood his ground. His clenched fists were evidence of his defiance, which didn't phase Commander Bodine.

"I'm afraid you've no choice in the matter, Blacksmith. There is a great threat against the kingdom, and we all must come together to fight for this common cause. You and your apprentice are being conscripted into the king's army."

"And if we refuse?" Tartan asked non-too friendly.

"You two will come willingly or unwillingly. If you continue to refuse or put up a fight, we'll take your young son too. I can always use another errand boy. At this point, I'm being lenient. Pray I continue to be."

"I'm going with you!" The girl exclaimed, as she grabbed Kieran's arm, speaking to him in a hushed tone.

They exchanged a look.

"Una, you can't!"

The commander made out Kieran speaking to the girl, but he ignored the private exchange, dismissing it as desperate lovers' spat." Had he looked longer, he would have noticed the young man's eyes strangely glazing over as if in a trance. He blinked and the moment was broken.

"I'd have you safe, here with Sara and Tarren." Kieran's pleading words died.

"No women except camp followers are allowed. I'm afraid one as beautiful as you would only be used in the most unspeakable of ways." Commander Bodine quickly interjected as his eyes drifted up and down Una's body as he spoke to her. His voice betrayed a hint of disappointment which he disguised with an impatient grunt.

"I can protect myself." Una warned them all in a voice that would tolerate no argument.

"I can't allow it. You would be a distraction to the men." Then the commander declared with finality, "this is war young lady, not an afternoon picnic."

"I'll go but leave Tartan here. He has a family to care for." Kieran tried to force the issue, but Bodine refused to be convinced.

"We need *all* men of fighting age, and his skills will be needed as well. Both of you report to our encampment just outside the village in the morning. Bring any tools you may need and all the weapons you have ready. See Sandoval, my sergeant-at-arms before noon or we'll come back and collect you, but mark my words, it will be counted as insubordination if you refuse to show. Punishment will be severe. We anticipate one major battle to put the outlaw threat down and then most likely, you'll be able to return home. For now, you have the rest of the day to prepare and report tomorrow as I ordered."

With a final lecherous glare at Una, the commander mounted his horse, and they rode away.

Sara flew into Tartan's arms with a sob.

Una pursed her lips and stared at Kieran with undeniable irritation. Crossing his arms over his chest, Kieran stared stubbornly at her and would not budge. After a brief stand-off, she turned away, heading toward the forest alone.

CHAPTER TWENTY-SIX

Garrion Swagger pushed his men and the horses at top speed for as long as he dared. His destination was Lady Rhiannah Dragahn's encampment. He and his men once stopped to catch a few hours' sleep and once slowed to covertly skirt the King of Lyndesea's army camped within Ten Thousand Mile Forest. Creeping by during the quiet night, it had been easy to sneak past the guards by circling far around. It took time but it was better than getting captured. While he rode toward the Lady to report his discovery, he contemplated long and hard what he would say to her. He felt in his bones that he had found what would at least set them on the path to finding the dragon egg his liege lady had sought all these years. He knew nothing about dragons or dragon eggs but knew it could be a treasure of immense value. The feeling in his gut that he was onto something was strong and he barely contained his excitement.

If truth were known, Garrion had not looked very hard during the many years while in Lady Rhiannah's service. He had made cursory inquiries around the various villages he had been through, and he brought her trinkets, icons, and magical treasures he thought might appease her voracious appetites but had little interest in finding a dragon egg he truly doubted existed. It was fortuitous timing now as the culmination of his ambitions seemed at hand. With the King of Lyndesea and Lady Dragahn at war, Garrion would be in the perfect position to exploit his knowledge and come out on top. Though he had not exactly worked out what it was that he found, the young blacksmith seemed as good a scapegoat as any and so he began to scheme.

He also knew that the Lady had a massive hoard she kept in hiding and if he gambled a bit, it could all be his. The tricky part was knowing exactly how to use this new information to its best advantage. The Ten Thousand Mile Forest and the king's army were between Lady Dragahn and her heart's desire and only after the war was won and he was crowned king, would he fully reveal what he knew, or suspected. The best part was that the lovely girl in Appleaid might also be his in the end, and it could all be accomplished with a few well-placed sword thrusts... when he was king.

Lady Rhiannah had been busy while Garrion was away the past few months. Their numbers had increased dramatically, and it was obvious that a few nobles had joined them against the King of Lyndesea. Riding through the encampment, he noticed a few banners flying that had not been there when he left. Doing a quick calculation, he realized she had possibly added another thousand men to their force.

It was early morning, and the haziness of campfires drifted across the cold ground. Men were just beginning to rise, and the day's activities began. Keeping the grin off his face, he rode toward the center of the encampment where the lady's black and red dragon banner hung limp in the still morning air. His stomach growled as he anticipated breaking his fast and then he would choose the right time to reveal the information he was sure would put him on the path to being a very wealthy *king* overall. He sat taller in his saddle just contemplating it.

The guards outside Lady Rhiannah's tent snapped to attention when he arrived. They exchanged nervous glances when he dismounted and approached with the intent of having his morning meal and an interesting discussion with his lady and then perhaps a quick tumble. Garrion immediately noticed the guard's nervousness and glared at them as they blocked his way. This was not a typical reaction to him who was second in command to the lady herself. Certainly, this was not how he was used to being treated. Scowling, he pushed past the guards and went into the tent.

"Lady Rhiannah, I…" Garrion's greeting died slowly, and his smile froze on his lips. His eyes narrowed and went cold.

Inside the tent he saw that his liege lady was not alone. A handsome noble dressed richly in gold and white, was sitting comfortably at the table laid with a sumptuous morning meal. Lady Rhiannah sat across from the man wearing only a robe that lay half open revealing a hint of her beautiful breasts down to her flat stomach. Her smile did not waver as the reality of the situation revealed itself to him. By their half-dressed state and obvious ease with each other, it was apparent that the two were lovers.

Garrion had not survived this far in life without developing the ability to quickly assess the obvious and use it to advantage. He may have been an outlaw since his youth, but as things had developed, he no longer led such a low life. At this moment, thinking on his feet, he held his reaction in check. If he acted the jealous lover, then the lady would have an advantage thinking he cared for her. If he acted as if he did not care, then she might not be averse to replacing him as not vital to her in any way. At this juncture, he felt it was best to check his emotions over finding them together and see how best to manipulate the situation to his advantage.

"Ah, Garrion," Lady Rhiannah purred, "you've returned. What news have you brought from the north?"

Not a hint of embarrassment or guilt crossed her lovely face, nor was she interested in anything but what he found on his latest hunt. She seemed unphased as if he had just left a day ago rather than gone a few months.

"Aren't you going to introduce me to your...guest?" Garrion couldn't keep the irritation from his voice nor his hand from resting on the knife hilt belted at his waist.

"This is Lord Stephan Arceneaux of Arcenaxe Castle. He is an old friend you might say, and joined the rebellion bringing almost a thousand men to support my cause." She smiled and reached for a gold cup. "I think he will make a great difference in my campaign and assure us victory."

"Stephan, this is Garrion Swagger, Commander of our military. He's been away on a mission in the north."

Garrion noted how her voice softened when she spoke the name *"Stephan"* with affection.

"Garrion Swagger," Lord Arceneaux tilted his head as if trying to remember something, "I believe, many years past, you and a band of thugs *appropriated* supplies from one of my outposts. You've come a long way from common thief to commander of an entire army."

It was at that moment that Garrion decided not to play the jilted lover but still claim his position, putting in motion the plan he had devised since that sunny afternoon when he met the lovely young maiden and impressive blacksmith's apprentice. Though upon first meeting Lady Rhiannah Dragahn, he felt a hint of magic drawing him to her as more than just a beautiful woman, that had long since worn off. Now his interest was strictly about gold and power. He gave the Lord a wicked smirk and shrugged a shoulder.

"If I recall correctly, your outpost was poorly guarded and sadly supplied. The place just begged to be raided, though I found very little worth *appropriating.*"

At this, he glanced at Lady Rhiannah, his eyes raking over her form for a moment before coolly turning back to glare at the petty lord. They both understood what he truly meant.

"Never mind the past gentlemen. We must come together for the good of our cause. What have you to report, Garrion?" Lady Rhiannah sounded impatient. "Have you any word of a dragon?"

It struck him that he had only been gone a few months and yet during that short time, she had already revealed to this simpering noble what it took her a year to reveal to Garrion. He grew more irritated by the minute.

"If Lord Arceneaux will excuse us. I do have information to relay, but it is for your hearing alone, my lady."

Lord Arceneaux turned his proud head and looked at Lady Rhiannah as if asking for permission to stay or guidance to leave. She smiled at him and nodded slowly, gesturing for him to take his leave. He rose, went to one knee in front of her, took her hand and kissed it before rising smoothly and heading on his way.

The scent of wind and rain with a hint of brimstone, smote Garrion and he suppressed a shudder of recognition and an alarm filled with suspicion.

"A word of warning, Lord Arceneaux," Garrion said over his shoulder as the noble passed, "you'd be wise not to anger me nor tread where I've already staked my claim."

Flashing perfect white teeth, he paused long enough to grin at Garrion's comment, then Lord Arceneaux ducked out of the tent. He could have sworn that the arrogant lord *growled*.

"Come sit down Garrion. Tell me what news you have?"

Garrion strode forward. A thrill coursed through him. This was the moment he waited a very long time for. His wildest ambition to be king of all Lyndesea sat smiling in front of him, anxious for his word. Though he was slightly enraged at what had just happened and obviously had been happening, he took a moment to collect himself. Grabbing a goblet, he poured some morning ale into his cup and gulped it down. He was thirsty, tired, hungry and very angry but needed a clear head to put his plan into motion. Plopping down in the chair just vacated by Lord Arceneaux he stared at the lady and shoved aside his jealousy and fear that he had been replaced.

"It was my impression, these many years that you and I have been together Lady Rhiannah, that our wants and desires were of similar nature. You wanted me to find the dragon egg you claimed was stolen from you and to exact your revenge upon the thief. As I understood it, such a thing could bring you great power, so I supported you in every way. I have worked tirelessly with every breath of my being. You have had my devotion, my bravery, my cunning, and the sweat from my body."

He paused for effect, pasting a wounded look on his face.

"I've given the last ten years of my life to further your cause. I did it because I want the power you offer and, as our forces have grown, I can see that my ambition to become king could, in fact, become a reality and you would have your thief as you wanted. Yet you have given me nothing in return for my labor except orders to tirelessly continue to do your bidding. I have served you well with the expectation that my reward was forthcoming. Finally, after all this time, I believe *I have found* what we have been seeking. *I* finally discovered the whereabouts of the thief who took your dragon egg."

"You've found the dragon thief!" Lady Rhiannah leaped from her chair.

Garrion did not look directly at her just in case she could detect his lie, or rather, the half-truth he invented. Instead, he affected a sorrowful look on his swarthy features and ignored her outburst.

"Now, on the eve of war, I return after a dangerous journey on your behalf, with terrible risk to my person, and in much anticipation of bringing you this good news, to find you've betrayed me with another man. A man opposite to me in every sense of the word, a man who looks down upon me as if I were filth on the bottom of his boot. Tell me Lady, what now is my incentive to reveal what I know?"

Lady Rhiannah's black hair swirled around her as if caught in a maelstrom and her face flushed red. The stench of magic rose in the air. She seemed to be struggling to keep herself from leaping at him. The look she gave him now was one of relief and triumph, hope and impatience.

He almost felt bad about lying and almost felt bad he did not have more to go on besides a hunch about a girl and a young blacksmith. Surely, the boy was too young to be Lady Rhiannah's dragon egg thief but there was the possibility that he might know something. Then there was the girl whose exotic scent was exactly like Lady Rhiannah's and that thrilled him in many ways. Garrion was always right when he had hunches, and this gut feeling was something to go on. He could work within the boundaries of truth and suspicion and by the time the lady found out, Garrion would already be king.

"Tell me everything! Where is he! Is he strong and cunning? Does he have men protecting him? Is he a mighty sorcerer? Where is the egg? Has it hatched? Did you see a dragon?"

"Ah-ah-ah..." Garrion wagged a finger at her, "first, what is in it for me? How much are you willing to *pay* for my discovery?"

The woman before him, he had to admit was quite spectacular in her rage, but then her skin began to flush burning coal red from head to toe, and her white teeth gritted in anger. He could swear he saw flame flickering in her eyes. She looked like a creature he'd never seen before, rippling as if fighting to stay in her skin. Then she flew at him with clawed hands, black nails going for his throat. Garrion pushed back in his chair, almost falling backward as she leaned over him. He had always feared that she was a sorceress of some kind and now he was seeing the proof because she was horrific to look upon in this evil state. Swallowing fear that threatened to make him spill everything he knew, he bolstered his courage.

"Tell me where me the dragon thief is, Garrion, or I will rip your throat out!" Her voice made a strange, terrible chord of sound that was both a woman's shriek and a low animal growl. Her sharp nails were digging into his throat. He choked on a dry gasp, but he held fast to his conviction that she would not kill him.

"Kill me now and you'll never know where they are." Garrion felt the blood rush from his face and could only hope he convinced her to spare him. There was always the fear of torture to consider as well but he had to follow through with the gamble he had taken.

"Whatever you tell me now, I know you've been in the north, so I know where to look. I can still kill you and find him."

"Yes, but the north is vast. There is wilderness and lands of unknown danger. I can spare you a lengthy hunt with my specific knowledge. Let us be calm, my love, and we can bargain. I reveal who your thief is in exchange for your treasure hoard. I know you have one."

Lady Rhiannah stepped back and took a deep breath. She calmed her anger and as she did, her skin paled slowly back to normal and though her face was still angry, she was able to speak in her feminine accent. Once again, she was the beautiful, elegant lady he knew. Her robe had come open and her breasts heaved but she didn't seem to care. He stared at her magnificence, recalling the many times he had laid his head upon those soft mounds.

"Is that it? All you want is gold?" She looked at him with astonishment and spoke with derision that could not hide her disgust.

"Oh, no. I also want to be the new ruler of Lyndesea. We will win the war and kill the tyrant currently on the throne. *I* will be crowned king, and you may be my queen. We'll find your thief and the dragon. You must have some power over one or you'd not be so eager to find such a dangerous creature."

Garrion smirked wickedly.

"Yes, Lady, I want it all, gold, power and the kingdom's rule. After the war, I will reveal what you so badly want to know, then together we'll go after your dragon thief."

CHAPTER
TWENTY-SEVEN

The wagons trundled along the road. Soldiers marched in lines or rode in groups on horseback. Many of the men were from Appleaid and some were from the surrounding villages. All had recently been conscripted into service and were headed to join the main force. The Kingdom of Lyndesea had been at peace for a very long time, and large contingencies of soldiers had not been needed until now. Older soldiers mostly returned from their ancestral homes and left their trades and families to resume military life. Because of this war, they had been recalled but more had to be forced into service to assure victory.

Lady Dragahn's legions numbered in the thousands, and rumors circulated that many nobles had joined her in the war against the King of Lyndesea. Horrifying whispers spoken around campfires at night told of her brutality, her sorcery and her habit of drinking men's blood. Other tales spoke of her endless plundering priceless treasures, ancient artifacts, and even her search for a live dragon, though no explanation was offered as to why. No one had seen a dragon for hundreds of years and so madness was also attributed to her list of cruelties and greed. Her wrath swept across the land spreading darkness, fear, and war with the stain of evil magic following in her wake.

Kieran sat next to Tartan on the seat of their wagon which was laden with tools from the forge and a small anvil they would need to apply their trade. He couldn't stop thinking about the argument he had with Una and how they had parted with angry words and hurt feelings. If he concentrated hard enough, he could find her with his mind but only by the barest thread of awareness as she did not seem to want to be found.

"You're awfully quiet." Tartan broke the silence. "What's eating at you boy? Being a warrior is all you've talked about since I've known you. I thought you'd be boiling over with excitement to be fighting in this war."

"I am Tartan. It is all I've ever dreamed of. I wanted to follow in the footsteps of the great Sir Kieran Cray and be a king's champion like him. To swing a sword and fight for king and country consumed me. I wanted fame and fortune, and a reputation as a great warrior. I've planned it and worked hard toward that goal."

"And now, you're on your way. If you go into battle, I've no doubt you'll make a name for yourself. What else is bothering you?"

"It's Una," Kieran scanned the sky, seeing if he could spot her camouflaged in the clouds above. "It was our dream. We were supposed to do this together. She's furious I wouldn't let her come along. We had a big fight and I'm afraid she'll never speak to me again."

"Ah, she'll get past it, lad. Una won't be alone; she'll have Sara and our children to keep her busy. She'll be able to accept that this was something you have to do, on your own as a man, and when you return hale and whole, it will all be water under the bridge."

"I know, but you don't understand her. She's *different* than most women and I don't know what she'll do without me. We have never been apart since... well, for a very long time."

He rubbed his thumb over the crystal set in his sword hilt. From the day she'd hatched they had been together, and he missed her.

"I've taught you well. Your skills with the sword are better than most of these poor boys. Sure, you're untried but you'll do well. Una should know you'll be fine for a short while without her. For my part, I'm hoping you'll never even see battle. I can make an argument to keep you with me and out of the fighting."

Kieran was about to protest but Tartan continued.

"I know you want to be in the thick of it and test your skills, but I wouldn't have you witness the bloody brutality of war. Nor would I have you live with the memory of taking another man's life on your conscience. It changes a man, Kieran. Just stick with me lad, I'll keep you safe. If I have my way, I'll keep you out of the fighting altogether."

"That's just it Tartan! I don't want to be kept out of it! You know this is all I've ever wanted since I ran away from home... everything I've worked for! I want to go into battle and emerge victorious and earn my name as a champion."

"Have you learned nothing from me boy?" Tartan sounded exasperated. "You're clever and talented for sure, you are big and have grown strong. I'm proud of what you've become but you're not a blood thirsty killer. Many of these old soldiers, these men of war, have given their lives to fighting. They have hard hearts and scars on the inside as well as the outside. Many more men have gone searching for glory but only found pain and death at the hands of someone on the other end of a sword. War changes a man, I'm telling you. You've built a good life, Kieran, don't throw it away for something as fragile as dreams and as fleeting as fame and fortune."

"I'm not a coward!" Kieran shook his head and growled, "and I'm not a little boy who has to be sheltered!" He was angrier than he'd ever been at Tartan. "I want to be more than a simple blacksmith!"

Tartan's jaw clenched shut and his face reddened with anger. He looked away from Kieran, going silent. His chest heaved as if he were holding in his fury at Kieran's insult.

Suddenly, the closeness of the wagon seat was too much. He'd just insulted the man who took him in and took care of him when he was at his lowest point. Kieran had enough talking and grumbled he would rather walk for a while. Leaping down from the seat while the wagon was still moving, he hit the ground smoothly and waited for it to pass. Then he fell in behind, keeping his indignation and anger in check before he said something more hurtful in his frustration.

Tartan's wagon moved on and Kieran watched it go. As he walked, to take his mind off the argument with Tartan, he relived his last conversation with Una in his head.

"Why can't I go with you?" she had shouted at him. Just like when she was a dragon and high emotions overwhelmed her, her skin flushed red, her hair glowed crimson like awakening coals, and Kieran thought she'd shift into dragon form or burst into flames. He was always awed by dragon magic, but this was different and even more intimidating. He held his ground.

"Because in war they have spears and arrows flying everywhere. You could be injured or killed."

"I will fly fast, and no spear or arrow can pierce my scales. You know everything I'm capable of. Everything we are capable of togeth-

er!" At the time, Kieran thought she sounded like a spoiled child, but he understood her frustrations. She hadn't been done.

"Dragons have been going into battle against humans for thousands of years. I've no other mate but you and I must keep you safe. If you go to war, I want to be with you. I must be with you!"

"It's been thousands of years since dragons have even been seen because they've all been killed by men! When I climbed up to your mother's cave, I wasn't even sure what I'd find there. I was thinking like a featherbrained little boy who listened to too many tall tales at tavern doors. I wanted treasure, but I found you. I didn't even know that big crystal I took was a dragon egg! Sure, we made glorious plans, but it was only make-believe. I never even intended on flying with you. I was a scared child. Not to mention if you're the last dragon, how can I risk you?"

"We are grown now, Kieran. War is here and it is time to give up childish ideas. We are faced with the reality of you fighting in the king's war. I will go with you and from my back, you will fight and be victorious against this enemy that threatens the land. Together we can bring back the glory of dragons and riders and we can have everything we dreamed of, but only if we are together!"

"I know all of this, Una. As a man, I must go to war and fight for the life we've built. Who knows what this enemy is capable of. The threat has been building for years and now is the time for us to protect our king and our country, but accidents happen, and you could be killed. War is unpredictable and you've never been in a battle."

"Neither have you!" she pointed a finger at his chest. "It's all we've dreamed of since we were young. We lived to go into battle, you as a legendary dragon rider and me as your dragon! Always, we were supposed to be together and now you'd leave me like some simpering human female."

"Una, how am I going to explain you to Commander Bodine and the other soldiers? How am I going to explain you to Tartan? They'll all see you. I'll be the only one with a dragon. Besides, it will not be me who gains fame, it will be you, the dragon! I'll just be along for the ride! And what about the enemy, you'll be in their sights to kill! You'll be the bigger threat."

"So that is it? Is that all you care about? Becoming a famous warrior? What we have, what we worked toward has all been a little boy's dream? I know dragon-kind's memories, and I've seen how it is done in battle. Though I am young, I could tell you tales thousands of years old. I can take you into battle and protect you, help you gain the renown you so badly seek, but your pride won't let it happen."

Kieran ran his hands through his hair then let them fall to his sides. Stepping forward, she stood within reach of his arms, and he wanted to pull her close and hold her. He looked into her emerald eyes and the love he felt for her as a dragon and a woman, was almost painful. His thoughts reached out and held her where his arms couldn't move. Conveying every feeling, every fear and every dream, he shared his inner turmoil.

"You're a woman now Una. Can't you just stay a woman? Let me, a man, go to battle, and you stay safe with Sara. There will be a time *for us to go to war together, but this is not that time. Let me do this on my own. I can't risk losing you!"*

Una's eyes had narrowed as they communicated without speaking, but she sensed the stubbornness, the selfishness and the anxiousness within him. She knew he wouldn't be swayed. Turning, she walked away. Her skin rippled and her hair lengthened, and horns grew, her form wavered in his sight, and she transformed into the dragon he knew and loved. Haunches bunching and tale whipping, she leaped into the air. Her colors rippled and changed, turning pale to take on the colors of the sky. The breeze her wings created as she flew away, caressed his face and Kieran was alone once again.

CHAPTER
TWENTY-EIGHT

Tartan sat by his fire with a bowl of stew some of the other men handed to him. He grimaced as it passed his lips, knowing it would be a long time before he got to taste Sara's good cooking again. The bread she packed for him with the rest of the provisions was crusty on the outside but soft on the inside. It reminded him of home. His heart ached. Not just for Sara and the children, but for Kieran as well. They'd had words and the conversation did not go as Tartan intended. He knew the lad was hurting, missing Una, and that he was torn between his loyalties. None of that mattered more than his safety in body, heart, and soul.

The caravan of men heading to join the king's army grew as more men joined the fight against the king's enemy. It didn't matter to Tartan that he hadn't seen the king in years; he was in it now. He paid his taxes, which were small, but that was almost all he had to do with the land's ruler. Kings were meant to protect their subjects from danger, but as the current situation showed, it was the *people* being called upon to protect the king's interest. Perhaps it was because Lyndesea had enjoyed peace for some time and as the land and people grew fat with prosperity, it became attractive to those who coveted its bounty.

Rumors spread through the camp about the enemy they were facing, but it was nothing he hadn't heard before, with all the gossip in the village. Lady Rhiannah Dragahn had gained a huge lawless army of thieves, amassed treasure and was threatening the rightful ruler of the land with a takeover. With the outlaw called Garrion Swagger, they swept mountains and plains and now headed north. If she was not stopped before reaching Ten Thousand Mile Forest, she would make her way through to overrun every village and city in between and beyond.

The sprawling capital city of Odessa lay to the northwest on the other side of the great forest. It was at least one hundred miles west of the Village of Appleaid, on the shores of Lyndesea Ocean. The king's plan was to stop Lady Dragahn on the other side of the forest and thus protect the capital and the villages and cities in between.

Another rumor was that Lady Dragahn had been tearing the countryside apart seeking a mythical creature, a *dragon*, though none knew why. Most men chuckled under their breath because dragons had not been seen in ages. Such monsters were only spoken of in legends and ancient tales. The hint that she was a sorceress added fear of magic and superstition, making the situation even more dire.

Tartan's story was simple. His father had been a king's soldier when he was a young boy. Tartan had been brought up to sword fight, fist fight and handle multiple weapons. He'd been raised and trained with a strong sense of duty and loyalty to the land and the king.

Now as he rode toward war, Tartan's words from the first day he met Kieran haunted him.

"Men fight with swords, but a true warrior fights with honor. He defends his king, his country and his family with his sword, his sweat and his blood."

Those had been the words of his father, drilled into him from the time he began to walk. Did he really believe those words now that they were headed to war?

"There is a lot more to wielding a weapon than just waving it around and hitting things. The problem is, most of the time if a man has a sword there is always another man who wants to fight him. It

takes a great deal of practice and skill to be good at wielding a sword so that you don't get killed."

Those had also been Tartan's words, learned from a life of tough lessons. Those were the lessons he wanted to drill into Kieran's head, but no matter how he tried to teach him the danger of being a warrior, the lad wouldn't give up his boyhood dreams.

The truly hard part was taking another man's life even if he was trying to kill you first. Tartan had tried to teach that to the lad above all the other lessons. Some tavern bard told his legends and fantastic stories, putting fire in the young boy's belly and no matter what Tartan taught him, the desire never left his heart. The dreams of victory and renown would not be left behind and the truth was, no matter how he tried to tell Kieran how ugly war was, how bloody, and terrible, the boy wouldn't relent. Tartan tried to give him new dreams built with his hands and earned by the sweat on his back. Blacksmithing was a good and noble profession. Sadly, in the days to come Kieran would learn the pain of war and the sorrow it would bring. The only ones who would profit from the battle ahead would be the enemy or the king who was sending these good men to their deaths.

Tartan looked at the sword strapped at his side. He recalled forging it himself, long ago when life forced his feet along the same path as his father. The long, straight, steel blade glittered in the firelight, and he recalled every strike of the hammer and every fold in the metal it took to make it. Soon, the smooth channel running down the middle would direct enemy blood away from his grip in a fight, as it was designed to do. It would protect his hand from slipping with the next blow. The double-edged blade was sharp enough to penetrate the toughest armor. Tartan took the black wood handle in his hand and pulled it free from the sheath. He recalled how, as a young boy, Kieran had touched the decorative carving with one finger and ran it along in the silver cross guard. He should have known then that the boy was too far gone in his craving to fight to be pulled back from the front line of battle. Suggesting to Kieran that he would keep him out of the battle ahead was perhaps not the best tactic.

Tartan prided himself on never lying, but that first day he had lied to the boy. He wanted the boy to understand the cost of taking another man's life. So, he told him the sword had never been to war and that it was an unnamed sword, unbloodied and untried in war and thus take away the glamour of fighting. He furthered the lie saying he wasn't a soldier and told only part of the truth. He truly had trained to become one when he was young. He was meant to follow in his father's footsteps, and now Kieran was following him. Tartan hung his head in shame and sorrow. His only solace was that Kieran was skilled and thus prepared for the battle ahead.

He had promised someday he would tell Kieran his story and as the lad trod out of the forest, Tartan realized that day had arrived. As the young man plopped down across the fire, he looked weary and dusty from walking. Tartan offered him the bowl of camp stew set aside for him earlier. Kieran took it and ate ravenously but wouldn't meet his eye.

"Kieran, I told you that first day you were my apprentice that I would tell you my story. Now is the time. I'd hoped to show what could come from learning the craft of a blacksmith, so you'd have a way to support a family, keep food on the table and possibly avoid becoming a warrior as you so badly wanted. Your skills surpassed mine when you made your sword and excelled at the craft. For years, I'd hoped you would never *have* to use it, but that day is coming despite my wishes and prayers."

Kieran's eating slowed as he looked up and gave his full attention to Tartan. He could see how tired he was, and how his brow wrinkled with worry. He set his half-eaten stew aside, rested his hands on his knees and listened.

"I was raised by a father who knew no other life than that of a soldier. He raised my brother and me to be soldiers like him. Tarrick and I were always competitive with each other, like brothers often are. Who was the strongest, who was the best swordsman and who was better at everything else made for constant competition. We trained, fought and were inseparable friends as well as kin. My father was proud of us, and we boasted and drank and lived as if every day was going to be our last. You have to understand Kieran; a soldier's life is not all glory and fame. Only a few earn a name or reputation like your hero, Sir Kieran Cray of the old legends."

There was more than a hint of sadness in his voice as Tartan told his story.

"You remind me so much of Tarrick. He always wanted more, wanted to be the best, and wanted notoriety he couldn't get as a foot soldier in the King of Lyndesea's army. One night we argued and said words no brothers should ever speak to one another. My father chose me to replace him and Carrick was furious. So, he left to pursue his dreams, and I stayed behind with our father. Years passed and when war came, as it always did, we fought an unknown enemy. They were fierce fighters, big and mean, and I did my best to protect my land and my king."

Tartan's eyes filled with tears as he spoke, and he wiped them away quickly before continuing. He grabbed a wine skin, took a long pull then threw two more logs on the fire to keep it bright. Kieran waited silently for the story to continue.

"During the last battle, I faced a warrior who was my equal in every way. He was dressed all in black armor and had a helmet with a shield hiding his face. I was convinced the enemy was evil. He attacked and we fought long and hard, trading blows that would have felled many smaller men. I was sure I had right on my side, so I fought with determination and gave every ounce of sweat and blood I had to defeat my foe. My final sword thrust to the warrior's chest ended his life. As he lay in the bloodied mud, I knelt to see the face of this great warrior who had almost beat me. I removed his helmet and recognized the man, though he was much changed. It was Tarrick. I had killed my own brother in battle. I found out later my father died that same day. He never knew what I'd done. I buried them side by side. Then, I left the king's army and went to find a quiet life as far away as possible."

Falling silent, the big man's shoulders drooped, and his eyes held a haunted pain that Kieran had never seen before and never wanted to see again. His chest felt tight, and his eyes were full of unshed tears. He waited for Tartan to go on. Many of the lessons Kieran learned from this man all made sense now and he understood what his mentor had meant all along.

"Kieran, I told you I'd never been to war, to hide my shame. I, who taught you lying was the worst evil was the one who told the biggest lie, but I knew the day would come that I'd have to reveal everything to you. Now, I have. I am sorry Kieran. Some stories are harder to tell than others, especially when they reveal the darker days of the past."

Kieran realized everyone had secrets they wished to bury. He also knew what it was like to live with lies and how it ate away at you over time. Now was his chance to tell Tartan the truth about Una and what she was, but the words stuck in his throat and would not come. This was Tartan's moment of truth, and he couldn't intrude upon the cleansing revelations and stomp on the man's pain, by trumping him with a bigger falsehood. All he could do was rise, go to Tartan and pull him into a tight forgiving embrace. There would be time in the next few days to tell Tartan that Una was a shapeshifting dragon.

CHAPTER
TWENTY-NINE

H e left her! Kieran had gone with Tartan to war, and *left* her there as if she were weak and needed to be sheltered and protected. She was a dragon and capable of more than he realized. The grief and the despair of being left behind threatened to drown her in a multitude of emotions of the human and dragon kind.

As a dragon, instinct would take over and Una would fly to Kieran, her rider and mate, and the war that awaited them. Eventually, it would be revealed that a dragon lived among them, and men would seek to slay her. There was little doubt that Kieran would be able to protect her even if they could convince every human that she was not a threat to them. The last thing she learned from her dragon memories was that humans were most dangerous when they were afraid.

The truth was, *she* was afraid to stay behind and wait for him. She was terrified of him going into battle on his own without her there to protect him. If he should fall, it would be the end of her anyway. Heartbreak would surely kill her. She paled and shook. There was one other secret she kept that even Kieran did not know and that was bigger than him, her and the battle ahead, but how could she reveal it on the eve of war. She had to find him and tell him but feared how he would take her news. He loved her but if he knew what she hid now, would that love withstand the test ahead?

The magic wanted to take over, change her from girl to dragon, and lift her into the sky to go to him. He had forbidden her to follow but he did not specify in which form and so her mind worked on ways to outwit him. Kieran was driven by his boyhood dream of becoming a warrior and it became her desire too, but the risks were greater than them both. Visions of ancient dragons accompanying their riders into battle and emerging triumphant had filled both their heads until it was unclear which of them wanted it more. As a dragon, she saw that this was the way it should be, the way it must be. As a woman, the fear of loss inspired only despair reflected by a color that must not come to light.

The wind caressed her skin, and she came to a decision. To stay behind would be inconceivable. She had to be by Kieran's side. Una's skin pulsed with life and took on the vibrant moonstone white opalescence that was her true color since she hatched. Her long hair swayed and flushed violet, her eyes stormed dark green and Una changed. Her dragon came to the surface with a roar, and she grew, transformed skin into scales, bones into horns, and arms into legs and wings until Una the dragon now stood where a girl once had.

Lifting off she made a lazy spiral upward to where the clouds billowed and promised rain. Flattening out she let her senses search and located her rider. With a flap of her wings, she sped high above the clouds toward him. Kieran had told her to stay home, but he would soon learn that she could not be ordered to do what went against her very nature. She had ways of dealing with men and...as a woman or a dragon...she would do as both her dragon heart and her human heart desired.

Across the campfire from Tartan Kieran tried to rest. Around them men slept in bedrolls, and some had tents. Others tried to keep warm wrapped only in their cloaks. The relative luxury of his bedroll was due to Sara's ingenuity and Tartan's experience of marching to war, so they were well prepared. Their campsite was a small distance off from the others and snoring and sleeping noises were faint.

Kieran had been dreaming of Una flying through white billowing clouds. The setting sun reflected silvery-white on her scales and glowed with the pinks, blues and the violet hues of evening light. He watched as she changed, hidden uphill in the dense trees of an unknown forest and walked down the mountainside toward him in her womanly form. She glided like a forest sprite, light-footed and silent, tiptoeing past the guards and sleeping men until she stood by his bedside. Smiling shyly, her colors shifting like prisms in the moonlight, she slipped into his bedding and with one muscular arm, he pulled her under him. They kissed and loved quickly and silently before drifting into a restful sleep and on the morrow, they would deal with the consequences.

The morning came and Tartan discovered Una. Shouting at them both, he and Una began to argue, and loudly ordered Una to return to Appleaid. She quietly refused while around them the shouts of men and the clank of armor and weapons indicated that the army was readying to move on. There was a bustle of activity and orders were given to march. All they could do at that point was pack the wagon and move out with the rest. Kieran was oddly quiet about her presence because he was part of her mind and understood her need to be there. Being apart was awful and made unbearable as the miles separated them over the past few days.

There was only one choice, they must take her with them as it was too far and too dangerous for her to go back and besides, she stubbornly refused.

Kieran lost himself in a comforting delusion. In his imagination, Kieran boldly confessed to Tartan that Una was a shapeshifting dragon. His voice was steady and his words plain as he revealed the truth. He told how he learned about the last dragon who lived in the land, had climbed the steep escarpment to the beast's lair in search of treasure to steal, but instead, had stolen the dragon's egg. He revealed how the egg hatched and told how they spent some time escaping the raging mother dragon.

The vision went swimmingly well as Tartan accepted Una and what she was. He even suggested ways that she, as a dragon, could take Kieran into battle flying on her back and single handedly win the war for the King of Lyndesea.

They sat in the back of the wagon and Kieran looked up at Tartan's rigid back. His love for Una collided violently with his loyalty to Tartan and both overshadowed his wishes, hopes and desires. Looking at her, the realization hit him like a hammer that it was time to stop having imaginary conversations and that his boyish dreams had to be set aside like boots he'd outgrown. Time to step into men's boots, take the hard path and tell the truth in reality. He and Una had never discussed revealing her secret because of the magnitude of it and who would believe them? Without Una shapeshifting and proving what she was, would Tartan believe their story? It was a time in the world when magic was all but dead, and dragons were non-existent. Kieran's hesitation was also for her. Would she want anyone to know, and would it endanger her?

When the regular halt was called and the three of them were again alone, he wondered. Could he truly reveal their secrets to this man who was more than a father to him and what would happen to Una if he did?

CHAPTER THIRTY

T here was no time or opportunity to have a heart-to-heart discussion revealing secrets. Officers of the king's army came demanding Tartan and Kieran stoke the fires of their make-shift forge and make repairs of damaged swords and broken armor. There was a lot of sharpening to be done. They worked through the night, not speaking to each other unless it was necessary and about the work they were doing.

Kieran pounded a dagger blade and after heating it one last time, plunged it into a bucket of water to harden it. When it was ready, he pulled it out and turned to find Tartan staring at Una by the fire. Feelings of contentment overwhelmed him, issuing from her and from his own heart because they were together.

"Kieran, leave that and come let us speak." Tartan looked tired but the clench of his jaw and the tenseness of his body gave an indication that he had something important to say.

Leaving his work, he followed Tartan's broad back to the fire where Una sat preparing their supper. By her side, he felt a flush of responsibility settle over him and he was determined that now was his opportunity to act like a man.

"I've come to a decision, and I want you both to know that I didn't come by it easily. I think you two should slip away during the night and head home to Appleaid." Tartan crossed his arms over his chest with his final words.

"No!" Kieran kept his voice low. His chest tightened and his anger rose.

"It is for the best. Una shouldn't be anywhere near the battle to come, and I don't want to even think about what would happen if Commander Bodine should discover her here."

Una stood at Kieran's side. He had an uncomfortable feeling and wondered why she was strangely silent and unmoved by this new development. Her mind was poised as if waiting. Kieran, beside her, straightened to his full height and looked Tartan in the eye. He took a breath and knew this was the moment he needed to reveal everything.

"Tartan, there are things you do not know, things about Una and me." Kieran began.

"Kieran, no..." Una began but was cut off.

"Una is..."

"Kieran, no..." Una said louder, her face flushed.

"Una is...*magic*." Kieran spat the last word out, but that was not what he meant to say. He gave Una a side-eyed look of frustration because she had taken control of his words.

There was a moment of silence in the camp, and the sun chose that moment to drop behind a cloud casting a gloomy light over everything. Tartan smacked his large hand over his face and swiped it down in a gesture that said he was at the edge of his patience, and he looked slightly disgusted.

"All women are magic boy but now is not the time for such matters. You've both forced my hand in this impossible situation, now take your wife and head home while you can."

"That's not what I was going to say!" Angry that Una had over-ruled his tongue, he turned to her and took her by the shoulders. "Show him whatever it is you want him to know." Leaving it up to her.

Una nodded, her eyes darting left and right while her mind spun. Images passed between her and Kieran but there was no resolution. It was obvious to both men that something was about to happen. Kieran had thought to blurt out the truth *'Una is a dragon'* but she had leapt into his mind and changed his words. Now, they were in a bind, but he realized the secrets were hers to tell. He could reveal his part in their deception to be completely honest with Tartan. She took a deep breath.

"I come from a long line of *exceptional* people. In the days of old, the women of my family went to war alongside their mates. Kieran has been teaching me to fight and I promise you, Tartan, that I can hold my own in battle. We fight together, two bodies, one mind, as if wielding one sword. Call it magic, call it skill, call it what you like. We will not go home, and I will fight by Kieran's side in this war and any war to come. I will protect him, and he will protect me as he always has."

Tartan did not look convinced. He took a deep steadying breath and looked back and forth between the two stubborn young people and then he had an idea.

"Alright, you say you can hold your own with a sword, then prove it." Moving to a pile of weapons he picked one and tossed it to the ground at Una's feet.

"Pick it up. You'll agree if I unarm you then you and Kieran head home tonight."

"Unarm or first blood." Una nodded. "Then you'll see, I will stay."

Kieran didn't know what to do. He spoke to her, *'Una what are you doing, you've never wielded a sword before! He could hurt you!'*

'I haven't, but you have, and you know all his moves. Trust me.' She answered calmly in a voice that would brook no argument. *'Stand out of the way, in the shadows where he can't see you and let me do what I must.'*

Kieran backed away with swift obedience and crossed his arms over his chest, watching from under a large oak.

Tartan shook his head and went to the wagon. Drawing the big sword he made, the same sword he killed his brother with, he moved to an open area where they could spar. Thinking this would be over quickly, he just hoped he didn't hurt the girl. Smoothing his hand down his face, he stepped forward and crouched into a fighting stance. The silver clasps in his beard caught the light as he gestured for her to make the first move.

Una closed her eyes and took a deep breath. The sword in her hand was well balanced though unfamiliar. She stepped forward and dropped into a fighting stance like she had seen Kieran do so many times before. Calming her mind, she reached for Kieran's and tapped into his memories of sparring with Tartan over the years. His skill became hers and as soon as Tartan stepped in range, she struck.

The diagonal blow would have surprised any other man, but Tartan was well prepared for a trick or a sneak attack and parried easily. He decided to get this ridiculous spectacle over with. Stepping offline, he moved to the side and stabbed out, his blade circled hers and he flicked it up, expecting it to fly out of her grip. Her blade went up but expecting the move she kept hold of it. Calling on dragon strength she easily held on to the weapon and made a quick counterattack.

Kieran watched from the side. He felt Una connected with his mind as she always did when they flew. He opened his memories letting her in. His sight swam and it was hard to tell if he fought Tartan or if Una did. As she said, they were two bodies, and one mind, wielding a sword against a man Kieran loved. He felt a surge as the force of Una's dragon swelled with strength and he saw through her eyes. In the shadows of the great tree, his eyes flickered with a green flame, and he stepped back, deeper under the cover of the branches. His left hand fell to his side and his right hand gripped as if he held a sword. His breath came fast as Una fought with his skill derived from muscle memory and years of practice.

Tartan employed every trick he knew to disarm the girl. It was strangely like sparring with Kieran, but he recalled the lad had taught her. Somehow, she knew his every move, every thrust and parry was met with an answering move. They circled and he realized she must be watching his face for any indication of his next move. Placing his back to the fire, the front of his body back lit by the fire's radiance, his face fell into shadow. Una was turned toward the fire now and there must have been a trick of the light because it looked as if her green eyes glowed with flames, catching him off guard and he almost got cut. He stopped playing nicely.

Una smiled and behind them Kieran likewise smiled because they knew she had Tartan's game. Her eyes narrowed and instead of being on the defensive, she attacked again as she had at first. She'd taken his measure and found the chink in his armor. Tartan was skilled, there was no doubt but after a few minutes she knew she had him. Her sword was the same hardened steel as his, but she had her dragon power. With Kieran's skills, together they were invincible.

Kieran began to sweat as the sword fight dragged on. He was breathing rapidly, not from exertion, but from excitement. His arms flexed and his thigh muscles twitched as if it were him wielding the sword, fighting Tartan for the right to stay and be considered worthy of the name warrior.

"Where do you want it Tartan?" Una asked barely winded, "Arm? Hand? Leg?"

"You sound overconfident girl." Tartan deflected a downward thrust. "Just like Kieran always is when we spar. It'll be your undoing. Come now, let's end this." He flew at her thinking to easily overpower the slight girl with his superior strength and rapid blows.

Just as when he fought with Kieran, she deflected every blow and danced gracefully out of the way. Tartan began to fear Una's skill. The look in her eyes was frightening, and he wasn't sure if she was trying to kill him.

Moving backward and then side-stepping, Tartan lunged and then retreated, making her come to him. Her sword caught a gleam of firelight as it cut from above, barely missing his head. She swept her sword across; he attacked from below. Switching to a diagonal thrust he parried and hit, she blocked and deflected his every attack. Tartan began to get winded, and his arm grew tired with the effort of softening his blows and thinking this was a no-win situation. He wasn't trying to hurt or kill her, but she had more at stake, and he knew one of them might get hurt should she grow desperate to prove herself. These thoughts had distracted him just enough that when the sting of the tip of her sword touched his temple, Tartan fell back in disbelief. His hand went up and touched the spot and he was shocked his fingers were smeared with blood.

Una took three steps back and lowered her sword, she had drawn first blood, now the fight was over. She smiled, quite pleased with herself that they had won. Sword fighting, she thought, was almost as exhilarating as flying at high altitudes. A thin line of blood now trickled down Tartan's face where she nicked him and she swelled with pride over her victory. Kieran stepped out of the shadows and walked toward her, sweat ran down his face, and wetted the front of his shirt as if he had just fought. He pulled her to his side and kissed her forehead then turned expectantly toward Tartan.

"You're bleeding," Kieran said meaningfully.

"Alright, she can stay, but I still don't think women belong in war... no matter how skilled they are with a weapon." Tartan pulled out a handkerchief and wiped the side of his face then started, his gaze jerking in a new direction.

Just then three men stepped out of the shadows. The ringing of sword blows must have brought them to see what was happening.

"I agree with the blacksmith." Spoke a very angry Commander Rothchild Bodine.

CHAPTER THIRTY-ONE

The three of them were escorted under guard to Commander Bodine's tent. He looked thunderous and after an explanation of why the apprentice's wife was in his camp and what the sword fight was all about, he looked even worse. No man in the tent could help but stare at Una and the commander was no exception. Glaring, he walked around her slight form and admired the swell of her breasts, the gentle curves of her hips and the way her men's trousers hugged her behind. Licking his lips his eyes gleamed with undisguised lust.

Kieran did not care that he was surrounded by the commander's guards or that they were in trouble, which included Tartan, he could not stand how the man was ogling his wife. Stepping by her side, he pushed her slightly behind him.

Commander Bodine looked at the big, young man and how he staked his claim for the beauty behind him. He knew they were married but that didn't always mean anything to a man of wealth and power as he was. The stray thought that he'd need to keep this girl from the king gave him pause.

This close to a crucial battle was not the time to tempt his liege lord or test the large warrior who revealed he would fight to the death for his woman. Bodine smiled, a lot could happen in a vicious battle; people could get separated from each other during the fighting. Unbloodied and untested, young fighters could fall to a well-timed sword thrust. He did not comment on the impressive skills he had seen the girl demonstrate during the fight he witnessed, nor did he mention the lad's sweating and obvious frozen fear that she could get hurt. It would be a detriment to the boy to have his attention divided between keeping her safe and the enemy trying to kill him.

He had a quick idea to keep these two young people close to him during the battle at the front line, and when the day was won, the girl would be part of the spoils.

Turning his attention to Tartan the Blacksmith, he observed him until something dawned on him.

"Tell me Blacksmith, why do you look so familiar? I hadn't seen it until I saw you fighting, but I think I recognize you from earlier days. Tartan is not a common name. It sparks my memory. I suspect you didn't grow up in the Village of Appleaid?"

"My name is Tartan MacLaren. My father was Sergeant Teigue MacLaren, he, my brother and I were in the king's army in my much younger years."

"Ah! Yes, you have the look of your father, now that I recall. You left the king's army to be a blacksmith?" Commander Bodine sounded disgusted.

"I left during a time of peace when fighting men were not needed. Smithing is an honorable profession and without me you'd not have swords to fight with on the morrow."

"True enough. Explain your combat with this intriguing young woman."

"It was...practice, Commander." Tartan hesitated to tell the truth that the battle was to test her skill and had she lost he was sending her and Kieran back home which would have meant desertion, and the punishment would be severe.

"Una wants to fight in the war, and I was testing her skill was up to the mark. I was making sure she wouldn't get herself killed in battle. I hate to admit it because I'd like her to stay out of danger, but I think she can hold her ground."

"There are a few female warriors amongst us. Though, I've always felt women are a big distraction in war. We shall see if *I* allow her to fight in the battle ahead."

"You're welcome to try and stop me." Una stepped forward with clenched fists, ready to fight then and there, but Tartan grabbed her arm and pulled her back.

"Will that be all, sir?" Tartan wanted them out of there before Una or Kieran did something even more rash.

Scowling, Commander Bodine reprimanded them for another half an hour about the need for discipline and the importance of following orders. He fined them half of Kieran's pay and told them to stay out of trouble. Tartan he tasked with finishing weapons and repairing armor and threatened him with dire consequences if the work was not completed satisfactorily. Finally, dismissing them, he pulled Sergeant Sandoval aside and spoke privately, giving his orders.

Tartan clearly remembered his father's lectures, and he was in no mood to speak to Kieran or Una when they returned to their camp and the wagon. He grabbed his hammer and went to pound steel, losing himself in the work. Kieran silently followed while Una gathered more wood for the forge fire. They worked until dawn turned the horizon gray before grabbing an hour or two of sleep. During Commander Bodine's yelling he had revealed that Lady Dragahn's army was a day's march away and let it slip that the war would officially start the day after tomorrow. It was his last command that they should be ready to fight with his guard at the front line that upset Tartan even more. Stabbing a finger at Una, he ordered her to stay close during the fighting or risk the end of everything she loved.

The next day it rained. As the columns of men and wagons traveled all day through Ten Thousand Mile Forest, the road became muddy and difficult to traverse. Wet leaves hung with raindrops, and the sweet smell of clean forest loam brought calm to the king's warriors but also served as a reminder of lives worth living. Cold seeped over them as if it tried to slow their steps toward the inevitable.

Professional soldiers, household troops, and more conscripted men joined the king's full force. They soon marched to a part of the forest where it opened onto long rolling hills. The rain fell out of plump gray clouds, and the thunder was deep and rumbling in the distance. This place was known as Hillside Valley. The advantage would be on the king's side as they hid within the forest edge and were poised to fight an easy downhill battle.

There was no sign just yet of the enemy, but scouts revealed that they were on the move, heading toward them at a swift march. Their ranks lacked the discipline of the king's army and there was a cheerful outlook that Lyndesea's organized force would prevail over chaos of the outlaws.

On the eve of battle, Kieran, Una and Tartan made peace with each other. Now was the time for unity, not sore feelings and anger. They listened as Tartan told tales of old wars, and they discussed strategy. The chances that the outlaws would adhere to any formal rules of battle was slim and so he told them what to expect from men who were greedy and desperate.

Una was strangely quiet, and Kieran tried to pry out of her what was wrong. She shut him out of her thoughts. He could not believe she was nervous about the battle, but when she went into the forest to cast up her supper, both he and Tartan exchanged a nervous look. It seemed maybe she was afraid, and they counted her sickness to it being nervous about the battle.

Kieran shook with excitement when a courier came ordering the three of them to the front line where King Odbalt Linden of Lyndesea would be. He was already there with his generals and commanders making plans for the war.

Tartan's hope was after one great engagement against Lady Dragahn, she and her force of outlaws would be put down like rabid dogs. Word was spread that the king also planned on marching to her castle called Dragon's Reach, deep in the southern mountains and taking back the loot she had stolen over the past ten years. All the outlaws were to be captured and hung for treason and crimes against the kingdom.

That night before the battle Kieran dreamed of ancient dragon warriors outfitted in scaled armor with flashing swords and sturdy round shields. His skin tingled with excitement and had he not exhausted himself forging weapons and later, in Una's arms, he would never have been able to fall asleep. She lay curled against him and sighed, contented that they were together. Her calm overwhelmed him and as one, they rested in confident peace and serenity.

Early the next morning, Una woke Kieran with kisses and soft caresses. Then, taking his hand, led him into the forest away from prying eyes. Without explanation she stopped in a small glen of aspen trees and, circling him with green flame flickering in her eyes, gestured and spoke in a language he had only heard her utter in their dreams. Magic flowed over his skin prickling sharply and with a soft rustling whisper his clothing *changed*. The rough homespun trousers hardened into sleek black leather as did his boots. The cream tunic he wore darkened deep violet-black and smoothed into a material as soft and as strong as spun spider silk. His vest became a scaled breastplate with a dragon rampant on the chest. The powerful pose of the dragon upright and ready to take flight symbolized the power, nobility and courage of a dragon rider in Una's dragon colors. Last, Una took his sword and breathed a stream of white fire over the blade. Now heat-treated with her dragon breath, it could not be broken by any man-made steel.

When Kieran opened his eyes, he was fully equipped and ready for battle and looked every inch the impressive warrior. Una's armor reflected his in every way, except that it was built for one of female stature and form. They looked like two halves of a whole. When they walked out of the forest together, Tartan stared in astonishment at what he saw. His face turned red with outrage. He had no idea where Kieran and Una had gotten or had time to make the armor they wore but to him it was an indication of untried naivety.

"What is this!" Tartan yelled. "You think to ride into battle and just win the war with fancy trappings!"

"Careful with your words, Tartan," Una said, "This armor is of the ancient design of my people. It will keep Kieran and I safe in battle."

Tartan looked baffled at Una as if she were a stranger. Moving over to inspect Kieran's new regalia, Tartan tugged and pulled, assuring himself that it was strong, protective, and serviceable. Inwardly he noted he had not provided Kieran with armor, so it was necessary. Exclaiming rudely under his breath when he didn't find any flaws, he found the scale mesh was tight over Kieran's broad chest but bent easily with his body and the strange material refused to rip. Drawing the sword his eyes grew wide as he noticed the changes to the metal and the gleaming edge that was vicious sharp. The stone in the pommel gathered and reflected the morning light.

"Where did you get all of this? I haven't seen any of it before." He did not want to admit the armor was above average in design, usefulness, and protection. He and Una began to shout at each other.

Kieran suddenly realized that both Una and Tartan were treating him like a child. His outrage grew as the two argued over the necessity of keeping him safe with armor and coddling. He stepped between them as their voices grew in volume and put his hands out to stop the quarreling.

"Listen to me, both of you!" Kieran's voice was deep with controlled anger. "You two act as if I think that I am going to a parade. I will go to war with my sword, my wits, and the skills Tartan has taught me. I will fight with a heart made strong by having my lady fighting at my side. If I win the day, or if I die, all I care about is being a good warrior and acting with honor for our king. Do not insult me by suggesting I don't understand the risks ahead nor the dangers we *all* face. Be assured, I do not go to make a fool of myself by showing off either."

Kieran felt embarrassed by it all and would rather have gone into battle with only his sword and sturdy boots had he not told Una he would wear dragon armor. He realized how fanciful and unrealistic his dreams were and now felt ashamed. He wasn't sure if he was convincing himself or chastising them.

"Tartan, you are a father to me, and I love you. I have become the man I am because you taught me to be respectable, not to lie and to be honest. Now, you must let me do whatever it is I am fated to do. Each of you must do your part to stay alive and I will do the same but stop treating me like a child to be coddled and sheltered. It is true, I am untried, but I am ready. Let us go into battle as brothers-in-arms and protect each other's backs from the enemy that threatens. Stop worrying about me!" Kieran stomped away leaving the two behind.

The sound of birds singing in the trees and the wind through the leaves surrounded Una and Tartan as they fell silent. In the distance a war horn called the troops to battle, and they knew they had to go. Una turned wordlessly and followed Kieran. Tartan nodded and went to don his own armor from days long past.

In the forest Kieran turned to Una. He grasped her shoulders.

"Today, I will fight bravely, but I'll not have you interfere. It is time for me to be a man. If I am killed, you will fly away to safety, Una. Do you hear me? While we both know what you are capable of, I'll not have you risk your life any further than you must, certainly not for my sake. Promise me, you'll do as I ask."

In his head he sent her a private message. *"I know you'd be safer in dragon form, but do not show your dragon under any circumstances."*

"I promise, but, Kieran, I will not let you die."

CHAPTER THIRTY-TWO

Lady Dragahn was prepared for battle as well. Armored in a black scaled breastplate with her long black hair braided down her back, she stood ready by a table with a map unfurled on it. Absently, she rolled a seemingly ordinary rock the size of her palm over the table. The same stone had been polished smooth by her motions over the last ten years, the same one she first found with the dragon thief's blood on it. A large ruby ring glittered on her pointing finger as her eyes darted across the map contemplating the battle ahead. Her dragon senses were tight, feeling as if this were the day she would prevail against those who would stand between her and finally reaching the dragon thief.

Earlier in the morning hours, she met with Garrion Swagger and the nobles who had joined her cause to discuss strategy and the placement of their men to the best advantage. They believed they were fighting a tyrannical king for the purpose of appointing a new ruler and for plunder. Lady Dragahn's driving force was to use the fighting and the plunder to keep her army moving north so she could find the thief. Though none of them knew that was the real reason she was there. If she could shapeshift into a dragon and fly north where Garrion hinted the dragon thief was, she would leave this all behind. The urge to kill Garrion was overwhelming and had to be tamped down frequently because she did need to know what lay in the north that would end her search. She was tired of waiting.

No matter how she tried to bribe or cajole or threaten, Garrion kept the thief's whereabouts secret. All she had to do was win the battle and hand over the entire Kingdom of Lyndesea to him. Her heart lurched thinking about the many years she had missed watching her young grow, that is, if it still lived. Gooseflesh rose on her arms and she tried not to despair thinking that the thief had possibly killed her young. One thing was certain, soon she would know. The waiting was maddening. A feeling that it would all be over today flowed within her and all she wanted was to be done with it so that she could finally get her thief and the precious dragon hatchling he stole. She would rip his heart from his chest, drink every drop of his blood and devour him whole, taking any strength or magic he had. After today, there was no place he could hide. She shook with anticipation and her mother's heart ached to see her youngling.

Lord Stephan Arceneaux came to collect her, and she smiled at his handsome face. He was an unexpected revelation these last few months, and she thought possibly she might miss him when this was all over, and she had what she wanted. His skill in bed was exceptional and if his muscled body was any indication, he would be unbeatable in battle which suited her just fine.

One thing was certain, he would be a far better king than Garrion Swagger and as she mounted her horse, she plotted an alternate strategy, one that would lead her to the thief and one that would punish Garrion Swagger for creating this war and making her wait longer. He had no idea what torture it was for her not knowing about her child, knowing that the end of her search was near. He dangled the information in front of her like temptation she had not the strength to refuse. In the end she promised herself, Garrion Swagger would understand what pain truly was: a torment equal to the anguish he had so graciously bestowed upon her.

They rode to the meeting place where they would bring the battle against the King of Lyndesea. King Odbalt was in the way of her getting what she wanted and though it was a necessary evil to get past him, she decided she would make him pay as well.

Facing the enemy was everything Kieran hoped for in terms of splendor and pageantry. Rows of the king's bravest knights and fearless warriors were impressive in shining silver armor under colorful flags waving in the breeze. Their weapons were held at a uniform angle and all the men turned in unison staring down the hill where the enemy gathered. Archers stood in two impressive lines with arrows knocked and fingers ready to release. Working in disciplined formality, the soldiers saluted the king and the nobles and cheered. The energy and excitement stirred the air, and it was mesmerizing.

Kieran, Una and Tartan took their places among Commander Bodine's guard as ordered. They would be with the rest of the warriors in the first line of attack. He was thrumming with excitement and intent upon making a name for himself. This was the culmination of his dreams.

The commander had raised an eyebrow at Kieran in his black armor and could not help but seemed to be impressed. When his eyes tracked to Una, the man had licked his lips and swallowed.

Every time he saw her, he flushed visibly, and it did not go unnoticed. Had they not been on the same side, Kieran might have run the man through for such lecherous stares at his wife, but then the king rode forward. Everyone's attention turned to him.

Odbalt Linden, King of Lyndesea, seemed impressive on the large charger he rode that was just as heavily decorated in gold as the king. Riding closer toward his nobles, his ornamental gold armor flashed polished to a shine. His belly was larger than a seasoned warrior's but was accommodated by the shiny breastplate. The cantle and pommel of his saddle were high, and the stirrups shortened to accommodate his short legs. Though he may have been handsome in the past, opulent living appeared to have taken its toll and when he smiled his crooked front teeth made him look comical. He addressed the troops admirably and spurred them on to fight for victory, for their homes and country.

From a distance, everyone spotted a beautiful woman in black armor mounted on a black horse. Flanked by two men and four guards, she rode toward the center field to parley. King Odbalt, three of his knights and Commander Bodine rode out to meet them. After a tense discussion, the attempt to resolve the conflict was abandoned. Though this mutual meeting was a chivalrous and practical way to avoid casualties, most knew that negotiations were futile. There would be no agreement or a truce, only the terms of engagement and no offer of surrender was forthcoming from either side.

Returning, Commander Bodine and Sergeant Sandoval resumed their places in the line where Kieran, Tartan and Una had been positioned. They advanced together with the commander's guard and would be among the first to engage the enemy after the first barrage of arrows. Sandoval was positioned just behind Kieran with his blade drawn.

When the first horn called the troops to ready for the charge, Kieran, Tartan and Una stood side by side. There were no last words of comfort, or advice given, and no farewells, or warnings. They each knew their part was to hold back the enemy from getting past them or taking the king.

Kieran looked at the enemy with sharp focus. This was the moment of destiny he had worked toward his whole life, but he felt oddly cold and distant. Much of this was how he pictured going into battle, but his vision always showed him riding Una, his beautiful white dragon and part of him was disappointed. He knew at any moment Una could take dragon shape and together, they could win the war, just the two of them, but that was not how it turned out at all. All his childish dreams of being a warrior were indeed coming to fruition but all he could think of was that death was at hand for so many of the men and the reason for this waste was kept between the king, the nobles, and the enemy.

When the second horn blared the battle charge was on. The whiz of arrows and drum of charging horses, the stamp of soldier's boots, and the loud war cries for king and country rang out as men raced forward. Tartan, helmeted and dressed in full armor, was one step ahead of Kieran, and he felt rather than saw Una at his right side. Then he saw the point of an enemy sword coming for his face. He dodged the thrust and countered, and the scream of his foe rang out before the thud of the body hit the ground. After that first kill, he lost all sense of time and clarity, he fought with skill and calm coolness. The faces of the men coming against him flashed for an instant and then vanished with his sword blows. There were very few who withstood his onslaught, none escaped.

Courage was one thing and skill another, but the driving force of survival was overpowering. At all times, the metallic shriek of steel on steel accompanied the stench of blood in a sickening thickness. The screams of the wounded were horrifying. Kieran did not feel the sting of any weapon. His sight had sharply focused like it did when he and Una flew among the high peaks of the dragon mountains. She was by his side and repelled every attack that went her way. Tartan's face was grim as he pressed forward. They were to head to center field to reach Lady Rhiannah Dragahn who was responsible for the deaths happening around them.

A group of Lyndesea soldiers accompanied the three people Commander Bodine had taken such an interest in. They each fought with calm intensity. Sandoval circled around behind when the fighting was thickest. His orders from Commander Bodine were clear, and he was intent upon obeying. He understood the commander's desire for the young warrior girl from the small village, and part of him fantasized that when Bodine was finished with her, he could have her for himself. So, when the young warrior Kieran was pressed by two enemies at once, he made his move. A quick blow to the back of his head and the enemy soldiers would take care of the rest. Sandoval was not a big man, but he was wiry and strong, and he expected to overpower and drag Una away from the battle. Any resistance would easily be dealt with.

Coming up behind Kieran quickly, Sandoval struck. The lad was much taller than Sandoval and the power of his aim was thrown off by the confusion around them. He meant to stab him in the back of the neck with the point of his sword but only succeeded in landing a blow between his shoulder blades. The strange armor the boy wore deflected his weapon with a spark, and thus he succeeded in nothing but a poor attempt to kill him. Then the boy turned in response to the strike and Sandoval turned pale.

Kieran finished off the two men in front of him and felt a heavy thump to his back. He whirled, sword thrusting out in defense to meet the attack from behind but instead he found Sandoval looking shocked and terrified. The man panicked and hacked awkwardly at Kieran's neck. There was nothing to do but defend himself against a man he thought shared the same loyalty. Sandoval seemed to realize he could not match his target's skill and so he turned with a strangled cry and fled.

Una shouted and Kieran returned to the fight. He did not understand what just happened but suspected the worst betrayal. The battle lasted late into the afternoon and though the sun tried to peak out of the overcast sky at times, the day was mostly gray and gloomy, swollen with heavy rain clouds. A storm gathered overhead, and the cries of the dying were so loud that they rose above the clash of swords, and the whiz of spears and arrows. The battle lasted until night fell and the darkness dictated a reprieve for both sides.

CHAPTER THIRTY-THREE

Throughout the night, the cries of the wounded and dying filled the air. Kieran and Una cleaned the blood from their armor, sharpened their weapons and together they tried to catch an hour or two of rest. What happened during the battle gnawed at him and, though he tried to find the glory in the day's fighting, his heart could only recoil in sorrow. The smell of blood was everywhere, and the consequences of war could not be denied.

Tartan had fought with efficient ferocity and word spread of his identity as the once-renowned Captain Tartan MacLaren, who was in the king's guard in days long past. He was called to King Odbalt's tent and was kept there discussing strategy late into the morning hours.

Kieran's only solace was Una. Her solid presence and calm demeanor helped him get through the night. Though death and pain were all around them, they found comfort in each other's arms and release in the tangle of their limbs. His tired body embraced hers and the rhythm of their lovemaking comforted him and reassured her. Words of love whispered in his ear with Una's sweet voice, bolstered his courage and when morning came, Kieran was ready to face the sun rising in the east and the day's battle ahead.

The king's army gathered for what they hoped was the last time. Tartan, Kieran and Una took their places in the frontline. The horn blew, the ranks formed and once again the archers took their places. There was no attempt to negotiate peace this day, it was straight into battle and the fighting quickly turned brutal. Fire arrows flew, making streams of black smoke through the air and competing with the whistle of hurtling spears. The screams of the enemy were distant but indicated the arrows reached their targets. The rise and fall of moaning sounded the death knell. The clash of swords on armor and the thud of axes on shields echoed in the morning mist until the noon sun bathed the land.

Finally, later in the day, the tide of battle turned when the ranks of men on the enemy side turned and fled. After the King of

Lyndesea's army won, rumors started immediately of the three warriors from Appleaid, one of whom was a woman. Whispers were that many people witnessed the two young warriors fighting in almost perfect unison. Also, many claimed to have seen green fire dancing in both their eyes. Claims of his unbelievable strength and suspicions of magic circulated like wildfire. Una was splattered with blood, but none of it was hers and she was treated as a warrior princess.

There was not much more time for talking about the strange trio, as they were called to the king's side so that he could reward their bravery and skill. Commander Bodine looked at Kieran with fury in his eyes. Sandoval never returned from the cowardly errand he had been charged with and was assumed to be dead. Bodine could not say anything, or he would implicate himself in trying to murder the impressive warrior who was swiftly making a name for himself. He met the young warrior's eyes and scowled at him.

The two-days of battle had been everything Kieran hoped for, until it wasn't. Flashing armor, troops of brave men marching in unison, gleaming weapons and flapping banners were all present. However, the strike and clang of sword on sword and the screams of the dying, the scent of blood and sweat-soaked bodies were not what he expected. The sight of men's faces frozen in agony, and the glazed eyes of his dead foes was the reality of war. There was no glory in it. Though making love with Una had been a sweet reprieve his heart was heavy with what he had seen and done. The bodies lay thick across the hill side and the plain ran with blood.

The war horn resonated through the hills calling the end of the war and indicated it was time to claim victory. Upon the hill the king waited in all his splendor, seeming to not care about the lives lost. Two days of battle had not affected him and his face flushed with anticipation and victory and the spoils of war.

It was not the glorious day that Kieran dreamed of as a little boy and anticipated as a man. Shame claimed his heart now that he had been so naïve. Finally, he understood what Tartan had warned him of that first day they met.

Kieran, Tartan and Una were eventually brought before the king. They were praised and promised glory, renown, and a small portion of the treasure King Odbalt expected to receive as victors. After being escorted to the side as champions, word came that Lady Rhianna Draghan and her men were willing to discuss terms of surrender.

CHAPTER
THIRTY-FOUR

G arrion Swagger had fought well during the two-day battle, but it proved to be too little, too late. Many of his men were overrun by the king's army or threw down their weapons in surrender on the second day when the battle was clearly lost. Nearly half of his outlaws had deserted. They had lost too many men, and the tide had gone against them. He wheeled his horse and galloped back to where Lady Rhiannah waited. His dreams of being king were swiftly sinking into the mud with his men's blood.

He found Lady Rhiannah arguing with Lord Stephan Arceneaux. They were standing close together gazing into each other's eyes with their hands clasped between them. She was begging and then ordered him to take his men, half of the gold and silver in their possession, and leave to avoid the wrath of the king. Garrion overheard her say that he was the key to her future which cast burning coals of fury upon Garrion's head. Lord Stephan Arceneaux was too noble to run and leave his lady behind, but she insisted. After a final passionate kiss, he did as she asked but whispered that they would meet again soon. Shortly, thereafter, Lord Stephan left the field taking his men and further weakening their numbers. The chance to regroup and fight on rode away. Garrion ground his teeth in jealous frustration.

The lady herself seemed calm and undisturbed by their losses. Only Garrion knew her interest mostly rested with finding the elusive thief and he had yet to figure out how best to continue to use his valuable information. It was a possibility to take the remaining loot and keep his head on his shoulders. He should be happy with that. Still, with his last card remaining to be played, he stuck by her and went along to discuss the terms of surrender.

Lady Rhiannah had removed her armor and unbraided her hair. Barefoot, she approached the king in a long sleek black gown that hugged her curves. Her beauty was undeniable. As if she had not just lost a second major battle, she acted as if she were in charge. Not a flicker of fear crossed her lovely features.

King Odbalt of Lyndesea, a few of his knights and nobles and guards waited for the approach of the losers. Wounded warriors were being helped, but many men still lay dead all around them. Lady Rhiannah Dragahn, Garrion Swagger and a few of his loyal men approached. He intently scrutinized the faces of the nobility in front of him watching for any sign of fear, treachery, or opportunity. That is when he spotted them. None other than the blacksmith and his apprentice stood beside the king. Both were outfitted in blood-splattered armor and standing with the king's men. They looked as if they had each spent their entire lives at the royal castle rather than in a small town hiding in the mountains. What this could mean was a mind-numbing curiosity and he struggled with this new development. He needed to figure out how to use this to *his* best advantage. Strangest of all beside them was the lovely maiden he had met on the bridge in Appleaid, and it looked as if she had just fought in the battle as well. These were the three Garrion suspected had information about or were in possession of the lady's dragon egg that she had spent ten long years hunting for. There was a possibility they could also prove to be the hidden advantage he needed to keep his head on his shoulders.

His attention was centered on the three people, and he was not listening to the negotiations. All he heard was that the lady and her lieutenants and all outlaws were to be taken and imprisoned and some would be hanged for treason. Lady Rhiannah seemed hardly phased by any of that and he was outraged when the agreement was made. Why she had given away so much so quickly without much of an argument was beyond his understanding. Before they could come and take him away in irons, Garrion made a desperate attempt to avoid the hangman's noose.

"My lady," Garrion interrupted the negotiations, "a word, please." He seemed calm on the outside, but on the inside, he was starting to sweat because he could no longer tell where her loyalty lay and he suspected the worst kind of betrayal. She nodded and stepped back to the line where her men waited.

"Before you negotiate away my life so easily, I suggest that the information you want is valuable enough for you to *reconsider* the king's demands and protect *me*. You and I know that you are a sorceress of some ability, and I think you intend on using that to your own advantage to get out of this mess. Leaving me behind. I suggest instead that you use the magic you have to save us. Tell them to set me and my men free, and I'll tell you the information you so badly wish to know." He smiled, knowing she would do as she was told.

Lady Rhiannah's amber eyes sparked flames and she lunged toward him grabbing him by the shirt front with strength he knew she possessed and he now counted on.

"Tell me now! Where is he? Who is he?"

Taken back by her crazed look, Garrion could not reveal that he only had vague ideas and was about to make a desperate guess. He surmised that is why she agreed to surrender so quickly. She knew *she* could escape, but those who followed her would not be so lucky. If she had any loyalty to him, he was not willing to risk his life on it. His only hope was to create some confusion and try and get away in the chaos that might ensue.

Behind them, the king and his men jerked when the lady turned on one of her own men and started shouting at him. It all was a bit comical. They truly did not understand any of what was going on but stood aside to watch, in fascinating surprise.

"Tell me!" her voice cracked with desperation then she threatened. "Your life is forfeit anyhow, so tell me and I'll be sure you escape with your miserably short life."

"There, beside the king are two people I discovered in the small village called Appleaid," Garrion pointed at Kieran and the girl beside him. "I suspect it is the young blacksmith's apprentice you seek and the girl in the strange armor... well, *she smells just like you.*" He pronounced his last words with as much surety as he could muster. The only hope he had to keep his head on his shoulders was that the lies he told would not catch up to him before he could escape.

He grinned as the lady slowly turned and looked where his finger pointed. Then she saw the young man and the girl beside him. Her vision focused and fixated on every detail about them. Their armor gave them away and she *knew*. The dragon rampant on the chest was the symbol of their crimes. She saw the crystal in the pommel of his sword and then she stared at his young face. Her brow wrinkled in confusion. Surely, he was too young to be her thief, and the girl? She drew Lady Rhiannah's attention with strong recognition though she had never seen her before. She could barely think past the girl's lovely face and what it all meant. Her body began to shiver, and she pointed at the young warrior.

"Give him to me! *Give him to me!*" Her eyes were wild and on fire as she shouted in a growling scream. Everyone could see, this was not just rage, it was insanity.

"Now see here, my Lady, you're not in any position to make demands and the terms have been agreed upon..." King Odbalt blanched, but his words were cut off by another scream.

"Give me that boy!" she stumbled toward Kieran, arms outstretched, claw-like hands extended, and her face contorted in anger.

Kieran felt the tide of fate flow over him. As the beautiful black-haired woman screamed and pointed at him, he knew in his heart that somehow his crimes had caught up to him. Next to him Una was frozen with a look of shock on her face. He turned to her, grabbed her shoulders, and thrust her into Tartan's arms.

"Hold her, no matter what happens." Tartan held Una who seemed to be in a trance of some sort and he stared at Kieran as if he had lost his mind.

Kieran boldly walked forward and stood tall and proud in front of King Odbalt, his knights and nobles, and every other person who had fought in this needless war. They all gaped at him. He was not sure what this woman wanted with him but felt as if this was part of his destiny. The weight of the dead and dying was his to bear, and he felt as if his time was up.

When he was within reach, Lady Dragahn's hand shot out, and she pricked him on the cheek then licked a drop of blood from her nail that cut him. She closed her eyes, shaking and then bent at the waist and began to wail. Her cries cut to the heart of everyone listening and more than a few men staggered back from the unnatural sound.

"You!" She breathed heavily, "You are the one! You are the thief!"

The lady roared, and her face turned red. An unnatural wind blew her black hair around like a tempest. Magic was called upon like these men had never seen before and many ran. She arched back and screamed at the sky in triumph. Men fell with their hands over their ears at the piercing cry, and the king and some of his men fell back as if struck. No one dared to ask what was going on, they just stood by and watched, suspecting this had nothing to do with wars or kingdoms.

"Where is it? Where is my egg?" She was in a rage and there was no telling what she would do.

Kieran understood immediately who this was. He knew because behind him was Una, the dragon shapeshifted into a girl. This, this insane woman who had clearly terrorized the entire kingdom to find him, the dragon thief, was the mother dragon shapeshifted into a woman's form. He had been found out finally.

The guilt struck him like a physical blow. All this death, the war, the terror, the corpses surrounding them, it was his fault. He dared not even look at the bodies now, or else he would be sick. This woman's madness, the full force of her wrath, was his fault. He finally understood she had ranged far and wide for ten long, endless years hunting *him*.

Strangely, Kieran felt a blush of relief that everything was finally revealed. The mother dragon had found him but now, she also found Una. His only thought was to defend her until his dying breath.

CHAPTER
THIRTY-FIVE

"Lady, I ask you to hear me out." Kieran's voice was oddly calm but loud enough to cut through her insanity. Lady Dragahn was panting furiously. Her black nails extended toward him, and her arms were turning to ruby red scales from elbow to fingertip. As if Kieran's words distracted her, she glared at him with wild amber dragon eyes. He went on.

"I was just a boy. I ran away from home seeking my destiny. When I heard that the last dragon's cave was high in the mountains, I took a chance and scaled the cliff to find it. It was dumb luck I did! I foolishly looked for treasure and gold so I could survive. Truly, I did not know the crystal was your egg! Then the egg hatched and..."

Kieran stopped and swallowed. Taking a few steps toward Lady Dragahn holding his hands before him in surrender.

"I don't ask for forgiveness or for your understanding. I just want you to know that I did the best I could to protect her and had no wish to harm anyone. I see now that my dreams of valor and glory were childish and misplaced, but I ask that no one else get hurt because of my mistakes. The responsibility is all mine."

"You were just a little boy! All this time I thought you were a strong warrior or a sorcerer who had taken my egg. Ten long years I've searched, a mother aching for her lost child and..." Lady Dragahn shook her head in confusion, then her eyes cleared and narrowed.

"Where is my youngling!" Her voice dropped to a growl, and she looked poised to leap at him again.

Tartan had been holding onto Una who watched in a state of horror. She seemed to wake up and struggled out of his grasp. Walking forward she went to stand beside Kieran.

"Here, I am Una." Kieran had never heard Una sound so scared or so brave.

The two women stood facing each other in shock and recognition. Everyone on the field could see that this was a momentous occurrence and no one breathed for fear of missing what would come next. A natural breeze blew across the field and caressed the mother's face. She turned toward the girl.

"Uuuuunnnaaa," Lady Rhiannah breathed, her face softening. "A daughter?"

She seemed stunned as if she did not know what to do next, then she came alive and reached forward, trying to grab the girl.

"Come! We are leaving!" She ordered.

Kieran drew his sword and stepped between them.

"She's not going anywhere."

The move was telling. Though Kieran had apologized and confessed his crime it was clear he would not give up what he had stolen.

"Neither man nor dragon will take Una from me." Kieran looked ready to fight.

"It is my choice, Mother. I will not go. I am Kieran's and he is mine." Una stood by his side.

"Nnnnooooooo!" Lady Dragahn wailed. "Don't you understand, our kind is fading from the Earth, we are the last. You must come with me, or all is lost. I am your mother!" Her last words faded on a choking cry.

"I chose Kieran years ago as my rider and mate. We cannot be separated. I am his wife." Una spoke loudly and lifted her chin in defiance.

"Leave with me now *or he dies!*" Lady Dragahn pointed a shaking finger at Kieran.

"I will not." Una revealed loudly. "I am carrying Kieran's child."

Kieran staggered back, then stopped stunned, frozen to the spot by what Una revealed.

Lady Dragahn turned on Kieran and her rage flared anew.

"I will shred you limb from limb! I will drink every drop of your blood and crush your thieving heart between my fangs. You have taken *everything* from me!"

"No Mother! I will not let you hurt Kieran. You must accept this is my choice. I will protect him from you and anyone else who would harm him!"

Lady Rhiannah had finally reached her limit. She tilted her head back and screamed at the sky. Kieran hadn't heard that heart-shattering sound for many years and cold sweat dripped down his spine, as she changed into a *dragon.*

Everyone gasped in shocked terror. The King, nobles, knights and warriors all ran for the safety of the forest. Tartan said something, but Kieran didn't hear because his head was buzzing from the shock of what Una revealed. Then everything fell silent and motionless.

The dragon was red as fire. Her long black mane lashed back and forth as her head tossed, and her transformation finished. Then the dragon rippled to black, roared, spitting a long stream of white fire into the sky until she seemed to run out of breath. After her change and her initial raging, the dragon lowered her horned head and growled at the humans standing at her black clawed feet. She swept her head back and forth and clawed the ground as if preparing to charge. Opening her jaws wide she struck out intending to snatch Kieran in one bite.

Kieran stood his ground with his sword in his hand and his eyes flaring with green fire. In a flash, Tartan was behind him and Una. He could only reach one of them and it was Kieran who he pulled out of the dragon's way.

King Odbalt behind them was shouting orders, calling for archers and spearmen. Men were screaming and shouting. Some went to protect the king while others were running away from the angry black dragon.

Una's form rippled and grew just as the mother dragon's had and then suddenly, there were two. The angry black and red dragon shooting white flame and a cold white dragon who spread large violet wings to protect the humans behind her from the mother's wrath.

The mother dragon took to the sky beating her wings until she hung over the groups of men on the ground. Her amber eyes were on fire. Her scales flashed and her belly glowed red as she searched for the dragon thief to incinerate him with fire. Una gained the same altitude and with claws outstretched, she swooped over the top and grabbed the back of the black dragon and held on. She pulled her mother away from the men below, away from where Kieran stood shouting up at her.

Tartan held tight to the young man he had raised and looked at him as if he had never seen him before. Above them, the two dragons began to fight, one to get back to the ground and the other to gain height in the sky. Their roars echoed across the sky.

"Why didn't you tell me, Kieran!" Tartan was yelling above the roars of the dragons.

Kieran stopped struggling and turned resolutely toward him and shrugged. "I guess we all have our secrets."

"I don't know what any of this means, Kieran but we must get you out of here. That black dragon means to swallow you whole!"

Tartan was tugging Kieran as hard as he could, but he seemed made of granite and would not budge. After that, Kieran only heard Tartan yelling and telling him to run. His flaming green eyes turned skyward to watch the two dragons fighting in the sky.

'Una, come and get me. This is my fight! I caused all of this. Remember, on the land and in the sky, we are one!'

'Kieran!' Una's mind screamed his name. He felt her uncertainty and something else that felt like sorrow and regret.

The black dragon fought the white dragon out of instinct and self-preservation. The white dragon was her daughter she knew, but instinct took over. In her rage, her claws sunk into the white dragon's back puncturing her scales. Dragon mother twisted and her head struck out as one of her horns sliced into scales and soft skin, she sunk her fangs into the white dragon's shoulder. They both roared and twirled, apart then clashing together in the sky. Red blood rained down on the men watching below. Then somehow, they separated and circled around. If either fought with deadly intentions or with halfhearted fervor, it was not certain. It was a strange battle between the two dragons in the sky and, as no one had ever seen a dragon before, no human watching could tell which was winning.

Kieran was shouting at Una and begging her with his mind to land and get him so he could fight with her as one. Streaking down, she snatched him up and with a toss of her head he landed on her back. The mother dragon was reorienting, poised to make a final attack. She saw the dragon thief on the white dragon's back and roared with indignation. Then they were level in the sky with her, and she paused to belch white fire at them both. The white dragon reared back and took the brunt of the flames on her chest and belly.

Once the mother dragon spent her flames, Una shot toward her like an arrow. Kieran reversed his sword in his grip and prepared to hurtle it like a spear into the black dragon's chest. They collided in the sky and Una sunk her talons into the mother's softer belly scales. He threw his weapon, and the sword he made with his own hands sped toward its target, embedding between the red scales of the mother dragon's chest. She roared in pain as it struck.

Una's wings beat hard, and she felt Kieran melding with her mind and heart, lending her his strength to push the black dragon back. They tumbled in the sky tearing and clawing at each other. With a final collision in the sky, they all fell. Una felt Kieran's remorse and sadness that it had come to this, and she felt the same. Una surged forward and the ground seemed to rush toward them.

The mother dragon's head turned, and her amber eyes saw them heading toward the ground. Whether it was motherly instinct or defeat, she twisted and crashed on her back into the grassy field. Spraying dirt and chunks of grass blasted into the air and she took the brunt of the impact. The white dragon crashed atop her. Their wings were outstretched with the violet wings of the white covering the black and red of the dragon mother. Both lay still. Kieran had been thrown off Una's back and landed with a practiced roll. It took him a moment to shake off the impact then he leaped up and ran toward the two dragons. He swiftly reached Una's head and was screaming her name. Their connection snapped as she went still.

The men of Lyndesea came out of the forest slowly and formed a circle around the fallen beasts. The archers raised their bows, arrows notched and ready. The spearmen took aim. The king raised his arm to give the signal to shoot but hesitated, watching to see if the beasts still lived.

No one cheered that the last dragons ever seen were dead, crashed to the ground in a war no one completely understood. Tartan started toward Kieran but fell back as the mother dragon's eyes slowly opened and her head moved trying to push the white dragon off and rise. Una's emerald eyes were closed and she didn't move.

"Una! No!" Kieran shouted. "Uuunnnnnaaaa!" Her massive body slipped to the grass as the mother dragon heaved up. He thought it was over for his beloved Una. He had stolen her egg, and she had given him love, a family and a future, but now it was all over.

The black dragon slowly rose, staggering to her feet. The sound of her raspy breathing filled the air. She took a stumbling step backward and her front claw grasped the sword in her chest and wrenched it from between her scales then tossed it aside. Once free of the stabbing annoyance, she turned toward Kieran, growling and opening her bloody mouth as she came.

"I'll devour your thieving heart!" The dragon mother gasped.

Kieran tilted his head up, holding his arms out in surrender and waited for the jaws to close and end him. If Una were dead, he did not care to live, and this was penance for all his wrongs.

The death blow did not come.

Una had come to and made a mighty lunge leaping at the black dragon and bowling her over. She had the mother dragon by the throat and was crushing her neck in strong jaws.

"Una, don't kill her!" Kieran pleaded loudly and screamed in her mind as well. *'It doesn't have to end this way!'*

Una released the black dragon and turned her great head to stare at him. Only the mother and Kieran could hear and understand Una's final words to the mother dragon.

'Mother, I choose my rider, my mate! Kieran and our child.'

The mother dragon lifted slowly, her blood streamed down her neck and snout and dripped onto the torn grass. She looked at Una with sad amber eyes filled with tears.

'Then you choose the end of dragons.' The mother dragon spoke to Una, but Kieran heard also.

Turning to stare at Kieran her head dipped once in defeat. Spreading her great black and red wings the mother dragon lifted into the sky. She turned toward the southern mountains and with a final chirruping message only Una understood, she flew away.

CHAPTER THIRTY-SIX

The king's men seemed to awaken from frozen fear and ran closer to surround the white dragon completely. Many of the men moved to protect the king. Someone shouted, "My King, your orders?"

King Odbalt watched the young warrior, Kieran, *speaking* to the white dragon. His soldiers were poised to shoot arrows and throw spears at the great beast who seemed to be paying no attention to him or the soldiers surrounding her.

The king raised a hand signaling and ordered reluctantly, "Stand down."

Kieran was staring at Una, and she was nodding her massive head as they communicated in a way that no one could hear.

Tartan picked up Kieran's fallen sword that was coated in dragon blood. Slowly, he approached Kieran and the white dragon hoping against all hope that she would not bite him in two or incinerate him. He tried to think of something to say to the boy he thought he knew and loved so much.

"What will you do now?" Tartan asked.

"I don't know," Kieran answered truthfully. "We can't stay here that's for sure."

"You'll always be welcome at home." Tartan's voice was strong, but his eyes betrayed his feelings.

Kieran poured all his love and admiration into one last look at Tartan as he handed him his sword. They hugged tightly. Nodding his head in thanks, he stepped away. Una stuck a front leg out and Kieran climbed onto her back. His sword was once again strapped to his side and the crystal in the pommel sparkled with radiant color.

"Kieran, why didn't you tell me?" Tartan shouted to Kieran upon the dragon's back. His face revealed he needed the answer to this last question before they parted.

"Hey, I told you she was magic." He shrugged one shoulder and gave Tartan a last half smile.

Then Kieran looked up as Una flapped her wings and they leaped into the sky. Una, the white dragon and her rider swooped and turned to fly into the northern clouds.

Behind him Tartan heard men start shouting and the King of Lyndesea gave more orders. All the other men who had been Lady Dragahn's soldiers, watched the last of the magnificent and frightening dragons fight then fly away. Some stood in stunned amazement, others bolted to escape the king's wrath. The battle ground was once again caught up in skirmishes as the king's soldiers fought to maintain their victory. Eventually, they gathered all that remained of the enemy, and the fighting stopped.

The king's men victoriously took Garrion Swagger prisoner along with his outlaw men and charged them with multiple crimes against the kingdom. The dead were buried, and the wounded were seen to. King Odbalt loudly decreed Commander Bodine should march on the lady dragon's castle. Their next mission was to collect the gigantic beast's treasure, as it was well known dragons kept a hoard of riches, gold, silver and jewels, magical armor, and silver swords in gilded scabbards.

Tartan stood staring, watching the sky until the white dragon and the boy he loved like a son, disappeared. He turned and headed back to his wagon. He wondered if he would ever see Kieran and Una, the last dragon, again. Tartan left the battlefield knowing, miles away on the other side of Ten Thousand Mile Forest, his wife and children awaited his return and his heart ached with missing them.

Months later, late one summer night, Tartan sat by his forge fire smoking a pipe. He was restless, haunted by dreams and memories that would not let him rest. When he returned home from the battle against Lady Dragahn, he told Sara the fantastic story of Kieran and Una. They were overwhelmed thinking that all those years, a dragon had been living up the mountains from them. Many things made sense to them now and they spent days speculating about all the secrets and lies mixed with the truth. The horses disliking Kieran's smell, him not agreeing to stay on the farm, and hiding Una from them all those years, now he understood. Even the fanciful stories about dragon sightings in the mountains by the people of Appleaid were confirmed by what he now knew was true. He had seen the transformation with his own eyes.

They learned from travelers that after the war, Garrion Swagger confessed the truth of the mother dragon's ten-year search for her egg and revealed his part in it. Despite claiming to be under the influence of her magic, he was hanged for treason.

There was a rumor that Lord Stephan Arceneaux, of Arcenaxe Castle, had disappeared. His part in the war was greatly disputed, and many discounted him as an accomplice of Lady Dragahn.

Many nights, the local tavern buzzed with talk and bards circulated the land telling spectacular poetic stories of the war at Hidden Valley and the battle between the black and the white dragon. Tartan neither confirmed nor denied those stories.

Songs were written of Kieran MacLaren's warrior prowess, and he became even more famous than his namesake, Kieran Cray, the King's Champion of old. One girl in the village even boasted of having kissed the famous Kieran McLaren when he was a young lad. After all that happened, Kieran's destiny to become a renowned warrior came true and they spoke of him with awe as the Blacksmith's Apprentice and the White Dragon's Rider.

Nights like this where the skies sparkled with stars, the wind was quiet and the only thing that moved was an owl up in the rafters of the barn, Tartan allowed himself to wonder what happened to the boy he had taken in. The boy he loved like a son. He also wondered about the lovely and mysterious Una and the magic that made her a dragon and a human. He shed a tear for the loss of their presence and sent up a prayer for their safety. Snuffing out his pipe and banking the fire, Tartan turned to go find his bed and his sleeping wife.

Suddenly, the horses in the corral neighed and reared trampling wildly to the opposite fence. Tartan looked around and a faint, familiar scent on the breeze reached him. He finally found the source of the disturbance. Two people came out of the night-darkened forest. One was tall and broad-shouldered; the other was smaller. That one leaned over heavily as if wounded or in pain.

Running toward them, Tartan reached Kieran and a very pregnant Una. She was gritting her teeth while birthing pains bent her over. He wordlessly helped the couple to the house and called for Sara who came running in her nightgown and kerchief.

Throughout the rest of the night, Una struggled to give birth. At times her eyes glowed with emerald flames, her brow glistened with sweat, and her moans echoed off the wooden walls. Tartan's children were awoken by all the noise and watched quietly from the bedroom doorway.

When the baby finally slid into the world, they all cried tears of joy and hugged each other with unbound happiness. Tartan grinned and patted Kieran on the back. Kieran was a proud father and Una reached for his hand as they placed the little girl in her arms.

"What are you going to name her?" Sara was smiling as she cleaned up blood-soaked cloths.

Una looked at Kieran, and held his gaze, and he nodded.

She smiled and pronounced, "Serene." Sara smiled and sighed dreamily at the beautiful baby girl.

After making sure Una was alright and the baby suckled at her breast contented, Tartan, and a very proud Kieran, went outside to sit on the well warn log that served as a bench. He poured them each a cup of ale and they toasted the new baby girl. It felt good to be back at the forge farm and the calm of the late night settled over them.

"Tartan, I suppose I owe you an explanation about a few things." Kieran began.

"Kieran, I love you like a son, and I don't care what you've done or where you've been, I am just glad you and Una, and now Serene, are safe and well."

"Still, I'd like you to know. I want no more secrets between us."

Tartan nodded and settled in with his ale and listened as Kieran's tale unfolded. He told of the stories he heard as a boy about the last dragon and her treasure. He went on about his dreams of being a warrior, obtaining fame and fortune, and how it fueled his determination to climb the cliff to the dragon's cave. The hard part was describing his desperation and fear after running away from home and how that made him act upon his dreams. The accidental theft of the dragon egg and Una's hatching was spoken of with reverence and guilt. He even told how Beck Dunn, his father and brothers, had found him and tried to take him back to the farm in Buttermilk, and that Una, as a dragon, had stopped them.

Last, he shared the final words of the dragon mother, *'Then you choose the end of dragons.'* Spoken to Una as a final revelation.

"I don't know if it is true or not that Una and her mother are the last dragons. I suspect not, but it seems likely. I just don't know." Kieran shook his head sadly.

"What will Serene become? Is she dragon or human."

Kieran didn't answer for a long time. Then he explained how dragons pass down knowledge through inherited knowledge of magic and dragon lore.

"It's in their blood." He said finally. "I don't know everything about dragons yet, but Una and Serene are hope for dragon-kind."

Tartan nodded with understanding but did not ask further questions on the subject.

Kieran went on with his story but didn't go into much detail about the last few months since the war but did say he and Una had nowhere to go. Since the forge farm felt like home, they could not help but return in their hour of need. He hoped that somehow, he and his little family would be welcomed back, and they could take up where they left off.

Tartan was silent for a while, then he nodded and refilled his ale cup before speaking his mind.

"Kieran, you should know, King Odbalt Linden has sent out a call for soldiers to join his army against another enemy coming out of the east. You've gained a name for yourself from your fighting skills and bravery in battle. After the war was over, I learned the king was impressed with you, and Una. He issued a decree that dragons are to be protected from now on."

Tartan hesitated and his voice was quieter as he revealed the rest.

"The king wants you both back. He's willing to offer you land, a title, and great wealth, if you will be his champion which of course includes, Una, as your dragon. The renown and the fame you dreamed of and the fortune you always craved can be yours. Or you can stay here, work the forge, and make a home for your wife and child. The king's offer is very generous. Will you take it?"

Kieran stood and turned to look out into the night remaining silent for a long time. Reaching into his pocket, he pulled out a long crystal shard broken off from the egg he had not meant to steal, so long ago. He stared at it, his eyes gleaming with unshed tears, his thumb lovingly caressed the smooth surface. The scant moon and starlight made the precious stone glitter. The warm light streaming out from the house illuminated his face. As he contemplated Tartan's offer, he gave a slight smile. Putting the crystal back into his pocket, he looked Tartan in the eye.

"I've no wish to pursue childish dreams, I think I'll stay here if you'll have us."

Tartan let out the breath he was holding, rose to put his hands on Kieran's shoulders, and grinned as he spoke.

"Aye, I will."

Kieran had one thing left to do. Later that night as his wife and child slept, he went into the forge barn. Lighting a lamp, he took the worn key off the wall and entered the back room. He unlocked the big trunk hidden in the shadows and lifted the lid. In the trunk lay Tartan's old sword. This was the same one he had shown the ten-year-old boy who had run away from home to pursue his dreams of becoming a famous warrior.

Drawing his own sword with the shard of Una's dragon egg in the pommel, he wrapped the blade in oiled cloth and set it inside the trunk. He closed the lid and locked his dreams inside.

The End

EPILOGUE

T hat same night, far off in the deepest forest of the southern mountains, the mother dragon lay on her side, straining and pushing. Her roars echoed off the cave walls, and she blew white fire as the pain grew, and her belly scales rippled. Holding her breath, she gave a final push. Out from underneath her long, glistening black tail and into the nest lined with thick black dragon hair...slid a shining black egg.

She breathed dragon breath on the egg and the smooth shape crackled, lengthened, and began to take on another form. At last, a glimmering black crystal now sat upright in the dragon hair nest and the mother dragon crooned softly to her egg.

Lord Stephan Arceneaux approached from out of the shadows and cautiously stepped over to the nest. The mother dragon looked up and turned her head toward him. He smoothed a hand over the long mane that fell between her eyes, and she gave a low purr.

"Well done, Rhiannah, my love. How soon until it hatches?" he asked.

The mother dragon's eyes held his, conveying a wordless message, flickering with flames.

Lord Arceneaux shuddered, and his gold armor split and peeled away, while his golden head shook with transformation. Huge gold membranous wings grew from his back, and his body grew, changed, morphing into a gigantic white dragon. His golden eyes flickered with flame and the scent of brimstone filled the air. Tossing his head back, roars of elation split the night air from the black dragon's mate.

The two dragons crooned over their egg and then the male went to stand guard in the cave entrance. The mother dragon watched and gave a satisfied grin.

Then she lifted her head, arched her neck back, and gave a roar that echoed through the shadows of the cave and out into the night. This egg would be protected by *two dragons*, and no one would ever steal from her again. She rested her head on her clawed feet and closed her eyes to sleep and await the fateful day when the beautiful black egg finally hatched.

ALSO BY WENDY L. ANDERSON

D ear Reader,

Thank you for reading The Dragon Thief's Heart. It means so much that you chose to step into the world I've created.

I hope you found yourself swept away by Kieran and Luna's journey and by the magic, danger, and the choices that shaped their fate.

Did you know your support, by posting a review, keeps me writing more dragon stories?

Please share your love of fantasy by leaving a review. Even a short review helps other readers discover this story and it means so much to me as an author.

Read more fantasy by Wendy L. Anderson.

***

The Kingdom of Jior Five-book epic fantasy romance series.

Of Demon Kind, book one
  Redemption of the Fallen, book two
  Heirs of Jior, book three
  Iron and the Arrow, book four
  The Last Ny-Failen, book five

***

If you love the world of the Kingdom of Jior, you'll love this new Spinoff Series!

The Legends of Everclearing!

Killian the Assassin
  Arianne the Mistress
  Tristram the Demon
  Conall the Strong

All available now!

***

Fall in love with these Viking Historical Fantasy Romances

A Cut Twice as Deep twin sisters fight to find happiness in a
ruthless world ruled by the sword and axe.
Solstice Child, a love triangle of the ages.
Valkyrie's Prey, a Valkyrie who doesn't want to give up a worthy
warrior to Valhalla.

***

If you like stand-alone books, try one of these fabulous fantasies.

Rapunzel's Tower a fractured fairytale that will sweep you away!

Ulrik   is a time-travel fantasy romance full of heart-stopping
action!

***

Remember - Share your love of fantasy books by posting a review. It doesn't have to be lengthy or complicated, even a few words make a huge difference. It is one of the most powerful ways you can support me and my writing is by leaving a review.

Even a short review will help other readers discover the series and help keep stories like this alive.

Thank you again, for being the best part of this journey.

***

My Gift to You

As a thank you, I'd love to give you a bonus story set in the world of Jior. It is a tale of two lost souls forced to cross dangerous lands in search of sanctuary.

Get your free story on my website www.wendylanderson.com

The Road to Jior

Stay connected with me for updates, new releases, and behind-the-scenes content:

Join my newsletter at: https://www.wendylanderson.com/about

About the Author

Wendy L. Anderson is a writer of passionately charged fantasy. Breaking the barriers of typical fantasy themes, she created the Kingdom of Jior epic fantasy series, a lusty and poetic five-book series that will have you wanting more in her Legends of Everclearing spinoff series. Inspired by authors such as Robert E. Howard and Morgan Llywelyn, Wendy went on to write other stand-alone works such as; A Cut Twice as Deep, Solstice Child, Valkyrie's Prey, Ulrik, and Rapunzel's Tower. These fantasy works break free from the usual boundaries of fantasy genres.

A Colorado native, Wendy decided it is time to write down the fantasies from her mind. Writing about everything from fantastical worlds to the stuff of her dreams she takes her stories along interesting paths while portraying characters and worlds she sees in her mind's eye. Her goal is to deviate from common themes, write in original directions and transport her reader to the worlds of her creation.

Wendy L. Anderson's fantasy has action, adventure, and suspense with just the right amount of romance!

Find out more at: www.wendylanderson.com